Wronged

Rin Sher

Copyright © 2022 by Rin Sher

All rights reserved.

The characters and events portrayed in this book are fictitious. Any similarity to real persons. living or dead, is coincidental and not intended by the author.

No portion of this book may be reproduced, or stored in a retrieval system, or transmitted in any form or by any means, electronic, mechanical, photocopying, recording, or otherwise without written permission from the publisher or author, except as permitted by U.S. copyright law.

ISBN: 9798411374209

Book Cover Photographer and Model @Justin Dube'

Contents

A Note From The Author	1
Dedication	3
Playlist	5
Prologue	7
1. Chapter One	21
2. Chapter Two	33
3. Chapter Three	49
4. Chapter Four	61
5. Chapter Five	71
6. Chapter Six	85
7. Chapter Seven	97
8. Chapter Eight	107

9.	Chapter Nine	117
10.	Chapter Ten	127
11.	Chapter Eleven	137
12.	Chapter Twelve	151
13.	Chapter Thirteen	159
14.	Chapter Fourteen	173
15.	Chapter Fifteen	183
16.	Chapter Sixteen	189
17.	Chapter Seventeen	211
18.	Chapter Eighteen	223
19.	Chapter Nineteen	243
20.	Chapter Twenty	253
21.	Chapter Twenty-One	269
22.	Chapter Twenty-Two	285
23.	Chapter Twenty-Three	289
24.	Chapter Twenty-Four	297
25.	Chapter Twenty-Five	309
26.	Chapter Twenty-Six	317
27.	Chapter Twenty-Seven	331
28.	Chapter Twenty-Eight	345

29. Epilogue	353
THANK YOU!	363
CONTACT ME	365
Other Books In This Series	367
Also By The Author	371
Acknowledgements	375

A Note From The Author

This book in no way depicts my thoughts or feelings on the matters contained in this book. The situations and characters in this story are fictional, however, research was done on real life accounts to get information on how sex offenders and those on the sex offender's list are treated under certain circumstances.

Triggers for this book include:
Drugging and sexual assault.
Sexual assault does not happen on the pages, however, it is mentioned throughout.
Unjust treatment.

This is to all of you who have been wronged at one point or another in your lives... Because justice is not always served, the bad are not always punished, and wrongs are not always made right.

Playlist

Never Say Never – The Fray
Ocean Eyes – Billie Eilish
Summertime Sadness – Lana Del Rey
Riptide – Vance Joy
I Feel Like I'm Drowning – Two Feet
Stay Alive – Jose Gonzalez
Sail – Awolnation

Prologue

Jacob

"Booyah!" I shout triumphantly to my friends. "And that, ladies, is how it's done."

My best friend, Campbell, rolls his eyes, almost hidden by his too-long black hair, as I nudge him with my shoulder and toss the controller onto the table.

There are varying degrees of snickers and grumbles from the other guys in the room, and I take a moment to gloat.

Instead of being at one of the crazy parties that have been going on every weekend this month, my four closest friends and I have been playing video games at Campbell's house all night. Most popular guys in the school, we are not.

I just turned eighteen two days ago, and graduation is in two weeks, so really, we *should* be out there living it up with the rest of them.

After hemming and hawing about it for most of today, I think I've finally built up the nerve to try to change things up and do something a little different tonight.

"I could probably beat you, Jakey," Mase says from where he's splayed out on the floor.

Jason pretends to cough into his hand, "Bullshit," which only causes my smirk to grow.

"No, it's my turn next." Neil swipes the controller off the table, and Campbell hands his over to Mase.

"I gotta get going now anyway," I reply as I get to my feet.

"Where are you off to at midnight?" Campbell asks after checking his watch. "I thought you were staying the night?"

I busy myself with collecting my shit, so I don't have to look at him or any of them. "Nah, I've got an early start at the store."

Technically, I *do* have to work at my parents' furniture store in the morning, but not nearly as early as I'm implying.

"Hmm, you wouldn't happen to be ditching us to head over to Seth's party a few blocks away, now, would you?"

My fucking cheeks get hot at being called out, and Mase happens to glance my way before turning back to their game on the TV. "Aw, shit, he totally is." He chuckles. "He totally fuckin' is."

I feign an exasperated sigh. "I'm not *going* there; it's on the way home. Can't help passing by it."

"Mm-hmm, and are you hoping to maybe run into someone outside the house on your way past, Jacob?"

Uh, only the girl I've had a crush on for about *forever*. Which they all happen to know about. Four pairs of eyes land on me, watching, waiting for me to squirm even more than I have been.

"Jennifer Lapmor *did* mention she was going to be there," Campbell says, raising a brow at me.

"She actually talked to you guys?" Neil asks, sounding more surprised than anything else.

I spin around, chewing on one of my nails, and try to find my phone. The sooner I get out of here, the sooner the shit-talking will end.

"No." Campbell laughs like it's the funniest thing. "I doubt she even knew we were behind her when she was talking to her friends."

Mase snickers. "Now *that* sounds more like it."

I finally find my phone buried in the couch cushions and turn to face Mase. "For your information, she talks to me all the time."

"Probably asking why you're staring at her."

"No," I huff.

She has asked me for a pencil, asked me what time it was, and said 'sorry' when she knocked a book out of my hand.

"She's said plenty." I ignore their chuckles and head toward the door. "Anyway, as I said, I'm just going to be passing by the party on my way home." And if somehow I'm invited inside, great.

"Wait, wait, wait, hold up." Mase pauses the game and jumps over Neil on his way to me. "Here." He reaches into his pocket, pulls something out, and then shoves it into my hand. "You know, just in case."

I look down at the condom in my hand, and Mase starts cackling as he walks back to pick up his controller. The others join in on the laughing while I grip the condom packet and scowl at my now *so-called* friends.

"Laugh it up now, boys, but you know what? She will be mine one day. I'll make sure of it. You just wait and see." I lift the packet in my hand and wave it at them. "And then I *will* need this."

They chuckle again as I turn around and walk out of the room with a smile on my face. I'm used to them giving me shit, especially Mase. And I usually give it back just as much.

It all depends on who's in the hot seat. I made myself the target tonight with my not-so-subtle plans to pass by the party and see what's going on.

I shove the condom into the back pocket of my jeans along with my phone before I reach downstairs. I'm not sure I'd like to have a conversation about why I'm carrying one around in my hand if I were to run into Campbell's parents. It's completely silent when I walk through the downstairs area and to the front door, so I didn't need to worry about it, anyway.

I step out into the cool air, take a deep breath, and then start the walk along the path toward my house. All joking aside, I really *am* hoping to run into Jennifer, even though she's not likely to be outside. And even if she were, she'd be surrounded by her group of friends.

I've had a crush on her all throughout high school. It started on the first day of school when she said 'hello' to me from her locker beside mine. I don't think I even responded to her because I was too shocked that someone as beautiful as her had actually spoken to me. I stood there frozen, with probably the stupidest expression on my face.

It didn't matter anyway, because she was swept into the popular crowd right after that, and I was kept firmly on the outside.

We're heading to the same college—which I happen to know because I overheard her talking to her friends—so I'm hoping we can start fresh and become friends.

And then, we'll go from there.

Just as I make the turn to cut through the field that sits halfway between Campbell's house and the party, a guy comes charging out from the darkness and bangs right into me, almost knocking me over, then continues running off without apologizing.

"Watch it!" I call to his retreating back. "Asshole."

Shaking my head, I turn and continue. But after several steps, an odd sound from nearby has me pausing and straining my ear to hear what the noise was. I realize it's a mixture between a moan and a whimper when it comes again.

Following the sound to where it's darker and where the grass is longer, I pull out my phone and turn on the flashlight so I can actually see.

My blood runs cold when my sight lands on a girl lying on the ground a few feet in front of me. She's face down, with her skirt bunched up at her waist and her underwear pulled down, wrapped around one ankle.

"Oh, shit!"

I quickly crouch down and roll her over, and a hazy fog clouds the edges of my vision when I see who it is.

No! No, no, no. Jennifer!

The large bruise forming on her cheek looks painful, her makeup is smudged, and her hair is a tangled mess, just like her clothes.

"Jennifer!" I cup her cheeks. "Can you hear me?"

She doesn't respond in any way. I run my hands all over her body, checking for blood or anything that feels like a broken bone. The panic and adrenaline mixing and swirling around inside my body have my hands shaking and my mind not thinking straight.

I start tugging at her skirt, trying to pull it down in my panicked state, but I end up scratching her leg with the uneven nail I was chewing on earlier.

"Shit. Fuck." I grip my hair. "Okay, okay, calm down."

Breathe in, breathe out.

"Jennifer," I say loudly. "Jennifer, wake up."

Even when I shake her a little, she doesn't move. In fact, I can't even tell if she's breathing right now. I fumble to find my phone that I had dropped earlier, and it takes me three attempts to dial nine-one-one.

I've never once been in a situation even remotely close to this, so I'm not sure how to handle it or what the best course of action is.

I know that the dispatch operator can track my phone to our location even if I don't say anything, so I throw it back down onto the ground and decide to try CPR.

Whether it's the right thing to do, I'm not sure, but I have to try something. I took a course about four years ago, and I think I remember most of what I'm supposed to do.

I shrug off my sweater, tossing it to the side, and then double-check that she has a pulse before tilting her head back. Pressing my mouth to hers, I blow one breath and then wait five seconds.

When I go to do it again, she lets out a muffled scream against my lips. I pull back, feeling fucking relieved that she's at least responding.

"Get away from me!" she shrieks with wide eyes, her words slurred. "Stop touching me!" She waves her arms in my direction, trying to hit me as if I'm attacking her.

I grab at them in an attempt to settle her down. "Jennifer, stop. I'm trying to help you."

"No! You fu—you fuckin' *raped* me."

"What?" The blood drains from my face. "No. No, I didn't. Shit."

One of her hands breaks free from my grasp, and she makes a swipe at my face. Her nail ends up making contact and slices my cheek, so I release her other arm to reach up and cover the sting. Wetness seeps onto my fingertips as blood escapes the wound. She got me pretty good, but I don't even care right now.

My phone's flashlight is still illuminating the area around us, and I watch as Jennifer shuffles back, trying to get away from me.

"It wasn't me, Jennifer." I try to make my voice sound soothing, but it ends up cracking.

My stomach revolts at the thought of doing something like that to her, *raping* her, and it fucking kills me to see her so afraid of me.

She fidgets with her fingers while her eyes flick all around us. Her pupils look huge in the light from my phone, which means she's either high, drunk, or maybe a bit of both.

Maybe the guy that did this to her drugged her or something?

Was it that guy who ran into me?

Her hand dips down to her upper thighs, and she rubs over the area, grimacing like she's in pain. I can see a streak of blood trailing along her inner thigh that I didn't see before.

Is that from what the guy did to her? Or is it from *me* when I tried to pull her skirt down? *Shit*.

This built-in need to comfort her has me slowly crawling in her direction. But as soon as she notices, she holds her hands up in front of her.

"No. Stay away. *Please*," she begs and starts crying. "Stay away."

My chest caves in at the sight of her so distressed, and it aches at the fact that she thinks I did this to her. I can't stand to let her think that of me.

"Jennifer, listen, it wasn't me," I try to say calmly and quietly. Meanwhile, I'm close to breaking down as well.

I can't even begin to imagine what she's been through tonight. If I'm feeling this fucked up about it, then what the hell must she be feeling?

The sound of sirens in the distance has her eyes swinging in that direction. A range of emotions, including relief, cross her face before immediately flitting her gaze back to me.

Her whole body is shaking from everything that's happened to her and the cool night air, her bottom lip quivering right along with it. I slowly get to my feet, picking up my sweater as I go, and then try to move closer again.

"Here, take this. You're cold."

Her wary eyes stay focused on me, but she seems a little calmer and doesn't tell me to stay away from her this time. Maybe she's feeling safer with the sirens getting closer. Or maybe she finally realizes that it wasn't me.

The closer I get to her, though, the more she starts shrinking back into herself again, and then her eyes get a wild look to them.

Suddenly, she launches herself at me, trying to attack me and claw at my shirt. She stumbles on some grass with her unsteady legs and falls to the ground, ripping my shirt on the way down and causing me to fall along with her. Then she's flailing around, freaking out and screaming, trying to hit me.

"Hey," I struggle to say. "Hey, calm down. I'm not going to hurt you."

I try to grab her arms again to settle her down, but she's too worked up and swings them at me as she did before. This time, I'm able to get out of her reach before she scratches me again, and then I jump to my feet.

Looking down at her, I feel completely useless. Helpless.

I can't even be mad that she's reacting like this after what happened to her. How could anyone be expected to act rationally in this situation?

When she starts crying into her hands, my heart cracks wide open. I can't stand to see her crying and so distraught. Out of instinct, I go to reach for her again, but a voice behind me stops me in my tracks.

"Step away from the girl and put your hands where I can see them."

I whip around to see a few police officers and paramedics walking toward Jennifer with a bag.

"You don't understand. I was trying—" The sight of a gun makes me stop talking.

"Put your hands up!"

I quickly lift my hands above my head. I'm sure this must look bad to them. A quick glance down shows my shirt ripped in one part. I also have scratches on my arms and on my cheek.

And shit, I scratched her leg. My DNA will be *all over her*, even on her lips. *Shit.*

I'm probably screwed. A cool chill licks at my skin at the thought of what might happen to me.

No. No, I can't be charged for this. *I'm innocent. All will be okay. I'll be okay. I'm innocent. I'll be okay.*

As one officer begins to put cuffs on me and reads me my Miranda Rights, I watch as another one reaches down to pick something up off the ground with gloves.

"This yours?" he asks, putting it into a baggie.

My stomach twists even further when I squint and see what it is—the condom Mase gave to me. It must have fallen out of my pocket when I pulled my phone out.

That's not looking very good for me. Still, it's not used, so that should work in my favor, right? They can't use it against me, can they?

As I'm led away in a kind of shocked state, I turn my head to look over at Jennifer, sitting with the paramedics.

With a look, I try to convey to her that it wasn't me—that I was just trying to help her, that I've cared about her more than she knows for years.

Doesn't she know I would never do anything like that to her? Or to anyone?

Doesn't she know that just the thought of it makes me sick?

If the look in her eyes as she tightens the blanket closer to her body is any indication, she doesn't know any of that at all, and it fucking hurts.

"I think he drugged me as well," she continues, talking to the paramedics while staring directly at me.

"It's okay," I whisper to myself. "I'm going to be okay."

She'll remember that it wasn't me, and they'll find other evidence on her that proves me innocent. I'll be let go by the morning.

They'll know it wasn't me.

They have to.

Chapter One

Remi – Present Day

Back and forth. Back and forth. I rub my thumb over the tips of my fingers, over and over, ending on an even number. It doesn't matter how many times I slide across them, just as long as it's an even number that I end on.

That's about the extent of my OCD. Which is to say, I *don't* have OCD. It's just a habit I developed throughout the years in uncertain, exciting, or nervous times.

This situation, I guess, would fall into all three of those categories.

I finally pause the investigative podcast I was listening to, pile my long black hair into a messy bun, and push open my car door. My eyes still linger on the beautiful colors painted before me in the sky as the sun sets over the ocean.

The scent of the seawater assaults my nose immediately—fish and salt. I can't say I'm a huge fan of it.

But I can't complain. If I do a three-hundred-and-sixty-degree turn, I *don't* see a single photographer around. Nobody is hiding in the bushes, ready to catch me in a weird shot they can manipulate and twist to fit their story.

That, unfortunately, has been my life with a highly publicized tycoon father and a socialite mother.

If it weren't for the fact that I look like an exact mix of my parents—my father's black hair and full lips and my mother's hazel eyes and nose shape—I'd think that I was switched at birth with how different I am from them.

Don't get me wrong. I lived that life—the one they do. I went to the parties. I posed for the pictures. I dated the well-known men my parents encouraged me to.

But I hated every second of it.

My phone pings in my hand, and I take a quick moment to lean against my car and check all the messages I received while driving.

My stomach instantly fills with dread when I see the first message.

Dad: Dinner at the Matron on Saturday night. I expect you to smile more this time.

Stanley Murdoch is not a nice man to most people, and the fact that I never told him I was leaving is not something that is likely to go over smoothly. Sure, I've threatened it several times, but I never actually followed through.

Until now, that is.

But I definitely didn't make a stop at my parent's place to say goodbye or even let them know via text.

I've told them numerous times that I was sick of it all and that I wanted to leave. They probably just thought I was having some sort of tantrum. It was never that, though. I refuse to continue on with a life that makes me more and more miserable with each passing day.

I drop my chin to my chest and try to remind myself that I'm a grown woman who is freaking twenty-six years old. I should be able to live my life however I want.

With that thought in mind, I look back at my phone and read the other messages.

Candace: Are you going to the party Friday night? Can you get me in?

Megan: Heard the papz will be at that brunch on Sunday. We should go.

Tony: Did you talk to your dad for me?

There are several more like that, that I don't even bother checking. Instead, I block all of them except my father and put my phone away again.

Fakes. Liars. Users.

I've been surrounded by fake people, fake friends, and fake boyfriends my whole life. All of them were just trying to get ahead by using mine and my family's publicity.

I had truly liked the most recent boyfriend, Nathan. I liked him enough that I even considered it when he suggested we should get married and make our families happy.

I'm glad I never actually agreed to it, though.

I suck in a deep lungful of the salty air and walk toward my new home. I picked this small beach town to begin a new life away from everyone and everything. Barely a dot on the map, it seemed like the perfect place to breathe, to start fresh, to be *free*.

Some of the stones on the path shift under my feet as I walk to the front door, and I can't help but think about how much my mother would hate that. Not me. A smile touches my lips as I look around.

Beautiful clusters of wildflowers grow along the path, which she'd also hate, but I happen to *love* wildflowers.

Peace and quiet surround me, sinking into my bones, and at the same time, a lifetime of stress and always being 'on' is purged out through my sigh.

This is what I was craving.

My new home is at the very end of the street, along the beach side of the road. It's also the smallest in this area.

Sure, I could have gotten one of the bigger houses that are around here, but this suits me just fine. I've never cared much about having money. I'm sure I would probably think a little differently if I hadn't grown up with more than I could ever spend, but I can't change that fact.

It's also true that having money has allowed me to escape and buy this house that has the ocean as the backyard—not many people can say that.

But I'd still give it all away in a heartbeat and live a simple life rather than be tied to the life that created the money in the first place.

I return my focus to the blue door in front of me and push my key into the lock. The door creaks open, and I get my first glimpse of the inside of my new home.

I'm instantly in love.

Despite the setting sun, the interior remains bright due to all the windows. Beach-themed colors and furniture fill the small space. Straight ahead is a set of French doors that lead onto a deck, with stairs that go straight onto the sand. I've only been to the beach once in my whole life, so to have it now as my backyard is surreal.

I tour the rest of the house: two bedrooms, one bathroom, a small kitchen, and a laundry room. Perfect. It's *exactly* what I was hoping for when I bought it without even looking at it first.

My phone pings once again as I reach into my bag to pull out the BBQ chips I got at my last stop. Stuffing a few of them into my mouth, I open the text from my mother.

Mom: I do wish you'd give Nathan another chance.

I let out a scoff, turning my phone off without replying.

"A second chance," I mutter as I roll my eyes.

I *did* give him a second chance. I'm a big believer in second chances.

We're only human, after all.

I gave him the benefit of the doubt when those suggestive pictures of him and another woman surfaced *more than once* since I've also been the victim of that type of thing.

But I drew the line at giving him any more chances when I walked in on him with Candace *and* Megan. The very ones who texted me earlier. None of them saw me. They still don't know that I saw them. But boy, did I get quite the show from the three of them.

At least it didn't break my heart—it wasn't in his hands to break to begin with. But any time someone else is chosen over you, it's still a hit to your ego, no matter what. He chose to screw my "friends" and who knows who else instead of me. Instead of continuing a life with me.

Then the asshole had the nerve to try to make *me* feel guilty about breaking it off with him and upsetting his parents. Mine, too, for that matter.

That was the last straw before I got a longtime family friend, Henry—who is *actually* a friend and not a fake—to find me a place here.

I bought myself an old Corolla to better fit in with my new life, filled it with my stuff, and left. No one but Henry knows where I am, and I know he won't say anything. He's always had a soft spot for me.

My parents will probably have a fit when they realize that I'm gone, and it's not because they want to keep me close to look after me—they're not exactly the loving and doting type. It's because they're afraid of me embarrassing them. Whatever I do or say reflects on them, and they don't like it when they're not able to control me.

I don't know what to expect living here. I've never lived far from my parents or the accompanying cameras, but I can already feel the pressure getting lighter and lighter with each breath I take.

From here on out, it's a new me. No. No, it's more so that I'm actually able to *be me* now.

With one final glance around, I make a mental list of things I need, grab my keys and purse, and head to the grocery store I passed by earlier. I'll need food for at least a late dinner tonight and breakfast tomorrow. But since I'm going there, I might as well shop for everything.

I love that there is no heavy traffic on the way to the store. I love that when I walk through the door to *Peaches,* the only grocer in town, no one seems to know who I am or my family.

The few people here still stare, but it seems more like they're wondering who this new person is in their town. I can't help but smile to myself as I grab a cart and start putting items into it.

"You must be the one who moved into the Cromac's old place."

Turning my head, I see an older woman stocking the shelves. She's dressed in a pair of high-waisted mom jeans and a long-sleeve black T-shirt tucked in with the logo of this store above her left breast. There is a friendly air about her that immediately makes me feel comfortable in her presence.

"Oh, I'm not sure. Did they live by the beach?"

"Smaller house at the end, on the shore-side."

"Well, then, yep, that's me. How did you know?"

"Just a feeling. Not too many passersby stock up on a week's worth of groceries." She nods at my cart.

Smiling, I hold out my hand to her. "I guess you're right. I'm Remi."

She looks me up and down before reaching out and grabbing it. "You're a pretty little thing," she says bluntly. "I'm Jolene. This is my store."

"So nice to meet you, Jolene."

She crosses her arms and leans against the shelf, tilting her head. The action causes her gray bob to move in perfect unison, making me wonder how much product is in it.

"You got a job yet?" she asks, skipping straight to business even though we just met.

"Uh, no, not yet. Is there anywhere in town hiring that you know of?"

The truth is, I don't actually *need* a job. I could live comfortably with the money in my account for quite some time. But I don't want to live my life not doing anything. I *want* a job. Besides not wanting to get bored, I want to contribute to this town.

Plus, working would help me get to know everyone better. I'm a naturally curious person, and I love getting to know people's stories, their pasts, what makes them who they are, or why they do certain things. It's one of the reasons why I like listening to investigative podcasts. It feeds my curiosity about what happened in a certain instance and why.

She nods. "I need someone here. If you want, come by tomorrow evening for an hour. I'll show you what the job entails, and if you're interested, you can start Monday."

I haven't even been in this town for half a day, and I already have a job if I want it.

I'd say this move is already looking successful.

"That sounds great, thank you. Is six o'clock good?"

"That's fine." She nods again, turning back to the items she was re-stocking.

I wonder what her story is. She's either in her late fifties or early sixties, and she's working here on a Thursday night. Does she have a husband at home? Grandkids? Or is this store her baby? I guess I'll probably find at least some of that out tomorrow night.

"Okay, I'll see you then."

By the time I make it home and put my groceries away, the weather has changed quite drastically. The once striking pink and orange painted sky is now filled with dark, menacing clouds, shooting flashes of lightning across the sky above the ocean. I can't decide which of the two I like better.

The deck at the back of the house is covered, so I find a sweater to put on and step outside to watch the now wild storm. Despite the wind and rain pounding against anything within reach, there's a calmness settling inside me. I know without a doubt that moving here was the right decision.

I can see some tiny specks of lights out along the horizon, and I wonder how those boats are fairing out there on the ocean during the storm. Just the thought of being out there on one of them has my stomach churning. I love that I live by the water, but I still much prefer being on land.

The other houses to my left don't appear to have lights on, so I assume the people living in them probably go to bed at a decent time, unlike me. I've been known to be more of a night owl, although that may change with a job.

My eyes wander back along the shore and then over to the right along the beach. Squinting, I can't tell if my eyes are playing tricks on me when I think I spot a small light flickering farther down the beach.

In the next flash of light, I can see the small shack-like structure where the light is coming from, so I guess I did see it correctly. I hadn't noticed it when I first arrived. It looks like it would be roughly a fifteen-minute walk along the shore to get to it. I wonder if it's a fishing shack or someone's home?

I think I'll have to take a walk down there one of these days and check it out.

Chapter Two

Remi

Besides the hour that I was at *Peaches* on Friday night, I spent the last three days unpacking, organizing, sitting on my deck, and swimming in the ocean. And by swimming, I mean standing in the water no further than ass deep. I can't actually swim, and I'm terrified to go any deeper.

I'll have to learn one of these days because it seems like an important thing to know when you live by the water.

It was a nice and relaxing weekend, but I'm more than ready to get out of the house and start work. I accepted the job from Jolene on Friday night before the hour was even up. Despite the size of this town, there was a surprisingly steady flow of people coming into the store. I guess being the only grocer in town has its advantages.

I was introduced to many people, and the ones who didn't introduce themselves still smiled at me in a friendly manner. At the very least, by working there, I'll be entertained by learning everybody's stories.

"You're early. I like that," Jolene says as I walk through the store doors.

She leans a hip against the candy rack by the cash register, and besides the floral pants she has on today, she looks exactly the same as on Thursday and Friday, with the same long-sleeved work shirt on.

She gave me a short-sleeved version of hers to wear today, which I paired with some skinny jeans. I've made sure to stick to my more casual style of clothing rather than what I would have had to wear in the past.

Checking the time on my phone, I see that I only have five minutes until I'm supposed to start. Do people actually turn up to work right when they're supposed to begin and no sooner? The only reason that I wasn't here even earlier was that I decided to walk instead of drive, and I hadn't calculated the amount of time it would take to get here.

"Did you get settled in over the weekend?"

"I sure did," I answer with a smile, thinking about how cute my place is. "Everything is unpacked and put exactly where I want it." Not where an interior designer or my mother would have put it.

"I bet that feels good."

"It really does." I make my way over to the register and prepare to take over for Jolene.

"You didn't bring a bag or anything?" She looks me over as if I might have one hidden somewhere.

"Nope. I just brought my phone and bank card." I gesture to my back pocket. "I figured that's all I'd need."

Jolene nods. "Okay. Well, if you want, you can secure them in that drawer there." She points to the one under the register. "And just hang onto the key for it until you're done."

"Okay, sure." I toss them into the drawer she mentioned and lock it. "Do you get much theft here?"

"Mmm, no, not really." She waves a hand in the air, as if dismissing the very notion. "But you'd be surprised at how many strangers we get in here. Either just passing through town or spending the day at the beach. Best to be safe."

"I didn't really think of that . . . people passing through to spend the day at the beach, that is. But it makes sense." I just hope it's not people who will cause trouble for me. It's my parents who are somewhat famous, anyway, not me, so maybe if I'm not around them, nobody will care about me anymore.

"You'll start to tell the difference between locals and strangers soon enough." She pats my shoulder as she passes me by. "I'll either be in the office or stocking shelves. If you need help with anything, just holler."

"Thanks, Jolene."

I hadn't worked a check-out before Friday night with Jolene. And even though I'm pretty confident I can handle it by myself now, the second she leaves me alone, I find myself running both thumbs over my fingers, anxiously waiting for customers to arrive.

The first person I serve is an elderly woman named Bertie, whom I met on Friday night. I remembered her name because she had told me how her husband's name was Bert, like hers, but that he often treated her like dirt. I wasn't really sure what to say to that except 'sorry'. She had just smiled, patted my hand, and said, "Don't worry, he's dead now." And then she left.

Regardless of that initial awkward moment, seeing the familiar face and having her tell me about what she plans on baking today calms any first-day nerves that I had instantly.

A few minutes after Bertie leaves, I see a cute little old man stepping toward the counter. Well, it's more like a shuffle that he's doing, hunched over and leaning heavily on a cane. I smile widely at him as he places two boxes of oatmeal in front of me.

"How are you doing today?"

"Well, I was going to go lift some weights at the gym after this, but I think I might skip it today." He adds a wink at the end, and I can't help but chuckle at him.

"Stop flirting with my new girl, Edgar," Jolene chides as she walks by.

"Oh, come now, Jo, don't be jealous," Edgar calls over his shoulder. "You know you can have a date with me whenever you like."

"Lucky me." Jolene shakes her head before disappearing down an aisle.

"She'll come around someday," Edgar says with another wink as he picks up his items. "Now, if anyone ever gives you trouble around here, you let me know, okay?"

I smile at him. "Sure. I'll keep that in mind."

The morning flies by even though it's not as busy as I was expecting it to be.

As a way of helping me remember people's names, I've tried to keep in mind something unique about them. Like Tim, the hardware store owner, has a really wide mouth. Luke, who works at the bank, has a big, bushy mustache to go with his bushy eyebrows. Wendy, the florist, has about five or six piercings in each ear. And so on.

When lunchtime comes around, I take my break in the office that has every available space, except for the desk and chair, used as storage, making sure to lock the door behind me as

Jolene instructed. The whole time is spent listening to another podcast while I eat a sandwich *I* made for myself, not some servant or maid.

When I get back from my break, Jolene is serving a girl wearing super short booty shorts, a baggy T-shirt, and has long red hair braided down her back. And although I'd never be caught wearing those shorts, they're kind of cute on her.

She's laughing at something Jolene said, but as soon as she sees me approach, she stands straighter and the laughter dies off.

"Jolene, you didn't tell me she was in the back office for her break. I would have gone in and said hello."

"You're not an employee here, so you can't just go back there, anyway."

The girl rolls her eyes. "I can't believe, after all this time, you're still a stickler for those types of rules."

"When you have your own store, you can make all your own rules. This one is mine."

"Yeah, I can't see me owning anything anytime soon." She shrugs.

Jolene turns to me. "Remi, this is Tahnee."

"Hi," I greet with a little wave.

Tahnee gives me a once-over. "You didn't tell me she was such a hottie, either, Jo-Jo." She leans on the counter and wiggles her eyebrows. "Hey. How you doin'?"

"Don't call me that," Jolene says to her. "And stop flirting with her. You're as bad as Edgar."

"Oh no, was he in here earlier?" Tahnee asks me with a chuckle.

I grin. "He was."

"Well, don't worry." Tahnee pushes up from the counter. "I was just joking around. I like meat in my taco, if you know what I mean."

"Oh geez, will you stop talking like that in here?" Jolene chastises while shaking her head and walking away. But you can see she's thoroughly entertained by it all.

I find myself laughing. "Yes. I think I know what you mean."

"Good, 'cause I can already tell we're going to be friends." Tahnee tosses a piece of paper in front of me. "Here's my number. Text me when you get a chance. Then I'll have yours, and we can hang out sometime."

I've never had a genuine friend before, but I can tell from this small interaction that Tahnee seems to be the real deal. And she's sweet, if not a little wild. And I like how upfront she appears to be, not like my old "friends."

"Okay. Sure, that sounds good."

"Talk later." She gives a small wave and then bounds out the door.

Shortly after my new friend leaves, I'm still smiling when a man walks through the door and goes straight for the rack closest to the check-out counter which holds all of your last-minute grabs. He's attractive in an older man type of way. I'd say he's about ten to fifteen years older than me, maybe even more, but very fit and healthy-looking.

When he places a single pack of gum in front of me, his brown eyes land on my face, and then they just stay there. He doesn't look away as I scan the gum, making me feel a little uncomfortable.

I've had plenty of people stare and watch me intently before. It comes with the territory of having "celebrity" parents. But there's something about the way he's doing it that seems odd. It's like he's studying or scrutinizing me or something, but not in a curious way. It feels almost slimy. He only looks away after I've told him the amount, and that's just so he can pull out a dollar bill from his wallet.

"What's your name?" he asks as he hands me the money.

This time, when I look at him, he's wearing a slight smile that gives off a completely different vibe than what I got from him a moment ago. The previous look is completely wiped off his face, which has me wondering if it wasn't all in my imagination.

I hesitantly answer, "Remi. I just moved here."

"Is that right? Well, it's nice to meet you, Remi."

"It's nice to meet you, too." I return his now friendly smile with my own. "And what's your name?"

"Grant. Grant Hubick."

"Nice to meet you, Grant." I hand him the gum—which seems kind of weird to be the only thing to come in here for—and then offer another friendly smile. "Enjoy the rest of your day."

"You, too, *Remi*."

The way he says my name and then holds my gaze a beat too long has those same weird feelings that I first had returning. I'll have to remember to ask Jolene about what his story is. Maybe there is something that will easily explain the oddness. He walks toward the door, does one final look over his shoulder, and then nods goodbye.

It's not until he's out of sight that it finally occurs to me that he might have seen my picture in a magazine or on the news at some point, and that's why he was looking at me so oddly. The realization has me wanting to slap my forehead for being such an idiot.

This place may be small and quiet, but it doesn't mean they don't follow any type of entertainment or business news. It's not like they're living under a rock.

I just hope that my whereabouts doesn't somehow make it back to my father. I don't think it will, but the thought is always there, lingering at the very back of my mind. It has me quickly scanning the magazines to see if there is any mention of my parents in them, but thankfully, there isn't.

A few minutes later, Jolene pokes her head around the end of the last aisle. "I'm just going to be restocking these veggies. If you're feeling comfortable, you can refill those drinks in the fridge." She bobs her head toward the line of fridges along the wall.

"Sure, no problem."

The afternoon continues at a steady pace, and in between serving customers, I restock the fridge. It's not exactly thrilling work, but it keeps me busy, and I enjoy chatting with my fellow townspeople. This is precisely what I was hoping for.

About an hour before my shift ends, an influx of people enter, keeping me stuck at check-out, and Jolene even has to come and help out at the second cash register opposite me until the line has gone down.

"Thanks for that," I say, taking a sip of my water bottle once I have a second.

Jolene waves me off. "No problem. That type of thing will happen here and there."

All of a sudden, when Jolene looks past me, her smile turns from pleasant and friendly to an icy glare that could freeze fire. I glance over my shoulder to see what could possibly inspire such a hostile look.

There's a woman about Jolene's age sifting through bags of chips at the end of an aisle, and I wonder if maybe they're fighting or something. I watch the woman for a moment, trying to see if there's any reciprocation of the clear hatred coming from Jolene. But the woman is happy in her own little world, searching for the right choice of flavored potato chips.

I'm still watching her when a guy comes into view, approaching my register. Even though he's wearing a hoodie, you can see that he's got some thick arms and wide shoulders underneath. His jeans sit low on his hips and fit snugly against his muscular thighs. When not covered, I bet his body is the type women would drool over.

It's not like I'm searching for a new guy at the moment or anything, but I could definitely enjoy spending some time staring at him. My body certainly likes what it sees.

His focus is down, and his hood is up, so I can't quite see his eyes. But I can see his nicely defined jaw, which is covered in a couple of days' worth of scruff. A muscle moves back and forth as if he's clenching or grinding his teeth.

Dirty blond hair peeks out from under his hood, and despite his rougher appearance, the strands look really soft. I have the weirdest desire to reach up and feel it for myself.

All the guys I've dated in the past have been *pretty*, never with a hair out of place. And they either wore suits or polo shirts with slacks. I realize now that I much prefer the more manly look, and I decide he's going to be my new eye candy while I get to know him.

Disappointment tries to sneak its way in like an unwelcome guest when I think of the possibility that he's just passing through town and won't be sticking around for me to enjoy.

He walks up and places his items down in front of me.

"Hello." I smile at him, but he's not even looking at me to see it.

Over his shoulder, I notice Jolene hasn't returned to stacking the shelves yet. She's there, staring daggers through the back of the head of the guy who is in front of me. Okay, I guess she isn't fighting with that woman, and this guy mustn't just be passing through town.

The way Jolene is glaring at him is like he's deeply offended her or something. She seems like such an easygoing person and I wonder what he could have possibly done to get on her bad side.

Maybe if I get him to speak, I'll find out that he's one of those douchey guys where nothing but shit comes out of their mouth, and you wish they'd never spoken.

"I'm Remi. I'm new in town."

Nothing. No acknowledgment. Just a shift of his feet. Well, I guess that's kind of asshole-ish behavior.

"Would you like a bag?"

A barely-there shake of the head is all the response I get. Well, if this is how he usually behaves, then I can see why Jolene might not like him. I happen to like surly, gruff people, though. I enjoy getting under their skin to see what's going on. There's almost always a reason for it.

And who knows, maybe he's just having a bad day? I've had plenty of those myself.

I total all of his items and give him the amount. "Are you sure you don't want any bags?" I ask while he pulls out his wallet. "It seems like a lot to carry."

The guy doesn't answer *again* but passes me the cash.

Okay then.

"Here's your change. Have a good afternoon," I tell the guy in my sweetest voice. Sometimes, layering on kindness is one way to get to them.

I watch as he starts picking up his packages and piles them onto one arm, my brows lifting higher with each item he adds. This guy seriously needs a bag. So, with one hand, I pick up his box of cereal while the other opens a plastic bag. But before I get the chance to put it in, the box is ripped out of my hand, and the guy is stalking out of the store.

"Uh, okay, see ya," I mumble to myself.

Jolene is still frowning after him when I turn my attention back to her, and then, to my complete surprise, she *spits* at him. Not actual spit with saliva, but the sound and action of it.

At my shocked face, she walks over to stand next to me. "You stay away from that man." She turns her head back toward the entrance. "He's on that sex offenders list. You know, that registry."

"What? Really?"

I join Jolene in looking out toward the man, who, up until a few minutes ago, I thought was simply a handsome jerk. Now I'm not so sure what to think. Registered sex offender? I guess that could be for any number of things, so maybe it's not as bad as I think.

The look on Jolene's face and her reaction does suggest otherwise, though.

As if sensing my thoughts, she says, "He's a rapist, Remi. They notified us all when he moved into town four months ago after being released from prison."

"Are you serious?"

I can feel my mouth hanging open. I'm surprised. Shocked. *Really* shocked, actually. How is it that he's allowed to live here in this lovely town? This beautiful, quiet place now seems tainted by his presence. My insides fill with revulsion, replacing all the lustful thoughts I had. So quickly, he turned into a despicable human being.

She nods. "We tried to get him out of here, talked to the sheriff and all that, but it didn't work. So now people just try to make his life miserable and hope he leaves on his own."

The guy approaches a pickup truck that I assume is his, pulls out a napkin from his pocket, and then uses it to open his truck door. Then he speeds out of the parking lot while Jolene and I stand here, still staring outside.

Chapter Three

Remi

After filling my mug to the brim with coffee, I stand out on my back deck, looking out at the ocean. I had a restless sleep last night after what Jolene had told me.

My mind just wouldn't shut off, replaying the encounter and everything Jolene said. Finally, after quite some time of tossing and turning, I ended up getting up and doing some reading on sex offenders and what they are required to do, whether they're allowed to live anywhere they want, that type of thing.

A lot of cases were different depending on the actual crime, but from what I gathered, he *is* allowed to live here, and they can't force him to leave. Unless, of course, he does the same thing again. It had me thinking all sorts of crazy things, like actually trying to get him to do it again. But then I felt sick at the thought.

At the very least, he has to be on the registry for ten years, and he would be on some sort of parole right now. I wonder if he has to check in with a parole officer on a regular basis? Jolene said that he had just been released from prison before he came here . . . I wonder how long he was in there? Did he only assault the one person? Does he regret it?

Damn, my curiosity.

I pour the remainder of my coffee into a travel mug and decide to start my walk to work a little earlier than yesterday so that I don't need to rush.

Now that people are getting to know me, I get random waves or honks as people drive by. People from my old life had done that as well, but for an entirely different reason. Here, it actually feels nice.

As I approach the end of the row of houses just before Main Street, I notice a SOLD sign hanging in the yard of one of the houses and immediately glance at the home out of curiosity.

An uneasy prickling sensation travels up the back of my neck when I see a dark figure standing in the window. It's too dark to make out anything other than the person is big enough to be a man, and they appear to be watching me.

My first thought is that it's *the guy* I found out about yesterday, the one who I thought way too much about all night. But I didn't really have any of *those* vibes from him in the store. Even looking back at our whole interaction, if you could call it that, there was nothing that had me feeling uneasy, just disgusted at the end after finding out what he did.

Facing forward, I pick up my speed, but then I shake my head at myself and slow my pace after a moment. I sneak a look back over my shoulder, and the window is now empty. The person was probably simply looking out at the street when I happened to walk by. I'm being silly, probably from lack of sleep and traces of paranoia remaining from the life I left.

The sun is already heating up my skin by the time I'm close to the store, and it's not even nine o'clock in the morning. A quick dip in the ocean and a walk along the beach this afternoon sounds like a really great idea.

Pulling out my phone as I cross the parking lot, I re-read the message I received from my mother this morning and contemplate replying. She was apparently completely shocked that I had actually left, despite me repeatedly saying that I wanted to.

Hesitantly, I click on her name and give her a quick call before I start work.

"Remi Jane Murdoch, what the hell kind of stunt do you think you are pulling?" she says by way of answering.

"Hi, Mom. Nice to talk to you, too." I look up at the sky and take a deep breath for strength. "I'm not pulling any type of stunt."

"After all we've done for you, you go and sneak off."

"I didn't just sneak off." Well, I guess, in a way, I kind of did. "I've been telling you for a long time that I was going to leave."

"Do you have any idea how bad this looks for us? You were meant to be with us for photos at the Matron, and you never showed. It was so embarrassing."

"I'm sorry, Mom."

"You're sorry? Sorry doesn't cut it . . ." She starts on about how I should be more considerate when it comes to her and Dad. How I shouldn't have left, and I have a responsibility to my family. I tune out most of it until she mentions getting my father to call me.

"Can't you just be happy for me that I'm happy? That I'm doing well here?"

"And where's 'here'?"

Of course, that's what she latches onto. Of course, she's more concerned with how it looks for her and Dad. But she's crazy if she thinks I'm actually going to tell her where I am. I bite down on my tongue to stop myself from saying anything I'll regret.

"Look, Mom, I have to go. I'm at work."

"Work?! Wh—"

I hang up before she can say anything more. She'd have an even bigger fit if she knew I was working at a store like this. I really shouldn't have said the word 'work' at all.

I shove my phone back into my pocket and try to do the same with the tension my mother has left in me as I step through the doors to the store.

Jolene greets me with a friendly smile, and all the crappy feelings I had tightening and squeezing my muscles drift away. People like her are the ones that I need in my life, people who are kind and loving and don't try to force me to live a life of unhappiness for their sake.

Yes. This is where I'm meant to be.

With a smile returning to my face, I head toward Jolene to start my shift.

The day is much like yesterday, with its busy and slow periods throughout, along with meeting new people, including a family that was just spending the day at the main beach area.

During one of the quiet times, I decide to find Jolene and ask her some more questions that have been bugging me about the guy from yesterday. I can't help it, my curiosity has the best of me.

She's stacking some pasta boxes on the shelf when I approach her. If she's not restocking something, then she's cleaning, always keeping busy.

"So, um," I start, then straighten some of the packages on the shelf in front of me. "That guy who was in here yesterday . . ." Her attention immediately swings to me. "You said he's been here for four months?"

"That's right."

"And he was in prison before that . . . Do you know for how long?"

Heavy creases form between her eyes, the subject of this guy clearly one that she does not like in the slightest. "Yes, that's right, he was, but I don't know for how long. Why do you want to know?"

I shrug. "I'm just curious, is all. Do you know if it—"

"Look," she snaps at me. "All you need to know is that he's dangerous, and you should stay away from him." Immediately, she lifts a hand to touch her chest and takes a deep breath. "I'm sorry. I guess it's just a touchy subject for me."

"It's okay, Jolene," I reply. Somehow, I know she wasn't getting upset with me. "I'm sorry for asking."

She fiddles with the boxes in her hand. "It happened to me, you know. What he did . . . when I was a teenager." She closes her eyes as if she's reliving it in her mind. "I was at a store, kind of like this one, and pushed into the office . . ."

"Oh, Jolene." I step closer, squeezing her shoulder. "I'm so sorry." That explains why she's adamant about locking the office door and not letting anyone else in.

She waves me off with a strained smile. "It's okay. It was a very long time ago. Just . . . just promise me you'll take care and stay away from him."

The fact that she's warning me away from him does little to quench my inquisitive nature. In fact, the rebel inside me wants to know him even more now that I'm warned away. And that's just messed up. Who wants to get to know someone who would do *that* to a woman?

No, it's not him *that I want to know,* I reason with myself. *But rather,* why *he did it.*

He's quite attractive from what I saw. So, was it just some sort of power trip for him?

I want to know.

To ease Jolene's mind, though, I answer, "Sure. I'll be careful."

This seems to placate her, and she returns to stacking the boxes again.

"Now, I know of a few good single men around here. What's your type?"

I laugh at her question despite her being completely serious. "I'm quite alright being single for now, thank you. But I'll let you know when I'm looking." I start to walk back toward the front counter again but stop after a few steps, turning around. "Just one last thing . . . What's his name?"

Her lips curl up in disgust again. "Jacob. Jacob Stark."

I nod and continue, repeating his name quietly. That kind of name belongs to a sweet guy, not a . . . well, I guess it doesn't matter. I won't be using it.

The weather has become almost unbearably hot when my shift is done. Sweat is practically dripping off me by the time I make it home, so I immediately change into a bathing suit and walk out onto my back deck toward the water. I *love* that my backyard is the beach.

The water feels nice, lapping against my feet, instantly cooling the inferno that was building inside me. Today, I push myself and make it to where the waves reach just above my waist before I chicken out and turn back.

As I dry myself, my gaze drifts to the little shack farther down the beach. I haven't really looked at it since the storm the other night, and now I notice there is also a dock there with a boat attached. I figure today is as good a day as any to take that walk and check it out.

That's yet another thing that I love about being here, away from my parents: having no schedule except for the one *I* set.

Throwing on my cover-up, I forgo any shoes and start my walk along the beach. The closer I get, the more I lean towards thinking it's not someone's home but just a fishing shack or something since it's so small.

There's one window and a door on the side facing me. And call me nosy, but I step onto the wooden path that runs along this side of the structure to see if I can look in the window.

Unfortunately, there's a curtain blocking my view of the inside. Do fishing shacks have curtains?

The wooden planks creak underneath me as I walk along the side of the shack toward the ocean. There's a slight breeze that sends strands of hair flying across my face as I walk. Once I push them back out of the way, the sight of someone standing in the water has me stopping, freezing mid-step just as I've turned the back corner of the shack.

It's not just anyone standing there, either. I'm almost certain it's Jacob Stark. He's the same build and height as him and has the same dirty blond hair that I saw peeking out of his hood.

Is this seriously *his* place? It must be.

Shit.

He's naked, too. Well, not naked; he's in boxer briefs, but otherwise naked.

Jacob is standing knee-deep in the water, with his head tipped back, looking up at the sky. His stance has the muscles in his back—that I had suspected were there when I saw him clothed—flexing in a tempting way, and I'm annoyed at myself for noticing them at all.

I force myself to look away from him and to the dock where the boat is attached, which is close to where he's standing. The boat is on the other side of the dock, so I can't see too much of it.

When my eyes drift back to him again, he's no longer looking up at the sky, but out at the ocean. His body, however, is slightly turned as if he's taking one final look before he's going to get out and walk this way. Shit, shit, shit.

I back up, quietly making my way back around the corner to the side of the house again. I'm suddenly very aware of my surroundings and how vulnerable I am. There is nothing else around here, no other houses or people.

No one would be able to hear me.

Is he on his way back up here right now?

I wouldn't want to find myself alone with him.

By the looks of the muscles I just saw piled onto his body, he'd have no problems holding me down and taking whatever he wanted.

A shiver runs through my body at the thought, and I decide it's time for me to get the hell out of here.

It's only now, as I go to leave, that I notice the camera high above the front door, almost hidden. Then, taking a closer look around, I notice another one about midway along the side of the shack, facing the direction I first came from. And another one above where I'm standing, facing the front door.

My eyes flick between the three as I walk slowly along the wooden planks, wondering what the hell he'd be using them for. As soon as it occurs to me that he'll know I was here, my heart starts pounding even harder against my ribcage. The thought doesn't scare me exactly, but rather, it pisses me off that he actually has me on camera.

Something that I have been avoiding.

It's one of the reasons for moving here in the first place.

Why does he need all of them? And from all the different angles? Maybe this is a way for him to scope out more victims.

Looking up into each of the cameras, I raise both hands and then flip him off, waving my finger in each one. You don't scare me, Jacob.

After that, I run off to the dunes and make my way back to my house as quickly as possible.

Chapter Four

Remi

I don't know whether it's a gift or a curse, but no matter what happens or who's at fault in a fight, I have this deep-seated need to apologize right away. To make things right. I'm always the one to reach out and say sorry first, even if I have nothing to be sorry about. I can't help it.

It's the reason I sent a text to my mom and apologized for leaving without saying goodbye.

And it's the reason why I still feel bad a week later, after flipping Jacob off on those damn cameras. It's so stupid, really. But whether he deserved it, I shouldn't have done it. I'm better than that.

I still don't think much of him as a human, but as I've said before, I'm a big believer in second chances, even for people like *him*.

Maybe he really is trying hard to turn his life around. And dammit, I'm still so curious about him.

A thunk on the counter behind me rips me from my daydreaming and absent staring out into the parking lot. And, *of course,* it would be *him*. I didn't even see him enter the store. It must have been when I was busy refilling some end shelves a few minutes ago.

Even though it would have been clear as day that it was me on the cameras, *and* I've been feeling bad about it and felt like I should apologize, I now decide to act as if nothing has happened at all. I blame it on the fact that I wasn't expecting to see him right this second and wasn't prepared to face him. If he mentions anything, I'll apologize.

"Would you like a bag?"

His answer is pretty much the same as last time: a barely-there shake of the head. There is no acknowledgment or indication whatsoever that he saw me on the cameras.

Maybe I was wrong about them?

Maybe they're just for show?

Or maybe he just hasn't looked yet?

He picks up his items, and before he walks away, at the very last second, his eyes flick to mine for the briefest moment. It's the first time he's made eye contact, the first time I've actually seen his eyes, and I have to say, I'm a little thrown off.

They're stormy blue-gray wonders that kind of surprise you if you're not expecting them. And I really wasn't.

It makes me wonder how I didn't notice them last time, even though he wasn't looking right at me. I guess they were pretty hidden under his hood. But today, he's only got on a ball cap.

It's pretty unfair that he'd be given such beautiful eyes. They're completely wasted on someone like him. His whole body is, really.

I watch as he walks toward his truck, frowning after him as if he'll be able to sense my disapproval of him. Once he gets to it, he pulls out a napkin and then uses it to open the door. That is so weird. He did that the last time as well.

Maybe he's a germaphobe or something? Then again, he touches things in here, and he handles money, so that doesn't really make sense. I hate to admit it, but it's just one more thing that has me curious about him.

When my shift ends, I agree to meet Tahnee at the juice stand in the middle of town. It's about a five-minute walk from the store. We've texted each other a few times back and forth over the past week, and she has also come to visit me at the store, so I've been getting to know her more.

The sound of crunching rocks beside me catches my attention about halfway through my walk.

"Need a ride?"

I turn to see Grant leaning out of his car window, waiting for my reply.

"Oh. No, that's okay, thank you."

"You sure? I'm heading in that direction." He nods down the road ahead of us.

I could be heading in any number of directions, really. Still, it's nice of him to offer, and his smile is friendly this time, so I return one. "Thanks. But I like the exercise."

"I can appreciate that." He looks me up and down. "You're in fine shape either way, though."

With that, he pulls back onto the road and drives off. I'm still not really sure what to make of that guy. I keep forgetting to ask Jolene about him.

Before I can think too much more about it, I spot Tahnee sitting on one of the picnic tables by the juice stand down the street.

Her bright red hair and bright white legs stand out against her surroundings, making me smile. Whether she's considered *out there* or not, it's nice to have a truly genuine and funny friend who doesn't want anything from me.

As soon as I'm a little closer and she sees me, she stands up and cups her hands around her mouth. "Hey, sexy! Get that fine ass over here!"

Her words have me literally tripping over myself and falling to the ground. Actually, it was the big rock I didn't see that had me tripping because I was busy chuckling at her silliness. Thankfully, I don't land on my face, but I do skid along on my hands and stomach.

I can hear Tahnee's, "Oh my goodness," followed by her laughter that she's clearly trying to contain. I laugh, too, despite being slightly embarrassed and the slight sting on my hands.

I look around the area while I'm still on the ground to see if anyone noticed me fall, and much to my dismay, I see a familiar truck close by and a pair of legs standing next to it. Attached to those legs is Jacob, of course, and he's wearing his usual scowl as he looks at me on the ground.

Any normal person would ask if I was okay or try to help me up. Not him, though. After another beat of him glowering at me, he pulls another napkin from his pocket and opens his truck door with it before getting in.

What is with the napkins all the time?

Tahnee arrives as I get to my feet and start dusting myself off. "I'm so sorry," she manages to get out between giggles.

"That's okay," I answer, distracted.

She nods when she notices me watching Jacob drive off and disappear around the corner. "Yeah. Don't ever expect any help from him. He doesn't do that sort of thing. Doesn't talk to anyone, either, and that's just fine by us."

For some reason, I actually feel sorry for him about that. It must be an incredibly lonely existence—having no one to talk to.

I've kind of been in that situation for most of my life, except with me, it was just being surrounded by fakes and parents who never had normal conversations with me. I wasn't living in a town full of people who hated me.

It makes me wonder if his parents talk to him at all.

"I noticed that he always seems to use a napkin to open his truck door," I mention as we start walking toward the picnic tables together. "Do you know what that's about?"

"Oh." Tahnee starts chuckling to herself. "His handle tends to get covered in spit every time he's around here. I guess he's more prepared for it now."

Spit? Every time? God, that's *horrible*.

She starts giggling again, but all I can think about is how bad I feel for the guy. And that's stupid, isn't it? Me feeling bad for him? I mean, he did something terrible, and now he has to pay for it. Right?

Only . . . he did pay for it already, didn't he? He spent time in fucking prison, and now he has no friends here as far as I can tell.

Will he be punished forever?

He hasn't proven to be a repeat offender.

Yet, I remind myself.

I keep wondering if I would feel even half as bad as I do if he were an older, sleazy-looking guy rather than the handsome young guy with a nice body and beautiful eyes. Truthfully, I know the answer is probably *no*, I most likely wouldn't feel bad.

I doubt I'd be one of those people spitting on his door handle, but I'd definitely make sure to avoid him at all costs.

And that's the opposite of what I find myself wanting to do with Jacob now, which is, weirdly enough, maybe becoming his friend. It feels wrong and dirty, and it's against what anyone else would probably feel or want to do. But I can't help it.

I drift back into the present and realize that I've missed most of what Tahnee has been saying, but from what she's talking about now, it appears to have just been about the drinks from the juice stand.

Since I do actually want to keep our friendship, I make more of an effort to pay attention to her. And I decide not to ask her anything more about Jacob.

Instead, she tells me about growing up in a nearby town, how she moved here during her senior year, and how hard it was for her at first.

Even though my initial intentions were to keep quiet about my family, I find that I trust Tahnee and want to talk to her about them. I tell her my story about growing up with the parents I have and why I'm here now.

"So, you're kind of famous? Does that mean I have to treat you differently?" She wrinkles her nose. "'Cause I don't really want to."

I can't help but laugh at her candidness. She's such a breath of fresh air, and I love it.

"Please don't treat me differently," I reply. "Besides, it's my parents who are, not me. And I wouldn't even call them *famous*-famous, just well-known."

We grab our juices and then sit at the table she was sitting on earlier.

"Well, I guess that explains how you were able to afford the house you're in." Tahnee slurps at her juice loudly and then swallows. "It may be small, but that bitch is right on the beach."

I smile, thinking about my cute little home. "Yep."

She tilts her head to the side in a thoughtful way. "But why are you working at *Peaches*?"

I place my drink down next to me and shrug. "I didn't want to sit on my ass all day. And I figured it was a good place to meet people." I absentmindedly pick at the chipped paint on the table. "Plus, Jolene is super nice."

"Oh, Jolene is a hoot. Especially after she gets a drink or two in her."

I let out an amused sound and take in that extra piece of information, storing it with all the other things I've learned about her so far. "I'll have to remember that."

"But seriously," Tahnee adds. "If you want to meet people, you should come work with me at *The Big Five*. No better place to meet people than at a bar."

"Nah. I'm good, thanks." I take another sip of my drink. "What does the name stand for, anyway?"

"Fuck if I know. I've tried figuring it out, but no one there knows, either. Not even the owner. Guess it already had the name when he bought it." She smirks, shaking her head as if she just thought of something dirty. "Anyway, you're liking it here so far?"

"I am," I say with a contented sigh, and then continue asking her some more questions.

We spend the afternoon chatting, and by the time I get home, the sun is just starting its descent. I make myself some easy pasta for dinner and take it and some wine outside to eat on the deck, watching the steady flow of waves coming in on a rhythm only the ocean knows.

Eventually, my eyes drift down the beach to the lonely shack that stands by itself. The plume of smoke and orange flicker tells me he might be having a bonfire or something on the beach beside his place. I swallow down a large mouthful of wine and hum while leaning my head back on the chair.

"What is your story, Jacob?"

Chapter Five

Remi

I tried talking myself out of this numerous times. Even now, as the waves push against my ankles, I keep telling myself to turn around and go back.

I don't listen, of course.

Instead, I just pretend that all I'm doing is taking a nice, leisurely walk along the beach . . . in the direction of Jacob's house.

Actually, now that I think about it, it may not even be *his* place. It could have been by complete coincidence that he was swimming in the water in front of it, in his underwear.

"That's so true," I mumble, trying to fool myself.

Even so, I continue walking in the shallow water in the direction of the shack and keep my eyes focused solely on the water. If someone *were* to be looking through those cameras, it would appear like I'm simply enjoying a walk in the water and sunshine.

When I'm practically in front of the shack and next to the dock, I have no choice but to stop walking. Then, as nonchalantly as possible, I turn my head to look around the area as if I have no idea where I've ended up.

From a quick sweep of the area, I can see remnants of a bonfire on the beach. There's another camera on the wall of the house facing the beach... *facing me.* And on the other side of the house is an empty driveway—there is no pickup truck in sight, thank goodness—and a little shed.

Attached to the end of the dock beside me is a boat, and I can't help but wonder if it's his as well. Even though I said it may not have been *his* place, I'm almost certain it is.

Before I can talk myself out of it—oh, who am I kidding, I wouldn't be able to stop myself if I wanted to—I step out of the water and make my way onto the wooden dock. It looks old but is still in good condition.

I start creeping along the wooden structure, treading lightly and quietly as if I'm not actually being filmed in broad daylight on the cameras, *again,* looking a lot like Edgar, the little old man with his cane, the way I'm hunched over.

There don't seem to be any signs that say 'no trespassing' or 'private property' around, so that means fair game, right? Public property?

With that thought in mind, I stand up straighter and continue walking down toward the boat like a normal person.

Grace is written in bold letters along the side of the boat. I wonder if he named it that. Or was it already named when he got it?

After taking another look back toward his house and seeing no signs of life, and no truck, I decide to step onto the boat. This is probably a bad idea. I know *this* isn't public property.

It still doesn't seem to stop me, though.

Nets, fishing rods, reels, buckets, and other fishing gear are neatly stored around the, uh, whatever the boat's main area is called. Obviously, it's primarily a fishing boat rather than a luxurious, cruising-around-on-the-water-and-relaxing type of boat.

I do one lap of the area above before descending the narrow stairs that lead into the cabin—I know that name, at least.

Luckily for me, the door at the bottom of the stairs is open. Slowly, I step into the little room and release a long, steady breath, trying to slow down my heavily beating heart. Besides the guilt, there is a certain thrill about what I'm doing right now.

This is new for me: entering someone else's property to snoop, and I blame my obsession with certain podcasts lately.

I thought about becoming a private investigator at one point, but then thought better of it. It would require a lot more schooling, plus it's not something my father would have ever approved of—not that he approves of what I've done now by leaving.

Turning back to my current illegal activities, I notice there's not a whole lot of stuff down here as I look around; a small bed that is neatly made sits on one side, while the other side has drawers and shelves with a small TV attached to it, and a . . . what is that? A PS3? Kind of old school.

There's also a map of the coast and a couple of old-looking photos on the wall. I take a step closer to get a better look, immediately recognizing Jacob and his beautiful eyes in the photos.

He's younger-looking and definitely not as muscular and rough around the edges as he is now—that's probably from prison. He looks like he's at that in-between stage where he no longer looks like a teenager, but is not quite a man.

In one photo, he's standing with an older man and woman in front of some furniture store. I'm going to assume they're his parents, since they share similar features.

I wonder if he still talks to them at all.

Did they visit him in prison?

What must they think of him now?

The other picture is of him and four other guys around the same age. They're all laughing, and Jacob is pretending to punch the guy next to him. He looks so happy and carefree.

What the hell happened to you, Jacob?

Well, if I needed more confirmation that this was his boat, these photos are it.

Since I'm already here, I decide to make the most of my criminal behavior and start opening the drawers and cupboards.

Do I feel bad about invading his privacy? Absolutely.

But does it stop me? Absolutely not.

There's not much of interest in the cupboards, just some food items and bits and pieces. The drawers mostly have clothes in them, but when I get to the last one, I find a stationary type of tray with some newspaper clippings in it.

Dropping to my knees, I start reading some of the headlines.

"TEEN CHARGED WITH RAPING 17-YEAR-OLD CLASSMATE"

"ALL EVIDENCE POINTS TO JACOB STARK"

"PARENT'S OUTRAGE OVER LATEST ATTACK AGAINST HIGH SCHOOL STUDENT"

"VICTIM IDENTIFIES JACOB AS ATTACKER IN LINE-UP"

"JACOB STARK PLEADS 'NOT-GUILTY'"

"VICTIM'S PARENTS SEEK JUSTICE"

"LAWYER IN RAPE CASE SAYS 'NOT ENOUGH EVIDENCE'"

I scan over some of the articles, feeling sicker to my stomach as I go.

"Parents of Jacob Stark, who once described him as a good, sweet kid, now shocked and disgusted by his actions."

"Many can't believe he would do this."

"Close friends say Jacob has liked victim, Jennifer Lapmor, for years and that he made threats pertaining to her on the night of the incident."

My gaze flicks back up to the wall at the photos. Something tells me that he doesn't speak to any one of them anymore—or rather, *they* don't speak to *him*.

A clunk and then a scuffle from above me on the boat has me letting out a yelp and throwing the clippings back into the drawer before slamming it shut and scurrying back on the floor.

Shit, shit, shit!

I restlessly run my thumbs over my fingertips while looking around me for a possible hiding spot, but come up empty. There's absolutely no place I can remain hidden down here.

What the hell was I thinking coming onto his boat?

There are a few more sounds from above, and then the motor starts.

Oh my god, I'm going to be trapped on a boat with him out on the ocean.

Before I think too closely about the fact that it's not exactly fear that I feel, I realize we haven't moved yet, so maybe there's a chance I can bolt up the stairs and jump onto the dock before he takes off. At this point, I'm willing to try, regardless of whether he sees me or not.

Blowing out a flustered breath, I get to my feet. Adrenaline begins filling my veins, urging me to move.

"Okay," I murmur to myself.

I start running for the stairs, climbing the narrow, steep steps as quickly as I can.

But I'm too late.

By the time I reach the top step, the boat is moving away from the dock.

"No!" My whisper-shout is swallowed up by the sound of the motor as I reach the 'back' of the boat.

The water churns and swishes behind it, and I lean over, briefly considering jumping in despite not being able to swim. But even just the thought of it has panic rising from the pit of my stomach.

Nope.

I'm not doing that.

We hit a wave or something, causing the boat to jerk, almost tossing me over the edge. Thankfully, I have a death grip on the railing and hang on for dear life. As soon as it's steadier, I push away from the edge and back up.

The next thing I know, I'm kicking something with the heel of my foot and falling backward onto the ground with a cry.

"Geez. Fuck!" A male's voice comes from somewhere.

I turn my head, still lying on the ground, and sure enough, there's Jacob, standing by the wheel, his cap backward and no shirt on with a confused frown on his face.

Within a second, I'm shuffling myself farther away from him, and he's cutting the motor and moving to the other side of the wheel.

"What the fuck are you doing on my boat?"

He rubs the back of his neck and glances around as if he's looking for anybody else who might be hiding on here as well.

Don't bother. It's just you and me out here.

"Well?" he prompts when I don't answer.

I go for a half-true answer. "Uh. I was just curious and wanted to check it out."

The hand rubbing his neck drops down to his side, drawing my attention to his naked torso that's on display. Somehow, I knew he'd have ink somewhere on his body. There's some kind of pattern on his forearm, as well as a Valkyrie across his chest—which is well-defined, by the way. I can't help but think of the amount of work that has gone into making such a nice form.

I internally shake my head and berate myself. It's definitely wrong to A) admire *his* body, and B) admire his body while in this situation. I pull my eyes away from him and notice the fishing rod perched against the side of the wheel. Clearly, I've interrupted a fishing trip of some sort.

"You were curious?" he asks.

There's irritation in his voice, and I almost want to say, *"Look, you think I want to be stuck on a boat with you? I only came on here because you weren't on here."*

But what I blurt out is, "Were you planning on doing some fishing?"

A muscled arm, the one with the tattoo, reaches up, and he rubs a hand over his face in agitation. "I don't need this shit."

It's when he eyes the steering wheel and then looks back at me that I realize he placed it between us and hasn't moved an inch closer. In fact, he almost looks hesitant to do so. That seems kind of weird, doesn't it? Or maybe it's a rule for him now?

"Do you have to stay a certain distance away from women now or something?"

He throws another scowl my way and then moves around the steering wheel to start the motor again, not bothering to reply to me. So, I guess that answers that.

Well, if there ever were a good time to ask him some questions, it would be now before we make it back, while he can't walk away from me.

For some reason, I'm not afraid of him. I can't tell if that's extremely naïve of me, or just plain stupid. But I went from being disgusted to intrigued and then feeling sorry for him.

I still feel all those things, but they're all coming together in some kind of confusing mixture that almost has me obsessing over him and needing to understand him.

We're not that far away from the dock, so I launch into my questions right away.

"So, you've lived here for four months?"

Jacob doesn't answer, but he does half glance over his shoulder, so I know he heard me. He turns the boat around, and we start toward the dock.

I try another question. "How long were you in prison for?"

Still no answer. The clippings he has in the drawer come to mind, and I think about the poor girl and what she must have gone through.

What was high school like for her after that happened?

Was she even able to finish?

The feelings of anger and disgust push their way back to the number one spot, and I glare at the back of his head. "What made you do it?"

I notice his back tense, but apart from that, I get nothing.

"Did it make you feel powerful, huh?" My voice raises the more worked up I get. "You liked her, didn't you? Did you just get sick of her saying 'no' to you or something? Get sick of waiting?"

The next thing I know, he's putting the boat in reverse and then cuts the motor before turning around, looking super pissed. In a low, menacing voice, he says, "Get the *fuck* off my boat."

Even I know I went a little too far with those questions and have obviously hit a nerve. I do actually feel bad about that.

Looking at where he's pointing, I see we're floating alongside the dock. We haven't quite come to a complete stop, but we're pretty close to it.

I lift myself off the ground where I had been sitting since falling backward and slowly walk over to the side where I'll need to climb off.

But it doesn't feel right to leave like this. Looking back over my shoulder, I see that Jacob is now staring at the ground, looking forlorn. Shit, I should apologize to him.

"Look, I'm sorry for what I—"

"*Off,*" he growls.

Well, it doesn't look like he's in the mood to hear anything more from me, so I step up onto the bench chair along the side, ready to hop across. But, instead of gracefully stepping up onto the dock, I move in the most awkward way possible, causing the boat to shift away from the dock.

And down I go into the ocean with a scream.

The panic is immediate when I hit the water, slithering up and curling its way around my chest and throat. I start flailing my arms, desperately trying to keep my head above water, but I only end up swallowing some seawater and choking, letting out a gurgled, "Help."

I'm vaguely aware of Jacob leaning over the boat's edge several feet above me. But in my mind, he's miles away and I'm all alone.

"You can't swim?" I don't answer him, as I'm too busy trying not to drown, with very little success. My head is under the water more than it is above it. "Grab hold of the life preserver!"

I hear him, I do. But he may as well be speaking another language because, right now, I'm too far gone. The sheer terror that I'm about to die has taken over, and it's removing all logical thoughts from my brain.

I feel like I'm kicking and thrashing as much as I can, but my movements are uncoordinated, all over the place, achieving nothing. I can hardly keep my head above water, let alone move toward a life preserver.

"Shit."

That's the last thing I hear before I feel myself sink too much. It feels like I've been struggling for hours, not minutes, or in reality, probably seconds. My arms are tired, and it feels like they're strapped with weights. My lungs burn from not enough air, and I don't have enough energy to keep fighting.

This is it. I'm done.

As soon as I stop moving my arms and legs, I sink deeper into the cold darkness. I've heard you're supposed to have some sort of life-flashing-before-your-eyes moment right before you die, but right now, all I can think about is how useless mine has been. I haven't made a difference in anyone's life.

Before I can delve further into how depressing those thoughts are, I'm being hoisted up above the water by a strong body. Jacob's arm is wrapped securely around my waist, holding me up, while his other arm slices through the water, pulling us toward the ladder on the other side of the dock. I splutter and cough, sucking in lungfuls of air.

He lifts me up onto the ladder, placing my arms over the rungs, still holding on to me from behind.

"You got this?"

"Y-yes," I answer, even though I don't know if I do. My arms kind of feel like jelly right now.

With a sigh, Jacob ends up climbing the ladder somehow while still holding me. I guess he figured I wasn't in any shape to pull myself up, for which I'm thankful. As soon as we reach the top, though, he drops me onto the sturdy wood and steps away, bending at the waist and breathing deeply.

"You good?" he asks, barely looking at me.

I nod my head, still trying to calm myself down.

I can breathe.

I'm not in the water.

He saved me.

"Thank you," I tell him, just above a whisper.

But I'm not sure if he even heard me because he's already jumping back onto his boat.

He starts the motor, turns it around, and takes off, leaving me in a pile of wet mess.

Chapter Six

Jacob

I lean back into the disgusting chair, placing one ankle on top of the opposite knee and making damn sure not to touch the armrests with my hands. For some reason, this chair is always filthy. I can only conclude that it's done purposefully to further degrade the person sitting in it. We are filth, after all, the scum of society.

How many times have I been told that over the past several years? And not even just from people like the guy in front of me, but from men who had actually *ended* other people's lives. To men who had no problem slicing someone open and watching them bleed out, *I* was the scum.

My gaze never leaves the man sitting across from me. I've already seen the shelves packed full of folders and papers. I've already seen the family photo on the wall with his wife's face covered with a picture of some exotic destination. I've already seen the certificates and bullshit with his name *Maxwell Myers* on them all over the wall.

The asshole takes his fucking time on purpose, stirring his coffee and then taking a long sip of it. Then, after placing the mug down, he leans forward, clasping his hands together above my file, in what is probably supposed to be an intimidating pose.

"You know the drill. Answer the questions truthfully, and then we can both get on with our fucking days." He doesn't bother waiting for a reply, though I wasn't going to give one, anyway. Instead, he picks up a sheet of paper and starts. "Have you been in close contact with any woman?"

"No." My answer comes out immediately, even though my first thought was of the boat incident and how I had my hands all over a beautiful woman while helping her out of the water. No way in hell am I telling him about *that*, though. It was a one-time thing, and I doubt she'll be talking about it with other people.

At least, I hope she won't.

"Have you been alone with a woman?"

"No." Isn't that pretty much the same as the first question?

"Have you been in contact with Jennifer Lapmor?"

"Fuck no."

"A simple 'no' will do."

"*No*," I grit out.

"Have you applied for work anywhere?"

"I have work already." The truth is, it's barely enough to keep me fed most weeks.

"Going fishing every day is hardly work."

"No one else will hire me."

"Well, you should have fuckin' thought about that before, shouldn't you?" he barks.

I clench my jaw so hard it hurts. I'm surprised I haven't ground my molars down completely by this point. It's the same type of shit he says every time I come here. I'm better off just keeping my mouth shut.

We continue with the stupid fucking questions until he's gotten all the information he needs, and my head is pounding from the base of my skull with a tension headache.

"So, you still need to come in monthly until—"

"I know."

"—the six-month mark. And then we'll reassess everything," he continues as if I never spoke, and like he hasn't said the same damn thing to me every time I've come. "Alright, now get the fuck out of here."

No problem. I get to my feet and step out of the tiny space my parole officer calls an office, not bothering to say goodbye. I want nothing more than to be done with this shit.

As soon as I get to my truck, I pull out a napkin and open my door. It looks fine this time, but I can never be too sure what's underneath the handle, and I don't have time to check.

I jump in and haul ass in the direction of the fish market. I was meant to stop there *before* my meeting, but one of my tires was flat again.

After the first two times it happened over the past couple of months, *and* after checking the cameras, I realized I didn't just buy a bunch of shitty tires, but rather, the 'welcoming' committee of this town was still 'welcoming' me with slashed tires.

Luckily, I picked up a few extra ones last month for cheap and was able to change it right away. But the delay meant that the cooler with fish and ice in the back of my truck had to sit longer than I wanted. The fish will be okay, but Ting, on the other hand, is always pissy later in the day.

I throw my cap on and then carry the heavy cooler down the aisles to where my usual guy is. If people are talking and pointing at me along the way, I don't hear it in this huge market. Many of these people aren't even from the same town as me, but news travels far and wide, especially about people like me.

Taking a quick glance around, I set the cooler down behind his tables and open it up. There are no greetings; we're not friends. He just leans down and takes out one of the striped basses, inspecting it thoroughly.

"I give you four dollar a pound."

"Four dollars? Come on, Ting, you're killing me."

Big commercial boats can bring in tons of fish. A single fisherman—actually, *fisherman* is a bit of a stretch—with not all the right equipment, only brings in a couple of fish each time, and this time it's after a few days of fishing.

"You take or leave."

Frustrated, I rub a hand down my face. "Fine, okay."

I don't exactly have any other options right now.

Ting takes the fish I brought in over to the weighing station, calculates the total, and then writes me a check.

"Thanks," I mutter, lifting the cooler that now only contains ice and water, ready to head home.

When he's in a good mood, he's offered as much as eight dollars a pound. Half of that won't get me very far, especially from just the two fish, but I'll have to deal with it.

I have the perfect view of the dock and my boat when I pull up to my place and park in the driveway. Immediately, I'm feeling like shit again. Although, admittedly, I've felt like shit ever since I was an asshole and ditched Remi on the dock, taking off right after she almost drowned.

Yeah, I remember her name from when she first told me at the store. It was the first time anyone had been nice to me in *years*. Obviously, she hadn't heard about me yet.

But of course, I was a dick to her. It was only a matter of time before everyone in town told her about me, so there was no point in being nice.

There's no point in trying to make friends here, anyway. They've all made up their minds about me. And even if I did make a friend, they'd just fuck right off when I needed them the most, anyway.

Being near an attractive woman is also asking for trouble, especially one as attractive as Remi. I remember what it felt like to hold her wet body against mine yesterday. I remembered in the shower last night when I took my dick in my hand and then again in bed. I'm obviously a sick fuck if I get hard over remembering the feel of her skin while I was rescuing her. It's messed up behavior.

It's not long after all those thoughts that I also remember the fact that she trespassed onto my property and all those questions she asked me like she had any fucking right to. Then I'm pissed all over again.

Still, it doesn't stop me from feeling like shit about it all, the weight of my actions sits heavily on my chest, and for some reason, I'd like to know that she's all right. And that just pisses me off even more.

Shoving my truck door open, I push away all those thoughts with it and stalk inside my home to find some painkillers. My head is throbbing, and I really should head back out on the boat again this evening.

I swallow down a couple of pills and stand at the kitchen counter, looking around the room. My place is small and has minimalistic furnishing, but it's all I need. One couch, one armchair, a coffee table, and a small round table with two chairs all sit in one room beside the kitchen. And then there's a separate bedroom and bathroom.

Feeling hungry, I decide to search the not-so-full cupboard for something to eat, settling on some cereal when I don't see anything else. After pouring some into a bowl, I head to the fridge for some milk, only to be met with an almost empty carton—definitely not enough for my cereal.

"That's just great," I mutter.

I had told myself yesterday that I'd get some today, and now I'm paying for it. The sound of me slamming the fridge door shut echoes loudly throughout the small space.

"Screw it."

I wasn't going to go into town today after already being out, but it looks like I'll be finding out if Remi is okay after all.

My head hits the headrest with a thump, and I curse out loud when I pull into the parking lot and notice how full it is.

Just what I need: a store full of people. I pick one of the only available parking spots by the entrance and jump out.

There's a long line at the check-out, so Remi doesn't see me when I first enter. Everyone else does, though. The entire atmosphere in here changes in an instant, like a vacuum sucked out all the cheerful conversations and laughter, leaving a quiet void. The chattering ends and glares filled with hatred come out.

Remi must notice the change around her because she looks up, and our eyes lock for a moment. She doesn't have the same expression as everyone else, though, and it kind of annoys me. I'd much rather her hate me just like the rest of them. It'd be easier to deal with.

I look away and continue to get my milk, ignoring every hushed whisper filled with venom along the way.

But, of course, with the way today has gone, I'm not surprised when I see Jolene, the store owner, restocking the very milk I need to get. There's no way she's going to make it easy on me by handing me one. I think she would rather see me starve to death than help me out in any way.

Seeing as she's almost done filling the shelf, I decide to stand off to the side and wait. I'm sure if she had noticed me standing here sooner, she'd have taken her time, but a few minutes later, she's finished and stacking the crates onto a trolley.

The scowl she graces me with as she passes me is lethal, but I just stare right back as if I'm looking right through her. It probably pisses her off even more so to think she has no effect on me.

There are four people in line when I make it to the check-out with my one carton of milk, and I don't miss the not-so-subtle step away from me when I get in line. The same type of shit has been happening since the people here found out about me.

Zoning out, I ignore everything around me until I'm next in line at the check-out. From a quick glance under my cap, Remi looks to be okay. And as much as I want to just leave it at that, the fucking guilt festering inside me won't allow it.

My throat almost burns when I clear my throat and force out the words, "You okay?"

I don't say anything more than that, but she must get what I'm talking about because she answers quietly, "Yeah. Thanks."

A head nod is all the acknowledgment I give back to her. She's fine. Now I can finally stop thinking about it, and hopefully, the little pricks of guilt will go away.

"That's two-fifty-two," she tells me after scanning the milk.

I pull out my wallet, but besides the check that I haven't cashed yet, there are only two measly dollar bills in there.

"Shit."

I feel around in my pockets for any loose change that I may have forgotten about, even though it's highly unlikely. Every cent is precious these days.

When I come up empty, I rub at the back of my neck, trying to relieve some of the tension.

Just fucking great.

Remi must read my face because, just as I go to pick up the carton to put back, she says, "It's okay." Then she reaches into her back pocket and pulls out another dollar, adding it to the ones I already gave.

What's more, she even tries to give me the change. I shake my head, mumble out a 'thanks,' and go to leave with my milk as quickly as possible.

Before I even get a few steps away, she calls out to me, "Jacob."

It's weird hearing my name said in a manner that isn't pure disgust. I turn back to face her, but almost wish I hadn't. I realize now that she wasn't saying my name with disgust because she was saying it with pity.

In her outstretched hand is a handful of tissues. From where she's standing, she has a clear view of my truck. She would have seen what they must have done to it. If I didn't actually forget to grab a napkin when I got out of my truck this time, I'd just ignore her and turn around and leave. But because today keeps getting shittier and shittier, I *did* forget.

I snatch the tissues out of her hand, well aware I'm still being an asshole, and get the hell out of there.

The day isn't done messing with me yet, though. After walking a few feet out of the store, a little boy comes running around the corner, tripping right in front of me. He looks to be maybe three or four, and the tears are instant.

Normally, I'd ignore him and keep going—nothing good ever comes from helping people, and this could get me into trouble. But just like yesterday, there is no one else around to help him, and dammit, I feel bad for him. So, I crouch down and offer my hand.

"You okay, buddy?" He grabs my hand instantly, pulling himself up. Snot and tears cover his face, and the sight of it has my insides twisting up. I don't like seeing it. "Hey, it's okay. You're a tough guy, right?" I ask.

When he stops crying and cracks the tiniest smile, I *almost* do, too. He's too young to be tainted by stories about me. Too young to form opinions on what I must be like. I give him one of the tissues Remi gave me, and he takes it without a care.

Whatever good feelings I had are gone in the next second when the mother—presumably—walks around the corner of the building.

"You get the hell away from him!" she shrieks, her voice high and shrill. Then she rushes to pull him away as if I was physically assaulting him right here on the sidewalk.

I'm once again reminded about why I don't bother. I get to my feet, turn away and walk to my truck, then use the remaining tissues to open the door before speeding back to the safety of my home.

If I had any alcohol, I might consider drowning in a bottle tonight, numbing myself to the extent that this cruel existence I find myself in no longer has its claws sinking into me in a deathly grip. But I guess the option of just plain drowning is still there.

Chapter Seven

Remi

After stepping out onto my deck and closing the door behind me, I switch the bag of goods into my other hand and set out in the direction of Jacob's shack. This time, with better intentions.

I've wrestled with the decision to do this ever since he came into the store the other day. I ended up deciding to bring him something as both a 'thank you' for saving me and a 'sorry' for trespassing onto his boat.

Sure, I had been a little upset that he took off and left me when I had almost died. But when he asked if I was okay the next day when he came into the store, I could tell it had bothered him as well or, at least, been on his mind. His eyes held a hint of concern that he couldn't hide even if he tried.

Seeing people spitting on his truck handle while he was in the store had actually been painful to watch, too. I had felt so bad for him. Add in the interaction between him and the kid outside, and now I've been feeling even more confused about him than I already had been.

This time, I walk up along the dunes in the softer sand away from the water, and the closer I get to his place, the faster my heart beats.

I keep wondering if I'm doing these things—breaking into his boat and going to see him today—because I want to see for myself what he's really like.

Am I somehow subconsciously trying to tempt him or provoke him just to get him to act in a way that justifies everyone's behavior toward him?

If I saw him as a monster, then I could stop feeling sorry for him, and the confusing feelings would go away.

It's probably partly true, but I also happen to see the loneliness surrounding him, and it calls to me. Somehow, I know there's some kind of goodness in him, and I want to pull it out and offer that part of him friendship. Of course, the fact that I even want to offer someone like him friendship probably means I'm messed up in the head.

The air is calm, the sky is clear, and nothing but the gentle lap of the waves can be heard. But inside my body is anything but calm and quiet. Contradictory feelings swirl and clash together, fighting against one another.

I approach his place, looking up at the cameras and wondering if he's watching me right now.

Walking to his front door, I take a deep breath and knock. There's nothing but silence that greets me from the inside. I wait another moment before knocking again, but still, there's nothing. With the mixture of thoughts spiraling inside me, I can't tell if I'm relieved or disappointed.

Instead of turning around, leaving, and forgetting about this like I probably should, I place the bag I brought down on the ground by the door and start walking along the side of the house to check the back toward the dock.

Just as I'm about to reach the end, a figure walks around the corner, almost running right into me, or rather, I almost run right into him.

"Oh!" I say, lifting a hand to my chest. "You scared me."

Shirtless again, Jacob looks up after stopping abruptly, and the surprised look on his face is quickly replaced with a scowl. He doesn't say anything but lets out a huff and takes a wide berth around me to get to his front door.

"I just wanted to say sorry," I rush to get out before he reaches the door, causing him to stop. "And to say thank you."

He glances up toward the camera ahead of him and then slowly turns around. "Why are you here?"

"I told you, I wanted to say—"

"No," he says in a low voice, cutting me off and taking a step in my direction again. "Why are you really here? Why do you *keep coming back*?" I swallow down the nerves and hold my ground, even as he steps closer. "Are you trying to get a reaction out of me?"

He stops when he's right in front of me, those beautiful blue-gray eyes looking dark and stormy as he holds my gaze, and yet even with the darkness in them, they're brightly lit from the sunshine.

In the next second, he raises his hand and wraps his fingers around my neck.

It's not a tight grip, though. It's just there, like a warning.

I can't help but wonder if this is it. Is this where he'll show me he's a monster?

Is this where his inner demons come out from where they're buried in the darkness?

I stand here, almost paralyzed, waiting to see what he'll do next. His muscular chest moves along with each breath he takes, and he's so close that all it would take is me lifting a hand, and I'd be able to touch his bare skin. I don't move an inch, though. I just hold his stare, barely blinking.

Waiting.

"Are you trying to see if I'll *take* you and *fuck* you without your permission, huh?"

I feel like any normal person would be afraid right now. Fear would be creeping along their skin, then soaking through, filling their insides. They'd be terrified of what might happen to them.

He could easily shove me against the wall or drag me inside and do whatever he likes to me. But for whatever reason, I'm not afraid at all—and that has me wanting to push him just that tiny bit further.

"Maybe," I answer.

The second I say the word, Jacob releases my neck as if it burned him and takes a step back. A mixture of emotions flicker across his face before he settles on the same scowl he's usually wearing.

"Just . . . just stay away from me," he warns, taking another step back.

I hear his words, and I see the stubborn set of his jaw that says, *stay away*. But it's his eyes that tell a different story, and it's almost like they're telling me to *stay*.

Not at this very moment, but maybe, just maybe . . . stay in his life.

As he turns around, his foot kicks the bag I left on the ground for him, and once again, confusion fills his features as he looks between the bag and me.

"I brought you some fresh-baked bread from the bakery and then decided to add some cheese and wine to go with it." I swallow, trying to wet my now dry throat. "As I said earlier, it's to say sorry and thank you. You know," with a wave of my hand, I gesture to the water behind me, "for saving me."

At that, I turn around and leave him standing there by his front door. It's better to leave him thinking things over on his own.

Plus, I'm feeling a little flustered, and I'm not entirely sure what to make of his actions, or my reaction to him, for that matter. I didn't feel threatened at all, which, considering the circumstances, I should have, shouldn't I?

It's just . . . I don't know. His grabbing my neck seemed like an act. A calculated move to try to scare me away, nothing more than that.

Maybe he really has changed?

Then again, maybe he's just scared of losing control once again, so he's pushing me away before that ever happens.

I reach up and touch where his warm hand was wrapped around my neck. It's still tingling as if his skin contained a toxin that was left on me, and my blood continues to thrum through my veins as if I'm still standing just inches away from him.

It bothers me that I can't get a clear reading of him. But I think what bothers me the most is that I feel like I *shouldn't* care about him at all. I *shouldn't* want to be his friend and make him less lonely. And I definitely *shouldn't* be physically attracted to him in any way.

I'm so lost in my thoughts that I don't see Tahnee sitting on my back deck until I'm walking up the steps.

"Oh!"

I quickly glance behind me, wondering if she saw where I was, but I realize there's no way she could have seen anything from where she's sitting.

"So *that's* how you keep your ass looking so good."

"Huh?" I walk over and take a seat on the chair beside hers.

"Your ass. Walking along the sand is really good for it."

I let out a half-hearted chuckle, still unsettled by what just happened with Jacob.

"Yeah, I guess."

"What's up with you?" Tahnee questions, apparently noticing my weird demeanor.

"Hmm? Oh, nothing."

"Aw. Is your mom giving you a hard time again? How many times has she called this week?"

"Just once, actually." I go along with what she thinks the problem is and try to get my mind focused on the here and now. "But I feel like I should probably call her and make peace."

"Well, you're better than me." She grabs a section of her hair and begins braiding it. "My mom will point out something dumb that I did, and then I'm too stubborn to talk to her for a week." She laughs at herself and rests her head back on the chair as she continues the braid.

To be honest, when it comes to my mom, I'm kind of shocked that it has only been the one time she has called this week. And even more so that I haven't heard from my father at all.

He's not the type of person who just lets people get away with doing something if he doesn't like it. I'm pretty sure he's resorted to some questionable conduct to get what he wants and have his way in his business dealings. I wouldn't be surprised if he did the same thing in other areas of his life. A lot of people are quite afraid of him.

I'm not exactly afraid of him. I just don't want him to come here and try to force me to leave with him because I *really* don't want to.

"Oh, I almost forgot to tell you. There are a couple of guys that want to take us out for a drink." She laughs again when she sees the skeptical look on my face. "Okay, okay, so, one of the guys I kind of really like, and he said he'd bring a friend if I wanted to bring one. And I want to bring you. What do you say?"

"Uh, I don't know, Tahnee."

"Come on. It's just a drink. There's absolutely no pressure for you to do anything other than that. I know you're not looking for a man right now, but you do want friends. Do it for me, please?" She clasps her hands together under her chin and pouts her lips, bringing a smile to my own lips.

I sigh. "Okay, whatever. For you."

"Yay!" She picks up the braid she just did and waves it at me. "I'll set something up for when we're all free."

"Where did you meet this guy, anyway?"

"He had work in town and stopped by *The Big Five* afterward when I was working. He lives twenty or thirty minutes away."

I nod. I should have known she met him at the bar.

Tahnee and I head inside after a few minutes, and I end up cooking us stir-fry for dinner. Our friendship has moved fast, and I feel rather comfortable around her, crazy and all. She's the type of friend I always wished I had.

Tahnee keeps me entertained with more of her insane stories as we eat, but I can't help my thoughts drifting back to the man down the beach throughout the rest of the evening and wondering whether he's eaten anything from the bag I brought him.

Chapter Eight

Remi

This is probably not a good idea. Those words are so familiar to me now. I know I've been saying them a lot lately, and yet they don't seem to stop me at all.

The moon reflects onto the ocean like a giant beacon of light, illuminating the darkness below. Tiny flickers of light are scattered across the horizon as ships and fishing boats move along in the distance.

I didn't bother putting any shoes on. I've gotten used to and even enjoy the feeling of sand between my toes. It feels cool on my feet after the warm day we had.

The flames burning ahead cast a warm orange glow on the surrounding area, including *his* face.

As soon as I had stepped out onto my back deck a minute ago and saw the fire down the beach, I knew I'd be coming here even before I registered that my feet were moving in this direction.

The closer I get, the more I can see the fire reflected in his eyes. It causes them to glow like a predator in the night. I feel like the moth being drawn to the flame, but I don't stop, even though I know it might be dangerous.

Jacob hasn't seen me yet, completely lost in thought, staring at the burning wood like it holds the answers to life.

The moment I arrive, I take a seat on the sand without saying a word. I'm not quite on the opposite side of the fire, but I'm not close to him, either.

I purposely don't look at him right away, needing a moment to collect my thoughts, and instead, focus on the crackling fire. When I do finally bring my eyes to look at him, I almost regret my decision to come here, and I begin to wonder why I did it in the first place.

It's clear that I've disturbed his peace. The calm look I'd seen on his face just moments ago is now replaced with an angry glower and a clenched jaw. And then there's his foot, tapping restlessly on the ground.

A puff of air blows past my lips. Well, I'm already here, so I might as well make the most of it.

"Hey," I finally say, and then immediately feel like an idiot.

He literally had his hand around my neck a few days ago and told me to stay away from him. And here I am saying *hey*.

He doesn't reply, of course; he doesn't even look at me. But he does rub his palms on his sweatpants like he's contemplating saying something.

Finally, he turns to me and says, "Ten years." At first, I'm confused as to what he's talking about, but then I remember that I had asked him how long he had been in prison when we were on the boat. He confirms that's what he's referring to with his next words. "You wanted to know how long I was in prison. Ten years." His focus returns to the fire when I don't say anything.

That is quite a long time. It's not just that he went to prison for ten years, but he actually missed that long of his life on the outside. It's kind of crazy to think about being out of the world for so long. He was in his late teens when it happened, which would put him in his late twenties now.

I'm a little surprised that he actually voluntarily told me something. But if he's feeling like sharing that with me, then maybe he's willing to answer some other questions.

I decide to go for it. "Wh—"

"Yeah, you see," he says, cutting me off. "I liked her for *years*, and I just got so sick of waiting for her, as you said. So, I drugged her, then took her to a field and fucked her." He turns his whole body so his entire focus is directly on me. "I made a couple of mistakes that night, though. One was not waiting until she turned eighteen so she wouldn't be counted as a minor. The other was hanging around the area too long afterward."

I know he's determined to make himself look bad. He's trying to appear as if he doesn't give a shit.

His words are meant to shock me, make me hate him more, and make me cower away from him.

They're meant to get to me.

And they do.

I hate what he did. It's absolutely horrible. Sickening.

But he doesn't know.

He doesn't know that even though he said those horrible words, even though his face looks angry and harder than stone, his eyes tell a different story.

He *hates* what he did.

He *does* regret it.

He's *not* that same man now.

But for whatever reason—well, actually, the obvious reason would be that he's treated like shit by everyone in town—he makes sure to keep everyone away.

So, I don't react to his words. I don't scrunch my face up at him or get up and leave. Instead, I hold his gaze until he finally looks away.

"Why do you keep coming here?" he asks after a few long seconds when he doesn't get the result he thought he would. The same question he asked me the other day.

I shrug. "I guess I'm here to be your friend."

He lets out a scoff. "Maybe I don't want a friend."

"True, you may not want one, but everybody needs one."

Jacob sits up straighter, an inner fire lighting his eyes this time like I just sparked something. "You gotta be fuckin' delirious if you think a friend is worth shit."

I wonder if he's saying that because of his old friends—the ones I saw in the picture. I can't really blame them for not sticking around, if that's what he's referring to.

And anyway, his situation isn't exactly an everyday occurrence for most people, either.

"I'm not delirious to want to spend time with someone."

He pokes his tongue into his cheek as if reigning in his annoyance before answering.

"Someone may spend time with you, talk with you, tell you what you want to hear, but at the end of the day, when push comes to shove, they're only looking out for themselves. They'll ditch you in a heartbeat if it suits them."

I shake my head at what he's saying. I don't know much about true friends, but I refuse to believe that it's all done out of selfish motives and not a give-and-take thing.

"I don't think that's the case for everyone."

"It is. You'll see. All you're doing is filling in some tiny space of their pathetic lives."

"Aren't we all just filling spaces in each other's lives? Whether you're a friend or not? And whether it's time that you're filling or an emptiness that was there?"

It's obvious he's had a lot of time to think deeply about this type of thing. Ten years, to be precise. I mean, who says things like 'filling tiny spaces in people's lives'?

"What's the point, then, if that's all you are to them? A space filler."

"Well, because they're filling *your* empty spaces as well."

I continue to hold his gaze, refusing to look away, all the while daring him to refute what I just said. The air around us starts to feel heavy, and I'm not sure if it's the words we've said floating between us or just his presence.

He finally severs our stare, looking back at the fire.

"You haven't been in town very long, so let me tell you how things are done around here." His voice comes out with a little less force than before. "I mind my own business and do my own shit. And everyone else does theirs and leaves me alone."

"Except they don't leave you alone, do they?"

He knows what I'm talking about. His mouth snaps shut, the muscles in his jaw twitch, and his eyes shift to the side. He doesn't like how they treat him. He tries to act like he doesn't care about any of it, but it affects him more than he lets on.

Those little actions he does, the looks his eyes give, they speak louder than any words he says. And they're always telling me a different story than his mouth.

My first thought is to say that he can't exactly expect anything different after what he did, but that's not why I'm here. I didn't come here to constantly point out or punish his mistakes, no matter how big they are. I came here to offer friendship.

Plus, I don't really agree with what the people in town have been doing.

And although I didn't do any of the things they did, I still went on his boat. I went through his personal property, and I also flipped him off in the cameras when he did nothing to me.

I feel bad about that.

We fall into silence again, each of us watching the fire blazing in front of us.

Occasionally, I steal glances at him, trailing my eyes over his features. If it weren't for the unfortunate circumstances, he'd have women falling all over themselves just to talk to him. I imagine they'd want to trail their fingers along his jaw and run their hands through his hair, all while staring into those beautiful ocean-colored eyes.

When he catches me looking at him, he immediately looks away again. "You can have that wine back, by the way. It tasted like shit."

I can't help it, I laugh. I'm not entirely sure why that's funny, but it is.

"What about the bread and cheese?" I ask while trying to hide my smile.

He rubs the back of his neck like I've seen him do before. "I ate it."

The fact that he looks simultaneously pleased with the food I brought for him and pissed off that he enjoyed it brings me another wave of happiness and satisfaction. He's trying so hard to be an asshole right now, but I just find it amusing.

As much as he's tried to make this whole evening an unenjoyable experience for me, I've actually liked being here by the fire with him, and I have a feeling that after the first few minutes, he's actually enjoyed it, as well.

Not once have I felt threatened by him, which further confirms the thought that he's a changed man and deserves someone to be nice to him.

I also appreciate the fact that he doesn't act all nice and polite just for the sake of it. After all the fake pretenses I've dealt with throughout my life, it's a welcome change.

I don't stay too much longer because I have work in the morning. But I also have a feeling that smaller doses work better for him when it comes to people.

Standing up, I dust the sand off my pants and give him one final look. "Thanks for the company. Enjoy the rest of your evening, Jacob."

He glances up from the fire and grunts. I'll take it. It's an improvement from completely ignoring me.

Chapter Nine

Jacob

As I store away the fifth and final catch of the day, I'm feeling pretty pleased about how successful the day of fishing turned out to be. One of those fish will be my dinner for tonight. My mouth waters at the thought of cooking it over the fire like I've done a few times in the past.

The warm air blows through my hair as the boat glides back toward the shore, reminding me that I need a haircut. I don't even remember the last time I let it get this long. I had always kept it shaved in prison, leaving no chance that it could be pulled from behind.

I grip the wheel tighter at some of the memories trying to worm their way to the surface, wishing I could purge them from my mind permanently, but knowing I can't.

As I get closer to the dock, I see a familiar figure sitting at the end of it, but not too close to the edge. It doesn't surprise me that it's *her* again. She's been here a few times since declaring that she was going to be my friend.

"Nice evening to be out on the water," Remi states as I pull in close to the dock and begin mooring my boat.

I don't bother answering her. Instead, I get the fish, step off the boat, and head toward my house. Of course, she gets up and follows me down the dock. No matter how much I've ignored her or how much I've been a dick to her, she's still like a fucking puppy that doesn't go away.

I guess that's not *entirely* true. She never stays too long, and she often brings me some sort of treat while never asking for anything in return. And, if I'm being completely honest, there's the tiniest little part of me that actually kind of likes it when she visits.

A part that starts to feel alive and jittery whenever she's near.

A part that had turned black and rotten over the years.

But that's just bad news.

Why would I ever want to bring her down to my level with the depraved and the evil?

So, yeah. I've tried to be an asshole to get her to leave me alone. I even put my hand around her neck to try to scare her off, for fuck's sake. But that only ended up backfiring and proving to be a mistake on my part.

Especially since I felt the softest, smoothest skin I have ever touched when holding her neck. Now, the feel of it is etched into my brain, along with the feel of her rapid pulse beating under my fingers. And I can't get it out.

I walk into my home, shutting the door behind me before she can follow me in, and put all but the smallest fish I caught into the deep freeze. I'll be taking the others over to Ting first thing in the morning.

Next, I pull out some tin foil and place the fish on it, adding some butter, salt, pepper, and lemon juice before wrapping it up. I've made sure, at the very least, to always keep those items stocked for this very reason.

I grab a fork before starting for the door, only to stop after a few feet. Retracing my steps back into the kitchen, I tap my fist on the counter a few times, contemplating, then blow out a breath. "Fuck it," I mutter and grab another fork before stepping back outside.

Remi is sitting on the sand over by the pile of rocks where I build my fires, as if she knew I'd be making one tonight, and she's invited herself to stay.

Looking up, I double-check that the camera facing that direction is recording. I feel relief when I see the little red blinking light and continue toward the pit.

That little part of me sparks with life the moment she smiles at me when I get closer, but I just look away, tossing the fish onto the chair I keep out here, and then get started on the fire. Once it's going well, I place the fish on some rocks that are out of the flames and sit back on the chair to let it cook.

"Did you catch that today?"

Taking a quick glance at Remi, I notice she's not looking at me but at the fire, and there's a peaceful look on her face. I can't help but notice how fucking gorgeous she looks with the warm glow of the fire kissing her perfect skin. It causes her dark hair and her hazel eyes—that seem to change color with the light and her mood—to shine.

It pisses me off that I'm noticing it because I don't *want* to notice.

Turning away again, I mumble, "Yes."

"I wouldn't mind learning how to fish," she replies contemplatively.

"You might want to learn how to swim first."

"That's true," she says a little more quietly this time, probably remembering the events of the other day when she almost drowned. I can't imagine that's something you easily forget.

When I look over at her again, she's lifting a handful of sand up and watching as the grains fall between her fingers, deep in thought.

It occurs to me that I have no idea who she really is. I don't know her last name. Why she's here and where she's from.

Nothing.

It's best that way, anyway.

Soon, she'll give up on me and join the rest of the town in their efforts to get me to leave—and I'm not entirely sure this isn't just part of some scheme as it is. I guess I'll find out, eventually. I just have to be shrewd until then and keep both eyes open.

"I know what it's like having to start over. Start fresh," she says after a moment.

"What, you were in prison as well?" I ask sarcastically.

I wasn't saying it to be funny, but she laughs anyway. And honestly, the sound isn't terrible.

"No, not in prison, like you . . . but it was a type of prison, I guess."

"Well then. I guess you know *exactly* how I fucking feel."

I feel like shit seeing the slump of her shoulders and downcast eyes. I know she's actually trying, for whatever reason, and I can't seem to stop being a dick to her.

Running a hand over my face, I push out a, "Sorry."

It's no surprise when she doesn't immediately respond. The silence stretches between us, causing an uncomfortable feeling to surface in me. Thankfully, after a few long seconds, she finally responds.

"I was merely stating that I came here for a fresh start as well. I didn't mean to imply that I know what your life has been like, because I really don't."

She's absolutely right about that. No one can possibly know what I've been through. But I appreciate that she acknowledges that, at least. She really didn't deserve my harsh words.

The fish should be done by now, so I find a stump that can be used as a makeshift table between the two of us, and then use two smaller pieces of wood to lift up the fish and put it on the stump.

"You can have some," I offer as I open the foil and push the extra fork toward her. "If you want."

Remi doesn't hesitate to get up from her spot and sit by the stump. Instinctively, I look over my shoulder at the camera for my reassurance before picking up my own fork.

When I look at her again, she's got another smile on her face, obviously taking my peace offering as I intended.

We eat quietly for a few minutes, with the sounds of the crackling wood filling the silence. But this time, the silence doesn't feel suffocating.

It's weird eating with someone like this. It's weird spending time with someone like this.

Especially a woman.

"This is really good. I've never had fish this fresh," Remi says, nodding. "You're a good cook."

"Hardly," I mumble.

"What else can you make?" she asks, obviously trying to make small talk.

Instead of shutting her down again, I decide to answer her question truthfully. It's not like it's anything interesting, anyway.

"Mac n' cheese from a box. Frozen dinners."

"Oh," she replies. "Didn't you get to do, like, courses and stuff in prison? Cooking classes?"

I almost scoff at her question. She probably thinks it was just like how it is in the movies. And maybe it is like that in some of the minimum-security facilities, but that's not where I went. Almost every day was a struggle against other inmates, the guards, or even my own demons to stay alive. It was filthy, it was cold, and it stunk. So no, I sure as hell didn't do any *cooking classes* in prison. And my mom never taught me before I went there.

"Nope. I've never learned."

Remi takes another bite of the fish and swallows it with a contented sigh. "Well, I'd be happy to teach you how to make some other things."

My eyebrows furrow. "And why would you do that?"

"Just because." She shrugs. "Spaghetti is pretty easy to make. Maybe someday you could come to my place since I have all the ingredients, and I can show you."

I look at her in disbelief. A fucking cooking lesson? Is she serious right now? She appears to be.

"No."

"No?"

"*No.*"

"Well, I guess I could come here instea—"

"No, Remi. You just don't get it," I mutter, cutting her off like I always seem to, while standing up. "Whatever friendship endeavor you're on right now is not going to work. You think if the people in this town were to see you hanging around me they'd still talk to you? You think they'd still *like* you?"

Her silence is confirmation that she hadn't thought of that, and she knows I'm right. Nothing good will come of this for her, and it's better that she realizes it now.

"Exactly." I leave her sitting there with the fish and start back toward my front door.

"I'm not going to stop," Remi calls to my back, causing me to stop and turn around. She stands up and dusts off her shorts. "I'm not going to stop with my *friendship endeavor*."

An ocean breeze plays with her hair, tossing it over one shoulder and then back again. There's a determined look in her eyes, but there shouldn't be.

"Then you're stupid if you're willing to risk giving up a whole town just to try to be friends with someone who doesn't even want it."

With that, I turn around and walk into my house, making sure to lock the door behind me. Why she doesn't just give up, I don't know.

Chapter Ten

Remi

Despite saying that I wasn't going to stop trying to be Jacob's friend, I haven't been back to see him in a few days. As much as I'm ashamed to admit it, what he said about the town treating me differently did get to me. The words had finally sunk in when I got home that night.

I feel like I've been on high alert for any behavioral changes from anyone I've spoken to ever since. Every sideways glance and every frown in my direction has had me wondering whether they saw me with Jacob and wondering if he was right.

Then I feel bad and even annoyed at worrying about it to begin with. Can't I be friends with whomever I want?

But the answer to that question isn't a simple one, especially when it comes to a convicted rapist. I mean, why the fuck do I even *want* to be friends with someone like him? I can't make sense of it.

He's not the type of friend I should be seeking out, yet my gut tells me to do just that. And that's where all those conflicting feelings come back again.

I came to this town to start fresh, to make new, real friends, and to be happy. So far, that is working out, and I don't want to ruin it. But I could still have that and be friends with Jacob, couldn't I?

These thoughts have been running through my mind for the past couple of days, and they continue to run through my head as I walk to work.

I speed up like I do every time I pass the last house before Main Street, the one with the SOLD sign *still* in the front yard. I've seen the dark figure in the window a few more times since that first time, but I can never tell what the person looks like, and it makes me feel uneasy. It feels like I'm being watched, and I don't slow down until the house is out of sight.

When I get close to the store, I see Tim Davis, the hardware store owner, walk out the door and head toward his car. He looks in my direction and offers a friendly wave. If he knew I was at Jacob's place a few days ago, would he still be waving at me? Would he still give me that wide, toothy smile that looks like it will split his face if it goes any wider?

I want to believe he would, but it's hard to say.

Jolene gives me her usual warm, motherly smile and greeting as I walk toward her at the check-out. When I first met her, I thought she was really friendly but maybe a little standoffish. But as time has passed, I've realized it is just something she reserves for people she's unsure of at first. She's shown she is anything but that when it comes to the people she cares about, me included.

That just makes me feel more guilty because she specifically warned me to stay away from Jacob. She said he was dangerous. And yes, I saw those news articles that had the words 'aggravated assault' in them. But besides his gruff attitude and asshole remarks, I just can't see any violent tendencies in him. Even when he put his hand on my neck, there was nothing vicious about it.

The simplest thing for me to do is to listen to Jolene, listen to *him,* and just forget about trying to be his friend. It would make things so much easier for me. It would also make the town happy—not that they know anything different right now—and life could continue on peacefully.

So why is it still the last thing I want to do?

Hours pass by, and people come and go. And still, the answer doesn't get any clearer as to what I should do.

When I finish up with serving Bertie in the afternoon and don't see anyone else around, I crouch behind the counter to grab some more plastic bags out of the box, and then end up cleaning up and sorting some things under there as well.

A couple of minutes later, I hear, "Hey," from above me.

I know the voice, but I feel like I must be hearing things. I don't believe it's actually *him* until I stand and see Jacob standing there.

It's funny how he looks kind of annoyed that he said anything to me. It is, after all, the first time he's been the one to initiate a conversation. Well, actually, there was the time he asked if I was okay after the boat incident, but that doesn't count.

This time happens to be after he told me not to bother trying to be his friend. And here he is, basically being his version of friendly to me. It kind of proves to me that, although he said he didn't want my friendship, I don't think he really meant it.

That has my indecision vanishing in an instant. I can't just give up on him.

"Hi," I answer with a smile as I scan his items. "How have you been?"

He gives me a look that says, "*How do you think?*" as he hands me the cash and then opens his mouth to say something. But then someone enters the store, and his mouth snaps shut. I watch as he retreats into himself—how his face hardens, and he refuses to make eye contact with me again.

Even when the person that came in heads straight to the back of the store and there is no one else around, Jacob still doesn't look at me or say another word. He just picks up his stuff and stalks out.

If I continue to pursue a friendship with him, I guess that's the type of thing I can expect to happen on a regular basis. Although he really only comes into the store once or twice a week, so I would be at his place the rest of the time. There wouldn't be any risk of people finding out about our "friendship" there.

I finish up my shift and grab some ingredients for spaghetti. I'm not going to try to teach him this time. I've decided I'll just make it at my place and then take it over to him already cooked.

It occurs to me while I'm paying for my stuff that Jacob has never bought anything other than the most basic food items. I wonder if that's just because he doesn't cook anything else or because he doesn't have the money for better-tasting things?

"Have a good night." I wave goodbye to Jolene and Micah, the high school kid she has come in during the evenings, and then head home.

Once I've showered and cooked the food, I take an unusually long amount of time deciding what I want to wear, and then end up chastising myself for being so ridiculous. Am I really trying to dress nicely for him?

I end up putting on a pair of denim shorts with a tank top underneath a loose T-shirt. It's been quite warm lately, so if I get too hot, I can always take the T-shirt off.

Halfway through the walk to his place, my phone rings from my pocket. The name *Dad* flashes on the screen when I pull it out, and my feet stutter before coming to a stop. I can't believe he's actually calling me after all this time. My first thought is to ignore it, but I haven't talked to him since before I moved here, and I know I have to face him sooner or later.

"Hello?"

"This nonsense has gone on long enough."

There are no warm *hellos* or anything, no asking how I am. Just like my mom when she called.

"What nonsense?" I ask, because none of this is nonsense to me. This is my life.

"You running off like that. I've allowed you to have this time, but enough is enough."

He's *allowed* me? "Dad, I'm twenty-six years old. I can do whatever I like and live wherever I like."

"You think that, do you? What about your responsibilities to this family?"

I sigh, closing my eyes and dropping my chin to my chest. "Dad, the life you and Mom live . . . I'm not cut out for it. Plea—"

"It's time you came home," he cuts in.

The thought of going back there makes me feel physically ill. There is no way I'm giving up my home here, and without thinking, I look up at Jacob's house ahead.

"*This* is my home now." I hang up and then quickly turn it off.

Staring at my phone, I take a few deep breaths and clutch it tightly in my hand. I can't believe I just did that. No one hangs up on my father. I shake my head and put my phone away. What's he going to do? He doesn't know where I am.

And I've got more important things to worry about right now, anyway.

When I arrive at Jacob's place with the food, the sun is starting to get blocked out by some dark clouds forming along the horizon. It looks like we'll be getting another storm later.

After knocking on his door, I take a step back and wait for him to open up. A few seconds later, he speaks from the inside.

"What do you want?"

Looking up at the camera, I take another step back and hold the bag of food up in case he's watching. "I brought spaghetti for dinner. It's already cooked, so you don't have to learn." *This time.*

When he finally opens the door, the conversation with my father is the last thing on my mind, and I have to will my eyes to stay focused on his face.

I have to admit, seeing him in black sweatpants and a black T-shirt that is strained against his bulging muscular form makes it difficult. I try to remind myself of what he's done and that it's wrong to ogle him.

It ends up being easy to do when he opens his mouth to speak and reminds me *exactly* who he is.

"You realize if you keep hanging around here, I'm going to have to give my parole officer your name, address, and phone number, right?"

"Why do you need to do that?"

He sighs, annoyed. "Because you're a woman hanging around a convicted rapist. They want to keep tabs."

That makes sense. I'm sure there are probably a number of rules for him now. Jacob crosses his arms and clenches his jaw as if he's challenging me or expecting me to turn around and leave. But he should know by now that I'm stubborn and not easily scared off.

There is, however, one thing I need to know, and I do kind of feel bad about having to ask it.

"Will he share that information with anyone else?"

"No."

I nod slowly. Okay. I believe him. The town won't find out I'm spending time with him, and my father won't find out where I live.

I hold the bag up in front of me again. "Hungry?"

Chapter Eleven

Remi

It's not surprising to me that he makes us sit outside by the fire again. I can't imagine he has anyone go inside his home. What *does* surprise me, though, is that he gives *me* the more comfortable chair that he usually sits on while he sits on a log.

He doesn't particularly look all that happy about it, but I suspect there may be a gentleman buried somewhere in there who is capable of doing many nice things.

I brought a couple of paper plates with me as well as two plastic forks in the bag, so I place them on the same stump we used when we ate the fish and then dish out our food.

Jacob grunts out something that sounds like, "Thanks," when I hand over his plate, and it makes me smile. He's still trying to resist this, but I can see that I'm slowly wearing him down.

We eat quietly, and I admit that I end up watching him more than I watch the fire. I'm curious as to whether he likes the food. *I* think it's great, but I haven't cooked for anyone else before.

My mother thought it was a ridiculous thing for me to be doing with my time, and both she and my father were displeased when I took hospitality during my senior year just so I could learn to cook.

None of my exes liked to stay in to eat, either, so I never made meals for them. Eating out was a way for them to be publicized, so they made sure to take advantage of that at every opportunity.

Fortunately for me, I think Jacob is really enjoying the food, even if he doesn't seem thrilled about it. His glower shifts between his plate, the fire, and, on the rare occasion, me. He ends up finishing his plate before I'm even halfway done with mine.

"You can have some more if you want," I offer.

He doesn't say anything but gets up and adds more to his plate. A smirk splits my cheeks at the fact that he likes it, but when he turns in my direction, I quickly hide it by taking a bite of my food.

"You want more?" he asks, gesturing to the spaghetti.

"No, thanks. This will be enough. You can keep the rest for tomorrow if you'd like."

He nods and takes his seat again, eating just as quickly as before. It makes my chest swell, and I feel good knowing he's enjoying it so much, even if he doesn't admit it out loud.

"Did you go fishing today?"

"Yup."

"Did you catch something?"

He still gives me that look that says he doesn't understand why I'm talking to him, but answers, anyway, "Two somethings."

"Oh, that's great! And you sell them, right?" I've noticed that he goes out fishing regularly, so I figure it's not just a hobby or anything, but probably his means of income.

"Yeah," he replies, taking his last bite of food. "I take them to the fish market."

"That's in the next town over, isn't it?"

"Yep. That's the one."

It's quiet for a moment while I chew and swallow, and then ask, "Do you ever listen to podcasts?"

"You and your fucking questions," he mumbles, but there isn't any anger behind it. "No, I don't."

I know I ask a lot of questions, but I can't help it. That's how I learn about people, delving into their lives and their pasts. It's how I learn about a lot of things, really.

Seemingly out of nowhere, a bright flash lights up the entire area, immediately followed by a loud crack of thunder that makes me squeal. I don't know how I didn't notice the storm approaching us so fast. I've heard the low rumblings over the last little while, but I wasn't really paying any attention to it. Now, it's right above us. We both jump to our feet, and within seconds, heavy droplets of rain start coming down.

"I need to run home," I say just as another bolt of lightning strikes even closer than before.

I peer at Jacob, who is shaking his head.

"No, I don't think that's a good idea. Shit. Come on." He gestures for me to follow him, and I do without any hesitation, grabbing the leftover food as I go.

As we run toward his house, the rain gets heavier and the wind picks up in an instant like a switch was flicked. By the time we make it inside, we're already soaked.

Standing just inside his front door, we take a moment to catch our breaths.

"You okay?"

I nod. I'm fine, but I'm glad he didn't let me run back to my place in this storm. It only seems to be getting worse by the second.

There's a brief moment where we lock eyes, and neither of us says anything. A defining moment, perhaps—the fact that he's let me into his home.

But, of course, Jacob is quick to look away.

He then turns and walks off into another room, so I take the opportunity to check out my surroundings. It's even smaller here than in my place. It's basically just one big room with very little in it. He doesn't even have a TV in here. But I do notice more cameras, which has me curious all over again. I kind of understand the ones outside, but to have some on the inside as well? That's just weird.

I stay in the same spot while I look around. Despite the whole thing with the boat, it feels wrong to go walking and snooping through his home now that I somewhat know him a little better.

"Here, you can wear this."

I turn to see Jacob holding up a black sweater. He's already changed out of his wet T-shirt and is wearing another one, white this time, that showcases his muscles just as much as the other one did.

"Thanks," I murmur, taking it from him and handing him the food.

Without thinking, I start taking off my T-shirt since it's a lot wetter than the tank top underneath, and Jacob immediately spins around, coughing uncomfortably.

"Oh, it's okay. I have something on underneath."

I feel like a jerk because it's clear that he keeps himself out of situations where he may be tempted to act inappropriately. Not that I think he can't control himself; I haven't seen anything that tells me otherwise.

He nods but still doesn't turn around. One of his hands reaches up and squeezes his neck before dropping to his side again.

"I'm dressed," I tell him once I'm wearing his sweater.

It's so big and comfortable and smells divine. I instinctively snuggle into it, taking a deep breath of the manly scent embedded into the material. I'm so immersed in the sweater that I don't immediately realize that Jacob has turned around and is watching me with an odd expression.

Embarrassment prickles at my skin, causing my cheeks to heat. "I, um . . . It's really warm. Thank you."

Clearing his throat, he turns toward the kitchen and says, "Uh, you can sit on the couch. Do you want water or something?"

"Sure. Water is good."

I take a seat, suddenly feeling nervous. Not nervous about my safety or anything, but nervous about what to say or do. My thumbs start their journey across my fingertips, and I rearrange my weight around on the couch. Why am I feeling like this?

Jacob brings me a glass of water and then takes a seat in the armchair, looking just as uncomfortable as I feel. The space is already small, but it feels even tinier with his presence.

The sound of thunder spills through the silence stretching between us, but after a few minutes, I speak up.

"No TV, huh?"

"No."

"Is that on purpose, or have you just not gotten around to getting one yet? I have two at my place, so you can have one if you want?"

He shifts in his seat. "I don't watch TV."

"Ah, okay," I respond with a nod. "I noticed that you had a PlayStation on your boat." His demeanor changes from uncomfortable to annoyed at the memory of me breaking onto his property, and I raise my hands, palms out in front of me. "I am sorry about that whole thing, you know, but I can't change it now." I shrug. "Anyway, do you still play it?"

"Yeah, sometimes."

"What games do you have?"

He shifts in his seat again. "Just the usual teenage shit. Call Of Duty, Battlefield, NBA, and a bunch of other ones. All the older versions, though."

"Mmm," I hum, as if I know what he's talking about. "I always wished I could play video games when I was younger.

I'd try to play on the ones they had set up in the electronics department for about two seconds before I was pulled away."

Jacob leans forward in his chair, seemingly unable to sit still. "You said you came from a prison-type life?"

It's the first real question he has asked about my life, and he actually remembered what I had said. It causes a weird type of flurry to ignite within me, and I want to keep this form of communication open for as long as possible.

"Let's just say it wasn't your average upbringing with Stanley and Jaqueline Murdoch as parents." I throw those names in there to see if there are any signs of recognition from him, but there's nothing. No indication that he's heard of them. "I was given a schedule to follow and was constantly under the spotlight because of my parents."

My life from before has started to feel more and more like a distant memory, with no one ever bringing it up.

He nods. "And you moved here to be out of that spotlight?"

"Yeah." A small, almost nervous smile hits my lips. "I did."

"Well, that's good," he says quietly.

The storm is raging outside. You can hear the rain pounding against the windows, but unlike that first night when I felt at peace watching and listening to it from my back deck, I feel anything *but* calm. And it all has to do with the man with ocean eyes sitting in the armchair on the other side of the room.

Another lightning strike hits close by just as I go to say something else, and then everything goes black. We're surrounded by nothing but darkness in here.

"The power went out," I state lamely, pointing out the obvious.

"Yeah."

I pull out my phone and turn it on to use as a flashlight, but notice that I only have eleven percent battery power left.

"Shit. I'm almost out of power. Do you have a phone? Or a flashlight?"

"My phone is out on the boat. No flashlights."

"Okay. That's okay. We'll just sit here, in the dark, I guess."

When I had set out to come here tonight, I absolutely did not think it'd end up like this: us sitting inside his home in the dark while a storm rages outside. And while I know it's because of the storm, I still feel like the fact that I'm in his home right now means I've made some progress with him.

Something that sounds like a car door slamming catches my attention even through the thunder, wind, and rain, and I stand up.

"What was that?"

Through the flashes of lightning from the storm, I see Jacob stand as well.

"I'm not sure."

I follow him as he moves toward the window, and then we both peek through the curtain at opposite ends of the window. At first, I don't see anything outside, but then some more lightning lights up the area, and I notice a car parked out on the street. There's nothing else at the end of this road other than Jacob's house, so they're obviously not here for anything else.

"Were you expecting someone?"

I see the face he pulls at me right before he answers, "No."

"Hmm, I didn't see anyone in the car. Where are they?" My question is answered in the next flash of lightning when we see a figure dressed in black standing next to Jacob's truck. It's so creepy and unexpected that I jump a little when I first see it. "What are they doing?"

I turn toward Jacob, and although I can't see him clearly, I see enough of his face in the flashes of light to know he doesn't look happy about whatever it is. His expression isn't one of anger or resentment, though, but rather, a look of resignation.

"Jacob?" His eyes meet mine, and they tell me that he knows exactly what the person might be doing, and it's *not* being a 'good Samaritan' and checking up on him during the storm. "What are they doing?"

He turns his attention back outside and answers in a flat, emotionless tone, "Most likely slashing my tires."

"What?" I gasp.

"Or maybe this time, they'll smash a window."

"Are you serious?" I ask as Jacob continues to stare out the window. "We have to stop them." He doesn't move an inch or even looks away from the window. I can't let this happen. It isn't right. Maybe I can reason with the person? I can't see who it is out there, but I've most likely met and spoken with whoever it is. "I'm going out there to stop them."

I start to walk away but am stopped by Jacob's hand wrapping around my arm. "No, Remi, you can't do that. Are you crazy?" I turn to look at him again, and with each flash of light, I see what appears to be distress on his face. "What do you think is going to happen if they see you here at my place, and sticking up for me, no less? You'd be fucked. Whatever life you've found here in this town would be over."

He's right. I know he is.

He already said this to me the other day, but I had thought at the time that he said it more so to be a jerk and push me away, whether it was true or not. But now, I don't think that was the case at all. I think he genuinely cares and doesn't want me to screw up my life.

The fight I had raring to go slowly drains out of me with my next exhale. And a moment later, in the softest tone, he adds, "I'm not worth it."

It's said so quietly that I'm not even sure I was meant to hear it, but I did, and it hits me in the chest, causing an ache that shouldn't really be there for a guy I shouldn't be hanging around.

All of a sudden, he's dropping his hand and taking a big step back like he didn't realize he was still holding my arm until just now. I notice his eyes flick up to something behind me, and then he takes another subtle step back.

"I'm not afraid of you, Jacob," I say quietly.

"Why not?"

He should know by now that I'm not like the rest of the town. Doesn't he see that I'm different from the person outside doing who knows what to his truck?

It's true that I still have conflicting thoughts about him. My mind constantly tries to remind me of his badness while my heart looks for and sees his goodness. There's also the constant guilt that plagues me, telling me I shouldn't even be doing any of this. But I can't seem to stop.

Jacob is nothing like I thought he would be, and his behavior is contradictory to what anyone would expect from someone like him. It makes me more determined than ever not to give up on him.

Looking at Jacob, I can see him staring at the ground, doing that thing with his tongue where he pokes it in his cheek.

"I'm just not." I shrug, even though he's not looking at me. "I just don't think you'd hurt me."

Another look flashes across his face, like my words *mean* something to him, something important, but in a second, it's gone, and then he's stuffing his hands into his pockets and walking back toward the window, ending the conversation.

After the storm dies down—which is soon after the person doing something to Jacob's truck leaves—I follow him outside to see what has been done to it. The air is still thick with moisture, and the temperature has dropped, causing goosebumps to skate up my legs.

As we step onto his driveway, my stomach sinks when I see the dripping red paint along the side of his truck that reads 'RAPIST.' Jacob stares at it quietly, a gloominess surrounding us that wasn't present during the storm.

I want to say something, but I'm not sure what. *Sorry* just doesn't seem sufficient. So, I end up keeping quiet while he gets a bucket with some cleaning mixture in it to wash it off. I offer to help, but he declines.

Fortunately, it was spray-painted on there while it was wet, so it's easy enough to remove.

*Un*fortunately, it's not the only thing that the person did. There's a pocketknife sticking out of one of the tires. That's not something that can just be washed away.

"Fuck." Jacob lets out an exasperated sigh, leaning against his truck.

I've seen a lot of things over the years that have upset me or affected me in some sort of way, but not one of them has left me feeling as awful as I do right now.

"Um, you can use my car if you want," I offer, and he looks over at me. His ocean eyes try to hide the frustration, along with the torment, that he feels but fails. "I mean, if you need to drive somewhere tomorrow or something."

This time, he holds my gaze, almost like he's searching for something, but for what? I'm not sure. Then he pushes away from the truck. "Thanks, but it's okay."

Jacob walks past me toward the shed, and unlocks it, then disappears into the darkness. A moment later, he walks back out with another tire and a few other items to change it. I stand off to the side and watch as he starts getting to work.

"Do you want me to do anything?"

He glances over his shoulder and then back at what he's doing. "No. It's okay."

I don't know anything about changing a tire anyway, so I just stand, watching him while burying myself deeper into his warm sweater I'm still wearing. I stand watching him change a tire late at night by the ocean . . . because someone slashed it . . . because he's a convicted sex offender . . .

And there is nowhere else I'd rather be.

Chapter Twelve

Remi

A large, warm hand slides down from my neck to cup one of my breasts in a firm hold, squeezing and caressing it while rubbing a thumb over my very hard nipple. I moan at the sensation sparking through my body. My neck still tingles where his hand was holding me in the darkness.

How long has it been since someone touched me like this? Paid attention to me like this? *Nathan sure as hell didn't care to bring me pleasure like this.*

His grip on my breast tightens as the pressure on my core increases. Deft fingers move over my throbbing clit in a perfect rhythm, as if he already knows my body and precisely what it needs.

Images of his muscles moving and bunching while he changed his tire filter into my mind, and I imagine his biceps tensing and moving as he works me into a frenzy.

I try to close the gap between us, needing to feel his solid form against me, but it feels just out of my reach. Like when you can see a fire when you're out in the cold but never get near enough that the flames actually warm your skin.

A sharp pang of desire shoots from my nipple straight to my center when he pinches it. I'm so close to the edge. I want to touch him so badly, but my arms won't move. They feel constrained somehow, but by what? I'm not sure.

"Jacob." His name flies from my lips as lust fills every point of my body. My vision blurs and pleasure consumes me. I wish his lips were on mine at this moment.

I want to taste him, bite him. I want to be surrounded and filled by him all at once.

He continues to bring me up, and up, and up with his fingers until I reach the crest and then go tumbling down with a loud moan as my orgasm washes over me.

Drowning me.

My legs tremble and my breath stutters in my chest. An array of feelings burst from within me and scatter in every direction.

And then, I really am drowning.

Dark water surrounds me.

Terror replaces the sheer bliss from seconds ago as I sink deeper, my arms not making a move to push me to the surface.

I open my mouth to let out a scream, and that's when I shoot up into a sitting position on my bed, my chest still heaving and sucking in lungfuls of air as if I really were underwater.

My body is covered in a layer of sweat, and one of my hands is inside my panties, coated in my arousal, while the other is still gripping my breast.

A dream. That's all it was.

I flop back onto the bed, freeing my hands and slowing my breath. Heat floods my cheeks when I realize I had a dream about Jacob.

It was *his* fingers I felt touching me.

It was *his* name I called out on the brink of pleasure.

Slipping into the bathroom, I get cleaned up and splash some water on my face. As I stare at my reflection in the mirror, I'm forced to finally acknowledge what I've been denying, even to myself—that I'm attracted to Jacob, and not just physically.

I feel like there must be something wrong with me because of it—nothing about this situation is normal. But even just the thought of walking away from him causes my stomach to twist and turn, so I know I won't be doing that, regardless of any negative thoughts.

Somewhere along the way of trying to fill in his empty spaces, I started to feel things for him. A kind and gentle soul lies underneath the rough exterior, and I find it so hard to reconcile him with the man I read about in those newspaper articles.

My bathroom window faces toward Jacob's home, so I lean against the frame, looking down the beach to his small, lonely shack. The sun hasn't risen yet, but it's starting to get lighter. It's light enough that I can see his boat is gone. He's already out there trying to make a catch so he can earn some money. It's silly how even something as simple as *that* increases my feelings for him.

I'm too worked up after that dream to try to sleep again, so I don't bother getting back into bed.

A coffee, a podcast, and my back deck sound like the perfect way to pass the time until I need to leave for work.

A few hours later, I head into *Peaches*, and of course, the day drags by. It always seems to be that way whenever I've woken up really early. All I want to do is crawl into bed and sleep the day *and* these feelings away, but I have to be here until five.

It's around three o'clock when I see a familiar truck pull into the parking lot. My heart rate slowly increases when the memory of my dream surfaces, and the thought of his hands on me has my legs squeezing together. A warmth spreads throughout my body, and I'm pretty sure my cheeks turn pink. I'm blushing, and I *never* blush.

Jacob pulls all sorts of feelings out of me without even trying. In fact, he's tried hard to keep me away from him. But what good has that done?

I watch him with a soft smile on my face as he steps out of his vehicle. I'm so glad the paint came off the side easily. You can't even tell there was anything on it now.

He's wearing jeans and a long-sleeved shirt, with a ball cap finishing up the look. And although it's nothing special, it's so different from what all the men I've known would wear that it makes it all the better.

"Remi."

I'm pulled out of my gaze by my name being spoken beside me, and I whip my head around to see Grant standing at the counter with a chocolate bar. He turns his head to where I was watching Jacob walk toward the store and raises a single brow.

My heart beats wildly in my chest at being caught watching Jacob, and *smiling* no less, but over the years, I've been taught to keep my face neutral no matter what is going on inside my mind.

When he turns back to me, I act as if nothing is wrong. As if I wasn't just caught smiling at the town pariah.

"Hi, Grant. How are you today?"

"Good. Very good."

I scan his chocolate bar, finding it odd that he only ever gets random things like this or gum. He must eat out all the time or go out of town for his groceries.

Out of my peripheral, I see Jacob enter the store, and I can feel Grant's stare burning into me as if he's waiting, watching to see if I'll acknowledge Jacob in any way.

I don't, though. I don't watch Jacob walk by or watch him move down the aisle containing the bread.

I finish getting Grant's change out and hand it to him with a smile on my face. "Here you go. Have a good day."

"Thanks."

He picks up his chocolate bar, looks over in the direction where Jacob went, and then turns around and walks out.

Even if he hadn't caught me watching Jacob, I would have felt uncomfortable in his presence. There's just something about Grant I'm not sure of, but I can't put my finger on what it is.

A few minutes later, Jacob comes to the counter with a handful of items, and the smile returns to my face.

"Hi," he says.

It's just one tiny word, but it's such a difference from what he would have done in the past—which is, ignore me—that it has my stomach doing a little somersault. Ever since I admitted to myself about the feelings I have for him, I've found it hard to keep them as just the background noise they were before.

"Hey."

"Are you, um . . . coming over tonight?"

My insides flutter at the fact that he asked me, even though it's more than likely to do with him preparing himself for me invading his space once again.

Movement over his shoulder catches my eye, and I see Jolene reorganizing some shelves at the other end of the store.

My loyalties are suddenly tugged harshly in different directions. She was attacked by someone just like Jacob. That thought has the flutters disappearing instantly, and it feels like the rose-colored glasses I was wearing were ripped off, reminding me again that I shouldn't be feeling this way.

I swallow the lump in my throat and answer, "Um, not tonight. I was up really early, so I need to have an early night."

"Oh, yeah, sure."

I know my ears didn't deceive me just now when I heard the disappointment in his tone. It has all the mixed-up feelings inside me pulling and pushing and clashing together.

I total his items in silence, hating the way I'm so torn. He keeps his focus down, much like he did the first time I saw him in here, and I don't like it.

I watch as he turns to walk away with his things, the knot around my stomach tightening further with each step he takes.

And then my mouth opens before I can think twice about it.

"Jacob." He turns his head to look over his shoulder. "I'll be over tomorrow night."

Chapter Thirteen

Jacob

I thought that was bad enough when Remi used to turn up at my place here and there and stay for only short periods of time, but it's nothing compared to now.

She's at my house almost daily, making it hard for me to ignore her, along with my growing attraction to her.

At first, when she was always asking questions, I would give a dickish response to try to make her leave me alone, but that didn't work. So, I started answering just to shut her pretty mouth up. Now, I answer because I've found that I like having someone to talk to after all these years.

I like her company, and that's a fucking disaster for a number of reasons.

The only other person I've ever felt anything for is the very reason my life is the way it is now. I don't know if I could ever truly believe that something like that would never happen again.

Besides, what kind of life could I possibly hope to give her? We could never go out anywhere together. I can barely afford food and shit as it is. How would I be able to get her any type of gift? I had to pick some flowers from the side of the road and put them in one of my drinking glasses for the table tonight.

I'm being a fucking idiot even thinking about that shit, anyway. Why the hell would she ever consider me like that? It's amazing she's even hanging around in the first place. I'm probably just some charity case for her.

There's still another thought I haven't completely ruled out as well: that she's working some scheme to get me to leave.

Still, I can't find it in me to keep pushing her away, so I let her come over. I let her hang around, and I just suffer with my feelings.

There's a knock at the door right on time. She's always punctual, which I really like. Everything was on a schedule in prison, so I've become accustomed to it when I have something planned.

After a quick glance at the cameras to ensure the lights are on, I head to the door. I have to fight to keep my eyes focused on her face when I open it up.

She's fucking gorgeous, wearing a cute little dress that shows the swells of her tits and perfectly hugs her curves. It seems like she's been wearing nicer outfits lately, but I could be mistaken and just reading into it.

What do I know about how girls act, anyway?

She lets go of a strand of hair she was playing with and smiles widely at me. "Hey," she says cheerily.

I still don't understand why she's so nice to me and actually seems happy to be here. After all the shit she's probably heard around town, you'd think hanging around me would be the last thing she'd want to do.

I step back to let her in and end up watching her ass move through her dress as she walks past, causing my dick to twitch.

Then I feel like a fucking dirty asshole because I've been jerking off to her *way* too much lately. I try to think about other things while I'm stroking my dick, but her face always ends up in the forefront. Of course, it doesn't help that thinking about her makes me hard in the first place.

"So, I know I usually bring already cooked food for us, but this time, I figured I'd cook it here and maybe teach you at the same time?"

Shit. I thought I'd avoided the whole learning-to-cook thing, but I guess it's something I really should learn to do. I can't rely on her to always bring me delicious food, plus it'd probably be nice if I made her an actual meal sometime instead of just cooking some fish over the fire.

I grunt and say, "Fine, whatever."

She actually giggles at me as she walks into my kitchen without hesitation, holding a bag that I'm guessing contains ingredients for dinner.

"So agreeable today. Lucky me." Remi starts taking some things out of the bag, but then stops and makes a beeline for my table. "Oh, these are beautiful! I *love* wildflowers." She places a hand on her chest and looks over at me, but I quickly turn around and busy myself so she can't ask if I picked them just for her. I guess I lucked out with my choice of flowers.

"What do you need?" I ask as she steps back into the kitchen.

"Um. A cutting board, a pot for boiling some pasta, and a pan for cooking the meat and sauce in."

She chews on her bottom lip while thinking of anything else she might need, drawing my attention to it. I resist the urge to stare at her lips, and instead get started on finding the items she listed. I don't even know if I'll have everything. I had just bought a bunch of random kitchen items to get me by when I first got this place.

"Oh, and a knife and a wooden spoon," she adds. "I figured spaghetti would be something easy and simple for you to learn. Plus, you seemed to enjoy it."

"I've liked all the meals you've made," I mumble as I take out a pot and pan. After all the prison food I've eaten, her food is like a gourmet meal every time.

When I turn around, Remi has a big grin splitting her cheeks. "That's true, you have." She takes the pot and pan from me. "Cutting board?"

I reach behind the coffee pot and grab the small one I have. "This big enough?"

"It'll do," she answers, giving me that smile again. "I only added onions and peppers last time, but you can decide what you do and don't put into it. We can add other stuff, like canned corn or hotdog chunks. I brought some just in case."

All of that sounds pretty good to me, but I'm not likely to buy any of that very often, so sticking to the basics will probably be better. She pulls the rest of the ingredients out of the bag on the counter, and I stuff my hands into my pockets.

"The onion and pepper will be fine this time."

"All right, I'll get started on cutting the pepper. Can you fill up the pot with water to boil?"

My kitchen really isn't that big, so I have to brush by her to get the water. The subtle smell of her shampoo permeates the air, and I find myself greedily taking in deep breaths to pull as much of it into my lungs as possible. It's certainly nothing like the piss mixed with disinfectant I had to put up with for years.

My arm grazes Remi's as I place the pot on the stove, and I notice goosebumps form on her skin.

"Are you cold?" I didn't think it was particularly cold in here, but she only has a small dress on.

Remi clears her throat. "Uh. No. I'm okay, thanks."

She moves ever so slightly away from me, reminding me not only of how close I'm actually standing to her, but also that she likely still sees me as the detestable human being who is capable of harming her, just like everyone else does. It's a fucking punch to the gut.

Her arm knocks the onion on the counter with her movement away from me, causing it to roll to the ground, so I step past her to get it while she resumes cutting the pepper.

I bend over at the waist to pick it up, and the next thing I know, there's a clattering sound, and Remi hisses out, "Shit." I turn around to see her gripping her finger. "I cut myself."

Frowning, I step closer to take a look. "Let me see."

She releases her finger, and I watch as blood trickles down her hand.

"I just looked away for a second," she murmurs, shaking her head, a slight pink tinting her cheeks.

Pulling her hand, I lead her to the sink to rinse it off under the water. I'm not sure how deep it is, and I can't see with the blood in the way.

We both watch silently as the water washes over her finger, making the cut visible. I lift it closer to my face to inspect, and Remi winces.

"Sorry." I lift my eyes to hers, momentarily getting caught up in the swirls of green, brown, and yellow. She's so close that I can hear her shallow breaths. Or are those mine? I lick my dry lips, and when her eyes drop down to them and her eyes widen slightly, I release her hand and take a step back. Shit, maybe she thought I was going to do something to her. "Uh. It doesn't look too deep. A band-aid should be fine; I'll go get you one."

"Thanks."

By the time I get back, she's stirring the meat in the pan and holding her hand wrapped in a napkin off to the side.

"Here." I make quick work of putting some antiseptic on and getting it covered with the band-aid.

"If you don't mind cutting up the rest of the pepper and the onion, I'll cook the meat and the pasta."

"Okay."

We both get to work, and she talks me through each step. Whatever tension I felt in the air is gone, and I'm glad she's at ease again, obviously not seeing me as a threat anymore.

I don't ever want her feeling like that, so I make sure to keep a healthy distance from her. Well, as much as I can in the small kitchen.

When dinner is cooked, I tell her to go sit at the table while I dish out the food and pour glasses of water. Then I take a seat opposite her at the table.

"So," she starts after a couple of bites of the tasty food. "Did you end up telling your parole officer about me?"

At the mention of him, the food I was chewing turns rancid in my mouth, and it feels like I was slapped in the face with a cold hand. He's a reminder of the life I live, which I briefly forgot about while spending time with Remi, making dinner.

My hands ball into fists under the table, and I'm tempted to tell her to mind her own fucking business because I don't want to talk about him. But I'm not pissed at *her*, and it *is* her business, very much so.

Plus, the genuineness of her voice and the way she takes a bite of her food and then looks back up at me with those beautiful eyes, waiting for my answer, further tamps down the anger.

"Yes, I did." My brows furrow when I realize she should have heard from him by now. "He hasn't called you?"

She chews on her plump bottom lip, and I find myself wondering if they're as soft as they look.

"I had a missed call from a number I didn't recognize. Maybe it was him? I'll call it back tomorrow."

I nod. "Don't expect him to be nice to you at all."

She grins, finding something funny about that. "I'm used to dealing with surly men."

I almost roll my eyes at that, but end up just looking back down at my food as she lets out a quiet chuckle. She's always smiling and laughing.

Since she's the one to interrogate me most of the time, I decide to ask her the next question instead to get to know her better.

"How do you like working at *Peaches*?"

She looks taken aback for just a second and then smiles like I just gifted her something. "I like it, actually. I know it's not the greatest job, and it's not doing something fun like fishing, but it suits me fine."

I don't tell her that I had tried to get a job there when I first moved here, but was swiftly rejected. Or that I only started fishing because I had no other choice. It's not that I don't like it; I'd just rather be doing it for leisure instead of necessity.

"That's good."

I ask her some more questions about what she used to do, where she's from, and things like that. And I don't know who's more surprised by my sudden interest in knowing her. Either way, she seems happy about it, and that has an effect on me.

After dinner, we both quietly clean up the kitchen, and although I've kind of gotten used to having her around, the whole night has seemed more intimate somehow, and *that* is something I'm not used to.

With the kitchen clean, I go sit on one end of the couch. It's not very big, so I'm kind of shocked when Remi takes a seat on it as well, instead of the single armchair.

"You know, if you had a TV, we'd be able to watch something right now," she says, turning to me with a wink.

I shrug. I've thought about what it'd be like to have a TV again since she mentioned it. I've thought about what it would be like to sit back with a blanket on a cold evening and watch a movie. And I can't deny that there is a warm body next to me under the blankets in those thoughts. *Her* warm body.

"And I'm still waiting for a fishing lesson," she adds, followed by a pointed look in my direction.

"Well, you'll be waiting a long time," I answer. When her eyes widen and she points at my face, I shift back, frowning, unsure of what she's doing. "What?"

"You smiled," she states as a grin takes over her face.

I shift a little again, uncomfortable. Has this couch always been so lumpy?

"No, I didn't."

Her cheeks only widen at my words. I don't have anything against smiling; I just haven't had too many things to smile about over the past decade. And I hadn't even realized I'd smiled at her.

"You did so," she says softly. "And it looked really good on you."

I feel my heart rate triple when she slides close enough to me on the couch that our knees press together. Out of habit, I quickly glance up at the camera facing us. Once I get the confirmation of the blinking red lights, I turn my attention back to her.

Her face is only inches away from me now. Did she get closer?

I'm confused by her actions, and I'm not sure how to respond. I can't read the conflicting expressions on her face.

However, when she reaches up and touches my cheek and then leans in close, her intentions become clear.

I clench my fists on my thighs to try to keep myself from physically flinching at her touch. The second her lips press to mine, a bombardment of random thoughts rush at me.

I can't believe she's fucking kissing me.

Her lips *are* as soft and luscious as I thought they'd be—softer even.

She smells so good.

My dick starts to respond to her closeness, and my hands itch to touch her.

When she starts to move her lips slightly, I begin freaking out internally because I have no fucking idea what I'm doing.

Should I grab her face as well? Tilt my head? Her head? Fuck.

Okay, I need to chill the fuck out. I've seen people kiss before. I just need to do what feels natural. I try to relax into it and unclench my fists, but the second I feel her tongue poke out and swipe my lip, I lose it.

Nope.

I stand abruptly, causing Remi to fall back on the couch, and then walk straight into the bathroom, shutting the door behind me.

I grip the sides of the sink and stare at myself in the mirror. "Fuck."

What the hell just happened?

Besides me panicking, she actually kissed me. Why would she do that?

She should be running in the other direction, not leaning into me, pressing those soft lips to mine.

I blow out a breath and adjust my dick before splashing some water on my face.

If I go out there and we end up kissing again, or I let it go even further, she's going to find out.

"Yep. She'll find out that you're a fucking twenty-eight-year-old virgin who has no fucking clue what he's doing."

I scoff at myself in the mirror. What the hell am I even thinking? I can't let this go any further. I'm a convicted rapist, for fuck's sake.

I can't bring her down into my world, no matter what I feel for her. I'll just go out there and tell her to leave. She'll assume I didn't like it and go.

My chest tightens at the thought, but it has to be done.

After another deep breath, I open the door, ready to stalk out there and be an asshole.

But Remi is standing there on the other side of the door with her mouth hanging open.

Chapter Fourteen

Remi

Virgin. Virgin. *Virgin.* That word keeps tumbling through my head as I stare back at Jacob's wary face. My mouth opens and closes a few times. *Oh my god.*

I came over here to apologize for kissing him, thinking I went too far and feeling all sorts of messed up about it.

But then I heard him talking to himself.

Virgin.

The only way that can be true . . .

"You didn't do it," I gasp, putting the pieces together. It all makes so much sense now. "*You didn't do it!*"

My breathing gets labored, the realization weighing heavily on my chest. An overwhelming rush of emotions fills my body as I come to terms with what that means. Not only the unnecessary guilt I've been agonizing over for feeling anything for Jacob, but of what it means for *him*.

I turn away and walk the short distance to the kitchen, grasping onto the counter for support. Tears prickle at the backs of my eyes.

"This whole time, you were innocent. You were innocent, and they sent you to prison *for ten years.*"

"I know," he huffs out, taking a few steps into the room. "I fucking know."

I watch as both of his hands slide over his face and then move to the back of his neck to squeeze the tension probably building there.

I just can't believe it.

They sent an innocent man to prison.

He lost his parents.

He lost his friends.

He didn't die, but he did lose his life.

A sob rips from my chest, and I feel like I might be on the verge of hyperventilating.

"Hey, don't do that," Jacob says, now facing me. "Don't cry." He shuffles his feet beneath him, looking like he wants to comfort me, but years of being treated like a vile piece of shit has conditioned him to keep his distance.

I close the space between us, gripping him in a fierce hug. His body stiffens beneath my touch, and his hands hang in the air for a moment, not knowing where to settle. Eventually, when I don't let go but rather bury my face deeper into him as the tears flow, his arms circle around to rest on my back, pulling me closer.

"Don't cry," he repeats softly. "I've never been able to handle seeing tears."

"I can't help it," I mumble into his chest.

His whole *life* has been ruined, and he didn't do a damn thing. This town *hates* him, having judged him with no option of redeeming himself in their eyes. Oh god, they do all those horrible things to him, and he doesn't deserve even an ounce of it.

I pull back slightly to look up at him. His face is blurry through my tears, but I still see him in a new light.

"How are you not more bitter?"

He lets out a small snicker. "In case you hadn't noticed, I am, most days." One of his hands slides up my back and moves to my face, then his thumb swipes gently at the wetness on my cheeks, an action that seems totally out of character for him . . . or maybe not. Maybe that is what he was like before it all happened. "But you make the days a little more bearable."

My insides melt at not only his touch, but also at his words.

My heart is feeling so many things right now. It's clear that it knew something all along, something that I had failed to see. Though I did always find it hard to believe and see him as the truly evil man he was supposed to be.

The blurriness in my vision begins to subside as I get a hold of my emotions. His beautiful blue-gray eyes come into focus, and I feel like I'm truly seeing them for the first time. Where I once thought I saw guilt and regret, I now see torture, pain, and anguish. He was ripped from his innocent teenage life and thrown into a pit of monsters, labeled as one himself.

As my eyes trail over his face and land on his lips, a thought suddenly occurs to me. "Was that your first kiss?"

He releases his hold on me while letting out a quiet groan and walks over to the couch, rubbing a hand over his jaw.

I follow and sit next to him. "What?"

"It's fucking embarrassing."

I place my hand on his arm, giving a gentle squeeze. "No. Please don't be embarrassed. I certainly don't think anything less of you. God, I mean, you were robbed of *so much*. If anything, I find you more attractive because of it." Then, stroking his arm a little, I add, "I feel privileged to be your first." When I realize how that sounded, my cheeks flush hot. "I mean your first kiss."

He actually smiles down at his hands in his lap, and I'm struck once again by how young and handsome he looks when he does.

"Why did you let me think you did it?"

After sighing, he says, "Remi, I spent months trying to tell people I was innocent. My own family, who had known me my whole life, and friends, who knew me for years, didn't believe me. Why would I ever think you'd believe me? It was better for you just to think what everyone else did, anyway."

"And why is that?"

He shrugs. "You don't belong in the world of the debased."

"Neither do you."

His eyes swing to mine. "The rest of the world would disagree with you."

"I don't care. And I'm not staying away from you. It didn't stop me when I thought you were guilty, but were a changed man. It sure as hell isn't going to stop me now that I know the truth."

I lean my head on his shoulder, feeling so incredibly grateful that I stuck around him in the first place despite my initial thoughts.

My sights settle on one of the cameras, and my burning questions pertaining to them come to the forefront. "Why do you have cameras everywhere?"

Jacob takes in a deep breath before releasing it slowly. "The biggest problem I had was not being able to prove that I *didn't* do anything wrong. If there had been proof, my life would be a lot different right now."

"So, the cameras are here so you always have the proof?"

"Yeah. I'm not exactly welcome in this town, so I like to be prepared in case someone tries to accuse me of something. It makes me feel better to have these in my home, even though I'm pretty much only around people when I'm in town where there are in-store cameras everywhere. I keep all the videos on my laptop."

A thought occurs to me, and guilt fills my insides, bringing me back to when I first stumbled upon his home. "Did you, um . . . see me in some of your videos?"

"Yes."

"I'm sorry."

He shrugs as if it's the least bad thing to happen to him, but I still feel bad.

I've seen him look up at the cameras occasionally when I've been here. I wonder if that's out of habit or if he's just making sure they're on.

"There aren't any on your boat," I point out. That's one of the things I remember noticing when I was on there. At least he wouldn't have had to watch me go through his things.

"Uh, actually, there is now."

"Oh." I sit up straighter, fidgeting with my fingers and the band-aide he put on me earlier. "I'm really sorry for going on your boat like that. And for all the bad things I thought about you. And for all the things the people in town do to you. It's *so* wrong."

"Remi, I've seen some true serial rapists over the years. Believe me when I say the people around here are behaving exactly how I'd expect them to behave toward any one of them."

"But you're *not* one of them."

"They don't know that."

"They should." I shift to face him again. "I wish there was some way to convince them."

"I've given up on anything like that."

I lower my gaze. I guess he's had a lot longer than me to come to terms with his life and accept the injustice.

Well, at least he has one person on his side now, one person who doesn't see him as an evil predator. It makes me feel good knowing I just might make a difference in his life.

"You fought so hard to keep me away. Are you angry that I'm here and know the truth now?"

He holds my gaze for a moment, and then the side of his mouth tips up the slightest bit. "No. I'm not angry."

"Good." I lean my head on his shoulder again, noting how he didn't tense up like the last time. "How did you ever survive in prison?"

"You and your fucking questions," he says on an exhale, but there is no annoyance in his tone. "I almost didn't survive. The first few months were the worst; I was scared, alone, and depressed. And I didn't know the rules."

"Rules?"

I feel him nod. "There are rules amongst the inmates, and I hadn't learned them yet. Rapists aren't exactly well-liked in there, either, so when I unknowingly crossed paths with the wrong person . . . well, let's just say I'm lucky to be alive."

"Seriously?"

"Yeah. Fortunately for me, my behemoth of a cellmate stepped in and saved me. He never believed that I was guilty. I don't know why that was; I never said it to him out loud. But, nevertheless, even though he hated me—he hated everyone—he protected me until I bulked up enough where I could take care of myself."

"That's . . . I just can't even imagine."

We sit for a moment in silence while I digest all this new information.

Finally, my thoughts drift back to the reason we ended up here in the first place—I had kissed him.

I lift my head off his shoulder and turn my face toward his. He's so incredibly handsome, and I must admit that my attraction to him has multiplied tenfold since finding out what he's been through. His ocean eyes meet mine, and there's no war within me now about what I should do.

I lift my hand and slide it along his neck, all the way to the back of his head, and then pull it close so that our lips can meet. This time, he's not as rigid.

He doesn't grab me and stick his tongue into my mouth—I suspect it may be some time before he does anything like that. But he does move his lips, quickly learning how I like it.

Thoughts of the world around us drift away as I get lost in his kisses. His pressure increases while moving his lips over mine, and I gently suck on his bottom lip. A low groan rumbles from his chest, and all too quickly, he's pulling away.

"It's, um . . . been, uh," he sputters in a gravelly tone while smoothing a hand down the front of his shirt. "You should probably take some time to let all of this sink in."

I nod, trying to slow my breathing and simmering the need between my legs. I don't need time to let anything sink in to know that this is what I want, but I have a feeling it's for him. He needs the time, and I'm willing to accommodate him. Tonight has been a game-changer for both of us.

I lay my head back down on his shoulder and place my arm across his stomach. He doesn't wrap his arm around me or anything, but that's okay. If I was his first kiss, then I doubt he has any experience with girls *at all*.

It's a little hard to imagine, with him looking the way he does, all bulky and manly.

Plus, I have a very nice view of the large bulge in his jeans.

I let out a happy sigh. "I like it when you're chatty." He's been pretty forthcoming tonight, and I've quite enjoyed getting to know him better.

"Don't get used to it," he grumbles after a few seconds, and I can't help the giggle that escapes.

Chapter Fifteen

Jacob

Thirty minutes. That's how long I sat unmoving after she fell asleep on my shoulder. I guess getting all emotional took a toll on her.

I couldn't stay sitting there, though. I started getting anxious, an itchy feeling spreading all over my body the longer I sat with her stuck to my side. I carefully pushed her to lean on the other end of the couch and then sat in the armchair for a while instead.

With my hands clasped under my chin, I leaned on my knees, watching the steady rise and fall of her chest and the pieces of hair that fluttered with each breath she took. She was so fucking pretty.

As much as I liked watching her, my mind still wouldn't settle. Talking to her had brought up a lot of memories, and all the thoughts that had gone through my mind at my lowest point swirled around in my head.

Instead of hanging around any longer, I got up and came out to my boat, and I've been out here on the water ever since, laying back on the bow. Being on *Grace* has always been calming for me. Or maybe it's just being out on the water away from everyone.

At first, I just stared up into the black sky, watching the stars move slowly, but now that the sun is starting to rise, I stare out at the endless ocean in front of me.

I can't tell what it is that's bothering me exactly.

Maybe it's because no one had actually believed me before.

No one has ever been so clearly upset by what I've endured.

No one has ever told me that they'd stick by my side and have me actually believe it.

No one has ever looked at me the way she did.

And I've definitely never wanted to fuck somebody as much as I do her.

I wanted so badly to grab her and sink my dick inside her pussy when she kissed me. But because I've been told that I was a disgusting pervert for so long, now even just thinking those types of things fucks with my head. I guess, in a way, it's hard to see myself as anything other than what I've been called, and I don't want to sully her.

At the same time, I *really* want to.

Sitting up, I decide to throw a few lines in while I'm out here. I should have already been trying to catch something, but my mind was elsewhere.

A couple of hours later, when I've made two catches, I turn *Grace* around and head back to shore. I wonder if Remi will still be there. I didn't leave her a message or anything and I guess I probably should have. I wasn't exactly thinking about it eight hours ago when I first left.

The fact that I didn't sleep all night starts catching up with me by the time I make it back to the dock and my eyes start feeling heavy. Glancing down the side of the boat, I decide that jumping into the cool water for a quick swim will help wake me up.

I moor my boat and then peel off my jeans and T-shirt, jumping into the ocean below a moment later as I've done many times before.

The cool water instantly awakens my body and drowns out the negative thoughts that were plaguing me all night. I stay under the surface, expending some energy by swimming in whatever direction I'm facing.

I finally push up to the surface to take in some air when my lungs begin to burn. As I breathe in deeply, I look back in the direction of my home to see someone leaning against my truck. And it's not Remi.

"What the fuck?"

I quickly swim to the shore and walk up the beach to my truck parked in the driveway, not giving a shit that I'm only in my boxer briefs.

The guy pushes off the hood when he sees me coming and then takes another bite of the apple in his hand. I don't particularly pay too much attention to the people in this town, so it doesn't surprise me when I don't recognize him at all.

People have been messing with my truck for months now, but they've never hung around to chat, especially not at this time of the morning, so I have no idea what the deal is with this guy.

"Can I help you?" I ask in an irritated tone.

"This your truck?" He jerks his head toward it.

"Obviously."

He smiles, but it's not a particularly friendly one. "I was just taking a drive around and saw it. Don't s'pose you're looking to sell?"

I eye him over. I highly doubt he's actually interested in buying my truck, but I can't tell what his intentions are.

"Nope."

He takes another bite and then speaks with a mouthful of apple. "Too bad. 2011 was a good year. For the truck, I mean, of course." My jaw clenches tight at his implication. Yes, that's the year of my truck, but it's also the year my life turned to shit, and I don't think it was a coincidence that he brought it up. "Anyway, I'll be on my way," he says, taking a step backward and tossing his apple core off to the side. "Let you get back to things."

Whistling, he turns around and walks back to his car parked on the side of the road.

Well, that was fucking weird, but if that's the newest tactic to try to intimidate me, it failed.

I start toward my house but then remember that I have a couple of fish to unload, so I walk back down the dock to the boat to grab them, and then *finally* head back to my house.

As I open the front door, despite all the thoughts that ran through my head during the night, I get excited at the possibility of Remi still sleeping on my couch.

I'm disappointed, though, when I walk in to find the couch empty. The bathroom door is open as well, so I know she's not in there.

The silence in here is something that I'm used to, but I find it extra quiet now after having Remi here so much and all the talking we did last night.

I notice a piece of paper on the coffee table, so I walk over and pick it up. It's a message left by Remi. I guess she's more thoughtful than I am.

"Good morning! I had to go home and get ready for work. I'll see you tonight."

I guess now I have all day to prepare for her to come back here again.

Chapter Sixteen

Remi

"Okay, seriously. Did someone make a deposit in the bank of Remi recently?"

I almost choke on my saliva and look over at Tahnee leaning on the counter. "You are so crude sometimes," I answer with a chuckle. "And *no*."

Unfazed, she settles in further and replies, "Well, something good happened. You've had this creepy, permanent smile on your face for a couple of days now."

"Uh, thanks for calling my face creepy."

She smirks. "I didn't call your *face* creepy, just the smile you're wearing like you're in one of those nineteen-fifties commercials where they're constantly smiling."

"Can't I just be in a good mood?"

I don't actually know why I'm feeling so happy. What I learned about Jacob a few days ago is anything *but* something to be happy about.

Of course, I feel bad for him, devastated, really. But the *relief* I feel causes a feeling of freedom to run through my veins. I feel so light now despite the heaviness of the situation.

Her eyes narrow as she looks me over. "I guess. Hey, don't forget we're having drinks with those guys, probably sometime in the next week."

"Yep, sure," I answer, not really paying attention.

"All right, well, I'm going to head out now." She straightens up off the counter and stretches her arms above her head. "Do you want to come over and watch a movie tonight?"

I busy myself with the rack at the counter while trying to come up with a satisfactory answer. I hate that I still have to hide the fact I'm spending time with Jacob. But until I can figure something else out, I guess I just have to suck it up.

I settle for the most basic answer when no good excuse comes to mind. "I can't tonight. I have some things to get done."

Being the awesome person that she is, Tahnee doesn't ask what those 'things' are. "No worries. Another time. I'll catch you later." She blows me a kiss, and I wave goodbye as she walks out of the store.

By the time my shift is done, I'm almost bursting out of my skin at the anticipation I feel about seeing Jacob again. I didn't get to see him last night since he had to do some evening fishing, and I had laundry to get done and groceries to get.

Tonight, I had planned on cooking something at my place and bringing it over to him, but I don't want to wait any longer to see him than I've already had to. So, I bag the ingredients for chicken quesadillas to take over there and cook instead, and go to my room to get ready.

After passing by my nightstand more than once, I decide to grab a couple of condoms and add them to the bag as well, just in case. I'm not exactly planning on sleeping with him tonight, but I'd be lying if I said that I didn't *want* to, and I do want to be prepared for anything.

Once I have everything, I set out toward his place.

The ocean-scented air that I once didn't care for is now so familiar that it has a calming effect against the waves of nerves and excitement flowing in my stomach. There's a little part of me that thinks maybe he'll purposely not be at home because he knows I was going to come over tonight.

We've hung out a couple of times since I found out the truth, but I didn't kiss him again until the last night that I was there, and it was right before I left. I hadn't wanted to rush him with anything. But that night, I just couldn't help it.

It had turned heated, and I guess that's why I feel like he may try to avoid me.

When he does open his front door, dressed in a white T-shirt that molds to his body and a pair of faded jeans, all my worries disappear.

My thumb brushes back and forth against my fingers as I stand in front of him, feeling relieved and excited to see him. "Hey," I greet him.

"Hi."

Jacob looks hesitant as he steps back to let me in, which causes apprehension to swim through me.

Did something happen? Is it because I kissed him again?

It's not until I smell the food and see two plates on the table that I realize why he seemed nervous. I walk into the kitchen, place my bag on the counter while taking a peek at the food on the stove, and then turn back to Jacob.

He stuffs his hands into his pockets. "I used the hotdogs and canned corn you brought the other night and added them to some mac n' cheese. Thought I'd cook you something for once." He shrugs. "Might taste like shit, though."

I smile widely as I walk over to pull him into a hug. He's only stiff for a moment before sliding his hands around my back, and of course, it makes me feel giddy that he's feeling more comfortable with me.

"That was sweet. Thank you." Jacob grunts, maybe at the fact that I said 'sweet.' Or maybe it's just because that's what he does. "And I'm sure it won't taste like shit."

"We'll see."

Heading back over to the kitchen, I say, "I had brought some stuff to cook quesadillas, but we can just have them tomorrow night."

"Sure."

I pull out the chicken, sour cream, and cheese from the bag and put them in the fridge. When I turn around, Jacob has tipped out the rest of the items in the bag and is staring down at something on the counter.

Shit, the condoms.

There, beside the quesadilla wraps, are the two foil packets.

I feel heat creeping up along my neck and onto my cheeks. Embarrassment at my assumption makes me want to shrink into myself. "Um . . ."

After what feels like an eternity, he finally turns away from the condoms to peer at me. There's something in his ocean eyes, a look, like a storm is brewing, a mixture of both uncertainty and *desire*.

I think he actually wants it, too. He wants to be physical with me, but after what he's been through, he needs me to be the one to make a move. He needs me to show him that it's okay. And *that* has the need to be close to him growing substantially, erasing any embarrassment I had felt just a few seconds ago.

The look he gives me pulls at me like a tether. I take the few short steps over to him and then reach up to pull his head down for a kiss.

Jacob is slightly rigid at first as my lips slowly coast over his, but then he gets pulled into the natural progression of things, finally making a move. His lips part, and his tongue makes just a tentative sweep of my lips to begin with, and then he's delving into my mouth, his tongue probing and exploring as he lets himself get lost in the moment. The kiss turns from experimental to heated in an instant.

His taste has my body reacting with wanton lust, needily arching into him. I moan into his mouth as my hands move from the back of his head to cup his cheeks. Every single nerve in my body lights up with the contact.

I can feel Jacob's hardness growing against my hip, and it only spurs me on. I shamelessly rub my body against his, earning a low guttural groan from him. All these pent-up emotions are coming together in an explosive way, driving the need to be intimate with him.

I break away from the kiss to trail my lips along his jaw—the jaw that's forged out of every woman's fantasies. His skin is warm, and his scent is masculine. The ragged breathing coming from him in my ear has me so hot and wet between my legs that I can hardly stand it.

I feel almost feral with desire. When he follows my lead and starts kissing my neck in return, all I can think is *yes,* and then my eyes fly skyward, only to land on one of the cameras.

"Can we take this somewhere where there aren't any cameras or turn them off?" I ask with a gasp. Not that I think he'd sell the video, but the thought of being filmed does not appeal to me at all, especially after the life I left behind.

As if coming out of a haze, Jacob suddenly jerks back and then maneuvers his hands between us, gently pushing me back. "I, um . . . sorry."

I instantly feel the space between us as his warmth is replaced by emptiness.

"For what?" Frowning, I try to take a step closer to him, but he dodges me, making his way around the counter to take a seat on the armchair.

He runs a hand down his face and along his jaw. "I just . . . I can't *not* have them on, all right? I can't fucking do anything without the cameras."

I brace myself on the counter, still trying to calm my breathing from just a moment ago.

"Why would you still need to have them on with me?"

I get why he has them. I really do. But if he still won't be around me without them, then what else can I conclude other than he still doesn't trust me after all this time.

He lets out a regretful breath before answering. "Because I need to protect myself."

Turning away from him, I lean my back against the counter.

"Ouch." The sting of his words causes a tightness in my chest.

It hurts.

Am I wrong to think he should be comfortable with me by now? Have I not shown him time and time again that I'm on his side? I mean, besides at the very beginning.

Does he really feel like he needs protection from me? I would *never* accuse him of anything like that.

My chin drops to my chest as I watch my toes wriggle on his wooden floor.

Ten years.

He hasn't had anybody to trust for that long. He couldn't prove his innocence back then, so naturally, he'd want to do everything in his power to be able to do that now. How could I possibly even begin to assume how he should feel? This is a big step for him, and if he feels comfortable having proof on his hands, then I should be able to accommodate him. If not, then I should walk out that door right now.

I angle my head to look over to where he's sitting and take him in. He's leaning forward and resting his elbows on his knees, looking at the ground. His biceps tense as he continues to run a hand along his jaw. His hair is adorably mussed up from me.

I know very well there is no way I could walk away from him now.

Even if it means being filmed having sex.

I push away from the counter, grabbing one of the condoms and slipping it into my back pocket before I walk over to him. His head lifts as I get closer, and he watches me intently when I step into his space.

Positioning myself between his legs, I gently nudge his shoulders with both hands, pushing him to lean back against the chair.

"Okay."

"Okay?" he asks skeptically.

"Yes," I answer before bending and placing my hand on top of his, rubbing my thumb along his knuckles, mimicking the action I do to my own fingers. "If you need them on, it's okay."

I straighten up, taking hold of the bottom of my shirt and slide it up over my head, then drop it to the side. Though it's warm in here, my nipples pebble against my bra when the air hits my skin. My jeans are peeled off next, joining my shirt on the ground.

Jacob's eyes flare, his pupils blown wide at the sight of me in only my underwear. Underwear that, if I'm being honest, I wore for him . . . just in case.

The heat that was brought to a simmer a minute ago begins to boil again as I look at the pure desire blazing in his eyes while he watches me.

Reaching down, I tug at the bottom of his shirt. I feel like if I don't do this right now, he'll change his mind and retreat back into himself.

He's hesitant at first and doesn't move, but then he slowly lifts his arms up, and I'm able to take his shirt off him. Relief mixes with the heat building in me, and I take a second to admire just how broad and sexy his body is. I've seen his chest a few times already, but being able to touch it? Well, that's something else entirely.

Goosebumps form along his hot skin, and his muscles tense as I run my hands from his pecs down to his abs, tracing over the patterns inked into his skin. Even doing something as simple as this feels special to me.

Stopping at the button of his jeans, I glance up at his ocean eyes. "Is this okay?"

He doesn't answer me, but he doesn't stop me when I slowly slide the button through the hole.

His grip on each armrest tightens, and he keeps his gaze focused on my face. It's like he thinks if he moves or speaks, he'll be woken from this dream.

I keep my eyes locked onto his as I slide down his zipper, then push my hands into the sides of his boxer briefs to try removing both his underwear and jeans at the same time. He lifts his ass up from the chair so that I can take them off, effectively giving me permission and telling me that he wants this as much as I do.

Finally breaking our stare, I get my first glimpse of his dick as it springs free, and I'm happily surprised by its thickness and how beautiful it is. My mouth salivates at the sight of it.

The guys I've been encouraged to date in the past had dicks that matched their personalities; bland and boring. Not Jacob's, though. Velvety smooth skin covers his thick, very hard length. A pulsing vein runs the length of it, leading up to a mushroom-shaped tip.

Knowing I'm the first one who will touch him like this sends a thrill rippling through my body, and it has me wanting to make this experience perfect for him.

Instead of touching it just yet, I reach around to unclasp my bra, shimmying it off before hooking my fingers into my panties and then pushing them slowly down my legs. Jacob's eyes track my every movement, heating my skin as they glide over it.

I'm not a prude, but I'm not generally this bold and forward when it comes to sex. Then again, I've never been this excited about it before, either. I've also never been with a man who looks like he could hold me down with just his pinky finger.

His looks and his body scream of raw sexual energy, and yet he has zero experience.

There's something totally heartwarming about that.

Feeling even more bolstered and like he needs me to continue taking control, I lean down to retrieve the condom I grabbed out of my pocket.

Jacob looks as if he's practically vibrating in his seat, but he's barely moved from his spot except to help with getting his clothes off.

I tear open the condom and then grasp hold of his rock-hard dick.

"Fuck," he hisses as I roll it down his shaft.

"This will probably be fast," I say softly. "But don't worry. That's normal for your first time." The side of my lip turns up as I think of something to lighten the pressure for him. "Plus, I'll be riding you, and I'm pretty good at that."

Jacob's eyes snap up to mine, ending his perusal of my body, and his nostrils flare. "While I appreciate you knowing what you're doing," he grates out. "It also means that you've been with other men, and I find that I don't fucking like hearing you talk about that right now."

A rush of warmth pools between my legs at his possessive words, and I nod. It's funny how something as simple as that has me falling even more in lust with this man.

I drop down, placing a knee on either side of him, straddling his thighs, and then take hold of his dick in my hand. His breathing becomes even more ragged, and his teeth sink deep into his bottom lip like he's holding back more curses.

Leaning forward, I pluck that lip from his teeth with my free hand and suck it into my own mouth like I'm stealing those curses from him, then kiss him deeply. At the same time, I slowly rub myself back and forth along his shaft, spreading my arousal over his length.

After a moment, I lean back again, wanting to watch his face as I sink down on him, wanting to capture this moment.

But then I notice his eyes drifting to the side above me. A camera is there. I'm losing him to his fears again, and that just won't do. Needing to bring him back, I reach up to palm his cheek, rubbing my thumb over his skin, gently bringing his face and attention back to me.

"Hey, keep your eyes on me," I say softly. "You okay?"

His eyes focus back on mine, and he does the slightest nod, to which I nod in return. Then, lifting, I make a few passes over my clit with the head of his dick, spreading my juices around even more before positioning him at my opening. And then, slowly, I lower down.

Jacob breathes out a stuttered breath and squeezes his eyes shut.

"Shit."

I angle forward, resting my forehead against his while still watching him, letting this moment sink in as our breath mingles together.

When he opens his eyes again, his pupils appear dilated, and there's a wild, primal look on his face that wasn't there before. Like I just placed the key in the lock to unleash the raw sexual man that I had thought he looked like before.

The look freezes me, holding me captive momentarily, and then releases me as I melt into a puddle. *I'm* doing that to him, and I *love* it.

The longer I look, though, I can see there's more than just desire swirling around his irises. They're brimming with emotion. This isn't just sex. This is much more. It's life-changing for him.

As much as I'm taking control, I'm also offering myself to him, and he's never had that before—never had anyone trust him one hundred percent like this, which I do.

Once I've adjusted to being filled by him, I slowly lift myself and then drop back down while resting my hands on his chest, keeping close.

We continue to keep our eyes locked on each other while I move, and I feel shudders move through him as I continue to lift up and down, again and again, a little faster each time.

It feels good. So good that I end up closing my eyes and dropping my head back, humming with pleasure. I'd love to get mine right now. Grind on him until I find my release. But I'm making myself hold back. My focus is on him this time, and I don't think he's going to last much longer.

This time, when I open my eyes, I find him staring at my chest, and it's only now that I realize he hasn't lifted his hands off the armrests. He's been holding back as well, but for different reasons.

It makes total sense. After being charged with rape and accused of forcing yourself on a woman, you'd want to do everything you can *not* to appear that way.

But I want him to let go. I want him to know it's okay.

"Touch me, Jacob," I whisper.

His eyes flick up to my face, and he swallows thickly before dropping them back to my chest again. And then he's lifting his hands. Warmth caresses me as he takes a breast in each hand, touching and squeezing, playing and discovering.

"Fucking beautiful," he says, more so to himself.

My nails dig into his chest as the sensations build in me, and I start moving my hips in a circular motion. Regardless of whether I come or not, I am thoroughly enjoying myself.

Jacob surprises me by dropping one of his hands to grip my hip and then begins to thrust in unison with me from underneath, finally letting himself move.

"This is..." Jacob begins, but trails off when he's pulled into the beginning sensations of his orgasm.

A few seconds later, I see him grit his teeth while his hands tighten their hold on me. He stills underneath me, the chords of his neck straining as he groans out his release and pulses inside me. I've never been so interested, so enraptured and turned-on by watching someone in the throes of ecstasy. It's a beautiful sight, one that will stick with me forever.

I watch as he comes back down to earth, fascinated and privileged to be the one who shared this experience with him. His other hand drops to my thighs, but instead of removing them quickly—something he would have done in the past—he gently rubs them back and forth.

"How was it?" I ask him after a minute. The low, rumbling, almost delirious chuckle he lets out at my question is so heartwarming to hear that it makes my chest swell. It affects other parts of me, as well—specifically, the area where he's still lodged deep inside me; the area that is still very much stimulated. I shift my hips slightly, my tone breathy. "I mean, it looked pretty good."

When he notices my movements, he's suddenly lifting off the chair with me in his arms, causing a startled sound to escape me. Holding me close, he walks in the direction of what I assume is his bedroom. I grab the other condom off the counter as we pass by, just in case that's what he has in mind.

When we make it into his room, he gently lays me on the bed and then uses a napkin from his dresser to take the condom off and throws it out. I eagerly watch as he returns to the bed and then lays down beside me on the covers. His eyes rake over my body, pausing on my pussy before returning to my face.

"I may not be experienced, but I don't think you got to come, right?"

I've never been one to fake orgasms or to just say what a guy wants to hear to make them feel better in the bedroom, and I don't intend on starting now. "No, I didn't, but I still enjoyed it." I smile. "Very much so."

His gaze flicks to my pussy once again before returning to my face. "Show me how to please you."

There's no question in his tone; it sounded very much like a command, and it has my nipples pebbling into hard peaks as an aroused breath escapes my lips. Jacob notices my nipples, and heat sparks in his eyes.

"Have you . . . watched much porn?" I ask, trying to get a baseline to go off of.

He looks to the side, almost like he's trying to hide his embarrassment.

"Not since I was seventeen. I wasn't allowed to have anything like that in prison, and even if I were, I wouldn't have touched it. Didn't feel right considering what I was in there for."

That same ache that I get in my chest any time I think of the injustices done to him returns, but instead of letting it fester and grow, causing the sadness to seep in, I focus on his words from a moment ago. *"Show me how to please you."*

Without saying another word, I take hold of his hand and guide it between my legs, wanting to bring him back to this moment.

With my fingers on top of his, I show him exactly how I like to be touched. His eyes stay glued to where our hands are, and it has the pleasure building at a faster rate than usual. There's something so sensual and erotic about him watching so intently. The entire time his eyes are on me, mine are watching his face. His jaw works back and forth, and his chest moves faster and faster, his breathing quickening along with our fingers.

No. Not *our* fingers.

I realize I've dropped mine to the side, and he's doing it all on his own. He expertly rubs them over my clit, just like I showed him, just like in my dream from the other week. It has me letting out a moan and reaching up to grab my breast, squeezing and rubbing my hard nipple between my fingers.

My eyes close at all the sensations igniting together, but then fly back open just as quickly when I feel him push my hand from my breast and replace it with his own. He copies my movements, placing even more pressure on me than I had. It has me coming undone within seconds. My body bows off the bed as I cling to the blanket beneath me and cry out, "Ohh. Yes, Jacob!"

I'm breathing heavily when I come to, my eyes hazy and at half-mast.

Jacob's ocean eyes are locked on me, looking dark and heady. "That was the best thing I've ever seen," he says quietly.

"It was pretty great." I smile up at him, lifting a slightly shaky hand to palm his cheek as he looks my body over.

"I really want to fuck you again," he says in that same low tone.

My eyes widen in both surprise and delight at his words while my pussy clenches tight, instantly feeling the need to be filled by him again, as if I didn't just have an orgasm.

I glance down at his dick, and sure enough, he's hard as granite again.

I'm not sure he would have actually said that to me if he weren't in some sort of sex-induced haze, but I will definitely roll with it.

I reach over to the nightstand and grab the condom I had placed there earlier. "I'd really like that as well," I answer, holding it up.

"Yeah?"

"Mm-hmm."

Jacob takes the condom from me, glancing back at me a few times between tearing it open and then taking extra care to make sure it's the right way around. Once he rolls it on, he turns to me, stalling for the slightest moment before moving to place himself between my legs.

He holds himself up by his elbows, his dick nestled comfortably between our bodies, and then locks eyes with me. I've never had this much eye contact during sex before. His gaze sears into me, trapping me in its grasp. The intensity has me wanting to turn away, but I don't. How can I deny him that when he's been denied so much in his life?

So, I keep his stare, wondering what he sees when he looks at me.

Do my eyes give away all the feelings I have for him?

After rocking his hips gently a few times, he leans his face down to gently kiss my lips and then pulls back.

"Thank you."

He doesn't elaborate, but he doesn't need to. I know what he's referring to.

This whole evening has been so significant to him.

I reach up to cup his cheeks, lifting my head off the bed to capture his lips with mine. They part instantly, the lust returning and consuming us once again. Our kiss turns passionate, needy. His hips rock harder against my sensitive clit, and I drop my head back, letting out a gasp.

With my neck exposed to him, he takes the opportunity to kiss and suck it, nibbling on the soft flesh.

I love that he's learning not only what *I* like, but what *he* likes as well.

Sliding my hand between us, I take hold of his dick and bring it to my opening, not wanting to wait any longer.

Jacob thrusts into me in one swift motion, and then drops his forehead to my shoulder, breathing out a curse. My eyes squeeze shut at the delicious intrusion.

We stay that way for a few long seconds, connected and tangled together but unmoving.

Finally, when he must have gained some control over himself, Jacob begins moving his hips, moving in and out of me in a steady rhythm. His lips start trailing over my skin, his hot breath heating the area as he goes.

At this moment, our pasts don't exist. Our families don't exist. The town doesn't exist.

And it's so hard for me to imagine him as the same guy I saw him as just a few weeks ago.

When he gets close to my chest, he pauses and brings his glazed-over eyes up to look at me. There's a question there. He's asking for permission, not willing to assume it's okay.

Instead of answering with words, I reach up to grip his hair and shove his mouth down onto a sensitive nipple. The second his wet warmth encloses around the nub, a shudder runs through me. A moan vibrates from my chest—although it could have come from him; it's hard to tell.

When he begins to suck, a spark of pleasure shoots straight to my core and has me clenching tighter around him, causing his thrusts to become erratic and my senses to overload. My orgasm skyrockets and bursts inside me in an instant, the feeling almost overwhelming.

Jacob grunts out at the same time, burying himself as deep as he can. The two of us cling together as we get lost in the ecstasy.

Sweat coats both of our bodies, and our chests continue to heave as we come down from the high.

While Jacob's head remains lodged in my neck, I lift my hand to run my fingers through his hair, loosening the wet strands from where they're stuck to his head.

My heart is feeling so incredibly full right now, full of him.

My poor, surly but sweet, tortured man.

CHAPTER SEVENTEEN

Jacob

There's a warmth wrapped around me.

It's calming, comforting in a way like a warm blanket.

I feel peace in this moment, something that has seemed elusive for quite some time now. I bask in it, dwelling in the feelings it evokes.

But slowly, those feelings change.

Morphing into the unwelcome, sinister nightmares that used to plague me regularly. The warmth is a trick, lulling me into a false sense of security.

I'm supposed to be sleeping with one eye open, but I let my guard down, and I shouldn't have. Anything can happen in here, especially to someone like me.

The warmth moves across my stomach, preparing for the attack. I wonder if the weapon of choice will be a toothbrush carved into a shank. It probably won't be sharp enough to slit my throat, which would be the quickest death. They've tried this before and didn't succeed.

My eyes pop open as they slide their hands up my chest, and I shove back, creating enough distance to defend myself.

"Hey. Hey, it's just me," a soft voice says.

I blink several times, my surroundings coming into focus as the sleepy daze disappears. My heart still pounds, ricocheting against my chest, and my muscles are tense, prepared for the attack that never came.

"Shit. Sorry," I mumble when my eyes land on Remi's concerned gaze at the other end of the couch. It must have been *her* warmth I felt on me, *her* body I shoved off me.

"Probably a little disconcerting waking up next to someone for the first time, right?"

I nod, rubbing a hand over my face because, yes, it was the first time I woke with a body sleeping next to mine, and yes, thinking she was about to attack me *was* fucking disconcerting.

I stretch out my arms and back and then sit back into the couch, trying to relax a little more. Remi shuffles closer to me a second later and then lays her head on my shoulder. I've found that I really like it when she does that.

As the remaining sleep fog fades, memories of last night start to filter in.

The sex, and how incredible it felt to finally experience it with someone. But not just anyone, with Remi.

I remember how incredible it felt coming *inside* her and not on my hand.

I remember how her face looked and the sounds she made when she came.

God, I could live off those memories for months, years even, and they'd get my dick hard every time, just like it's starting to get now.

Finally, I remember us eventually eating the dinner I had made, then sitting on the couch where I learned more about her childhood. And as painful as it was, I ended up sharing with her what happened that night all those years ago.

We must have fallen asleep on the couch together at some point, which, in itself is amazing, considering it usually takes me quite some time to fall asleep in a comfortable bed.

"You hungry?" I ask after a minute, wanting to make sure she's comfortable and happy to stay.

"Not yet," Remi says with a yawn. "Hey, do you rent or own this place?"

"Again with the questions." My lips find the top of her head, gently pressing a kiss onto it. And although I've never done that in my life, it felt so natural to kiss her like that. I find myself leaning into her a little more, the scent of her shampoo floating up into my senses with each breath I take. "I own it. Bought it right after getting out."

"I hope you don't mind me asking, but how did you afford it?"

It's not hard to figure out that I don't have a lot of money these days. She sees the shit food I get from the store. She's seen inside my home. She's seen in my cupboards. So it's not surprising she'd ask.

"I used to work at my parents' furniture store." A bitterness tries to snake its way in when I think about my parents and how they believed I was capable of . . . I shove those thoughts away, not wanting to spoil my morning. "From thirteen onwards, and I got paid well for it, saving almost every penny. It was all put into a high-interest-rate account, so there was enough to buy this place and the boat that went with it after years of it just sitting there. The truck I already had from before."

"Wow, that's great. Well, I'm glad you picked here to live here."

"Me, too."

At first, I had thought a small beach town was the perfect place to hide away. I thought the fewer people around, the better. But really, the fewer people around, the more they talk to each other, and the more they want to get rid of what isn't a part of their community.

I'd most likely be better off as a nobody in a large city.

Even so, I'd move here all over again if it meant finding Remi, who is as beautiful as she is stubborn.

Remi places her hand on my thigh in what I'm sure is supposed to be a comforting gesture, but my dick responds by instantly perking up again. Like now that he's had a taste of what it's like to be with her, he wants it all the time.

I have to admit, it has me feeling a little concerned. What if I turn into the very thing that I hate? What if I try to force her when she doesn't want it?

A second later, those thoughts float away, making way for the anticipation of what's to come when her hand slides up higher toward the bulge forming in my pants. Shit, there's no way Remi hasn't noticed, but she doesn't seem bothered by it, either.

Her hand continues all the way up until she's cupping me through my pants and rubbing back and forth. My head drops to the back of the couch, and my eyes close.

"Remi, what are you doing?"

I know she only brought two condoms with her, so I didn't think we'd be having sex again. She shifts away from me and then drops down to the ground on her knees between my legs.

"Well, I thought I might give you your first blowjob." My dick jerks and hardens further at the word. My eyes drop to her lips as she licks them, and fuck, just the thought of them wrapped around my dick has me ready to come in my pants. Remi reaches for my waistband and then pauses. "At least, I assume it's your first time?"

I clear my throat, trying to calm my wildly beating heart, and buy myself a few extra seconds to ensure my voice comes out steady. "Yeah. It'd be the first one."

The beaming smile on her face is fucking gorgeous. It appears that the fact I have no experience doesn't bother her at all, but rather, it seems to make her *happy*.

She continues pulling my sweats down, and my eager dick pops out, swollen and ready with pre-cum seeping out.

"Mmm." She hums as she takes hold of it and strokes up and down a couple of times, then she brings it to her mouth without another word.

I hiss out a breath when her lips close around the tip, the rush of excitement traveling through me in the form of a shudder. My eyes want to close at the overwhelming sensations, but I don't let them. I don't want to miss any of this.

Her tongue swirls around the tip while her cheeks hollow out, and it feels beyond amazing.

I can't help the loud groan that passes through my lips when she starts bobbing her head up and down, while using one of her hands to massage my balls gently.

"Fuck, Remi."

I have the strongest urge to grip her hair and shove my dick as far as I can into her mouth, but I don't think that's appropriate. So, I ball my hands into fists and keep them seated on my thighs.

"You taste good," she murmurs, licking from base to tip before returning her mouth to where it was.

She continues with a mixture of movements, sucking and swirling and licking while humming. Saliva dribbles down the side of my dick and onto my balls, and the sight is so dirty and erotic it has them drawing in tight. I have no idea how I've managed to last this long.

Remi shifts on her knees and brings both hands onto my thighs. When she notices my clenched fists, her eyes flick up to mine. The next thing I know, she's picking up one of my hands, forcing it open, and bringing it to the back of her head, all without breaking rhythm or eye contact. And fuck, that has something in me snapping.

I tangle my fingers through her silky black hair and push her head down. The feeling of my dick hitting the back of her throat has me ready to explode.

Tingles start from the base of my spine, senses firing in every direction. All the muscles in my body tense, and I push my hips up as I hold her head down.

My eyes squeeze shut as my cum shoots deep into her throat. I groan out loud and long, getting lost in one of the best feelings of my life, where none of the shit from the past ten years exists.

After being milked dry, I finally open my eyes to glance down at Remi. Her cheeks are flushed pink, and tears trickle from her eyes like she can't breathe. Horror fills me as I realize I'm the one doing that. "Fuck, I'm sorry." I frantically pull my dick from her mouth and cup her cheeks. "Are you okay?"

She takes a few deep breaths, all while nodding and wiping her cheeks.

"I'm sorry," I whisper, leaning forward and pressing my forehead to hers.

"Hey," she coos, grasping my hands on her cheeks. "Stop apologizing. You did nothing wrong."

"I lost control, and you couldn't breathe."

"No, you did exactly what I wanted you to do. That was all normal for a blowjob. It's called deep-throating."

Still not feeling completely convinced, I begin to pull away from her, but she doesn't let me. Instead, her hands move from the outside of mine to the back of my head, holding me in place.

"Jacob, believe me when I say that I loved every second of it. There was no point in which I was afraid. Okay?"

I search through the greens, yellows, and browns of her eyes, noting that they're leaning more toward a forest green today—and look even more beautiful this close—and find nothing but honesty in them.

"Okay." I nod, accepting that she's telling me the truth.

"Good." She smiles. "Now, for someone who just had their mind blown, you're pretty serious looking."

She coaxes a chuckle from me, further relaxing any lingering tension I felt. "It was pretty fucking fantastic."

She's the one to giggle this time and then closes the few inches between us, pressing her mouth to mine. I feel like I've gotten much better at this since that first night. I angle my head, sweeping my tongue across her bottom lip until she opens for me.

I can taste myself on her, and it has another spark of arousal shooting through me. The feeling of coming down her throat was phenomenal, and I want her to feel that way as well.

I pull back from her lips. "Will you show me how to please you . . . with my mouth?"

A groan escapes her throat as she drops her head to my shoulder, but it sounds more like a groan of frustration. "I would *love* to do that right now," she says, smoothing a hand over my chest a few times. "But I need to get home and get ready for work."

"Oh."

I'd been so caught up in Remi and all these new experiences that I had successfully shoved the outside world and all of our obligations out of my mind. But now, the reality of life is trickling into my bubble, and I can't help the disappointment I feel.

Right on cue, Remi's phone dings from the coffee table, effectively bursting the bubble completely. I get to my feet, pulling my sweats up as I go, and head into the kitchen, leaving her to check her message.

"Oh, shit," she says with a sigh.

"What?" I ask, taking out a box of cereal.

She looks at me with wary eyes, making me pause my movements, waiting for the bad news to come.

"Well, I promised my friend Tahnee I'd go for drinks with her and a couple of guys. Her text just said that it's tonight."

My stomach instantly sours while unwelcome thoughts and emotions invade my mind. They're potent enough that it has all the good feelings from a few minutes ago vanishing.

Something must show on my face because Remi quickly stands from the couch and makes a move toward me.

"It's not like that." She tries to reassure me. "Tahnee likes one of the guys, and he suggested to each bring a friend. I'm just support for her, nothing more. She knows I'm not interested."

I drop my gaze to the cereal in front of me, suddenly not feeling very hungry. She doesn't need to explain anything to me. Yes, we fucked, and yes, she just sucked me off, but that doesn't mean I have a claim to her, does it?

We haven't talked about any of it, and I know people do that type of thing all the time without it meaning anything. I don't know why I was letting myself get so caught up in it.

Suddenly, she's wrapping her arms around me from behind and leaning her head against my back. "I'm sorry I didn't tell you about the drinks thing earlier. I agreed to it before . . ."

I don't know if she means before we fucked, or before she knew the truth. Either way, it doesn't matter.

"It's fine," I reply a little more harshly than I intended, reverting to my asshole mode. "I mean, fuck. It's not like I can take you out for drinks or anything."

"Jacob," she says, as if she's talking to a child. "I don't need to be taken out places."

"You say that now, but you won't always feel that way."

"Yeah, I think I wi—"

"You better leave now so you're not late for work."

I detach from her and walk into my bedroom, shutting the door behind me. I need to get dressed and ready to go out on the boat, anyway.

This itchy, uncomfortable feeling inside me is growing, and I don't like it one bit.

It doesn't help that when I step out of my room, Remi is gone.

And I have no one to blame but myself.

Chapter Eighteen

Remi

"Remi, this is Damien," Tahnee says, gesturing to the cute guy before me. His hair is medium-brown, neat, and tidy, and he has blue eyes. But they don't look like the ocean, and they don't cause tingles to run through me when I look into them. "And this is Justin." She motions to the man she can't seem to take her eyes off of.

I have to say. I'm a little surprised by her choice. Simply because he's a little *tamer*-looking than I ever would have expected for someone she likes. His hair is black like mine, short, and he has a short, neat beard to match. There's nothing . . .

extravagant about him. Both guys are simply *nice* looking, and each are dressed in a Henley and jeans.

"Hi, nice to meet you," I greet, holding out a hand to each of the guys.

They each say a variation of, "You, too," and then we all stand awkwardly outside *The Big Five* for a moment.

"Should we head in?" I suggest.

Tahnee stops her obvious ogling of Justin to agree with me. "Yep, come on."

She loops her arm with Justin's and begins walking in, leaving me with Damien.

He turns to me and smiles. "After you."

I'm already regretting that I agreed to this whole thing in the first place, and I can tell that Tahnee is most likely going to be in her own little world the entire night, leaving me to entertain Damien.

But I couldn't exactly cancel on her at the last minute, even if I'm still not entirely sure why she needed an extra person with her. It may have been Justin who needed it more so than her.

Entering the bar, we find a seat at one of the high tables. Tahnee takes the stool opposite me, meaning Damien has to sit next to me, and I give her an unimpressed look, to which she widens her eyes and gives me a 'give it a chance' look in return.

I can't completely blame her for trying to encourage me to get to know this guy better and have a good time. She has no idea that I've been spending time with Jacob, that I slept with him.

Or that I'm in love with him.

Wait... in love?

I lean back on my stool while I mull over that thought in my head. I liked him *before* I knew the truth. But now that I know it all and know what he's been through, the type of person he really is...

Yeah, I think I love him.

I always want to see him.

I want him to be happy.

I want to be the one to *make* him happy.

That look in his eyes when I sank down onto him his first time—the one that gives me shivers just thinking about—I always want to see *that*.

And I want to help mend some of his damaged pieces. I say 'damaged' because I don't think he's broken.

If he were truly broken, I don't think he would still be here trying to make a life in this town. I don't think he'd look at me with such expressive eyes like he does. And I don't think he'd be concerned about hurting me or how the town would treat me if they knew I was his friend. I also doubt he'd bother making me food or ask whether I was okay.

So, yeah, he's definitely damaged, but he's not broken.

And I think I'm in love.

It hasn't been all that long, but I've heard once before that sometimes it can take only a moment, an instant in time, for that connection to be made, a bond to be formed. And I think we have that.

I admit that his reaction to me coming here for drinks tonight was a little upsetting, but I can't say I blame him. I don't think I'd like the idea of it if the roles were reversed. And the fact that he reacted that way tells me he at least cares about me, too.

"Remi?" I'm pulled from my thoughts by Tahnee saying my name.

"I'm sorry, what?"

"Damien asked what drink you'd like. They're going to go get us some."

I look at the guys who are standing next to the table, waiting. I hadn't even noticed them get up.

"Oh, sorry. I'll have a glass of red wine, please. It doesn't matter which type."

"No worries," Damien says with a smile in my direction. "Back in a minute."

As soon as they're out of earshot, Tahnee leans forward. "Gah, I'm sorry if I've put you in an uncomfortable position. I just get so, so . . . I don't know. All I can think about is what it'll be like to have sex with him."

"Oh my goodness." I chuckle. "Why does it not surprise me that you just said that?" She shrugs in response, her lips curling into a smile that I return. "And it's okay. It's just a couple of drinks, right?"

"Yes," she answers. "But I do think Damien is a nice guy. And he's been staring at you pretty much non-stop."

"He has?" I hadn't noticed at all, but I've been pretty preoccupied thinking about Jacob.

"Yeah. And you have to admit, he's pretty cute."

"He is," I reply. But as cute and nice as he is, he isn't what I want. So this definitely won't be going any further than this evening. Unless, of course, friendship is all he wants.

The guys return with our drinks, and now that Tahnee has mentioned it, I do notice that Damien's eyes linger on me as he passes over my drink.

"Here you go."

"Thanks."

He gets settled in beside me, and I notice when he shifts his chair slightly closer. Whether it was intentional or not, I'm not sure.

"So, Tahnee says you haven't lived here that long. Do you like it here so far?"

"Yes. Yes, I love it, actually."

"Well, if you love it here, you'll definitely love Morro Bay, maybe even a little more." Damien winks and then takes a sip of his drink. "You guys should come for a visit."

"Oh! We should take a trip there next week," Tahnee interjects, apparently no longer wrapped up in only Justin. "It's only about a half-hour drive. We could go on your day off." She looks at me expectantly.

"Maybe." I offer a polite smile to both of them.

"You live right on the beach, right?" Damien turns to me. "I bet you're always in the water."

I take another sip of my wine. "Not nearly as much as you'd think."

"Well, I do a lot of surfing. If you guys come, I can give you a lesson."

I smile at him with a non-committal answer and take another big sip of my wine. I feel like it's going to be a long night. It's not that I don't like the company. I've established that he's a decent enough guy and easy on the eyes, and I always enjoy spending time with Tahnee. It's just that it's now clear that he's interested in more than just drinks with me tonight, and I'm definitely not.

One drink turns into two, plus some wings and fries. The conversation has flowed easily between the four of us, but my head has been elsewhere for most of the night. I've tried to make sure I don't give the wrong impression or lead Damien on in any way, but I'm not sure if he's taken the hint.

At one point, I started to wonder what it'd be like if it were Jacob here instead of Damien. Then I remembered that he would probably never be in this situation, and it hurt my heart. Not because I would never get to experience it with him, but simply because *he* never would. He'd be forced to leave the property before he barely stepped through the door. Not that he'd ever put himself in this situation, anyway.

I wonder what he's doing right now?

Letting my mind wander some more, I rest my chin on my palm and lazily look around the bar. Just as my eyes reach the front entrance, I catch sight of a figure outside the large window.

What the . . .

My pulse picks up when I notice it's someone who looks an awful lot like Jacob in the shadows. At least, he has the same build as him. They're standing at the very edge of the window in the darkness so as not to be seen, which is something I can see Jacob doing.

I stand from my chair, drawing the attention of the others. "Uh, I think I'm going to head out now, sorry. I have to work in the morning." I drop a couple of twenties on the table, even though I know the guys were planning on paying for everything. "Thanks so much for the lovely evening."

"Oh, um . . ." Damien begins to stand, but I stop him with a hand on his shoulder.

"It's okay. You guys enjoy the rest of your night. It was really nice meeting you."

I give Tahnee's arm a squeeze as I hurry out of the bar, not really giving any of them a chance to respond. The second I step out into the night air, I turn in the direction I thought I saw him, but there is no one there.

"Jacob?" I walk a little farther over until I'm standing right in front of the alley that runs down the side of the bar. "Jacob?" It's pretty dark down there, but I'm sure I see some movement. "Hell—"

"Remi?" I twist around at the sound of my name being called and see Tahnee, Justin, and Damien standing outside the door to the bar. "What are you doing?"

I glance back down the alley, but when I don't see anything, I turn back to the others.

"I just thought I saw something." Then, walking back toward them, I ask, "What are you guys doing out here?"

"We thought we'd walk you home," Tahnee answers, throwing her hair up into a bun. "Can never be too careful at night, especially with a *certain someone* on the loose here."

"Yeah, I heard you guys have a rapist living here," Justin adds with a scrunched-up nose.

Damien moves to stand beside me. "All the more reason to come visit our town."

It's a struggle to keep my irritation under wraps when my protective feelings for Jacob surface. I keep telling myself that they don't know any better, that they don't know Jacob is innocent, that they don't know him like I do.

But I still feel that not one of them has the right to talk about him at all.

Somehow, I manage to bite my tongue, and we start walking in the direction of my home. Tahnee and Justin move a few steps ahead, leaving me to walk beside Damien. I glance once more over my shoulder down the alley behind us but still see nothing. I must have just imagined him there.

"So, what do you do in your free time?" Damien asks after a few steps.

"Oh, I like to go for walks along the beach." I shrug. "And just whatever else comes up, I guess."

Actually, most of my free time lately has been spent with Jacob, but I can't imagine that answer going over very well.

I ask him what he does in return, and then we continue to make small talk for the rest of the walk to my place.

Just when I think I'm going to be free and maybe get a chance to go see Jacob tonight, Tahnee turns to me in front of my house. "Can I use your bathroom while we're here?"

"Actually, I wouldn't mind that, either, if that's okay?"

"Me, too."

On the inside, I'm wondering why the hell no one bothered using the bathroom at the bar, but on the outside, I just smile and nod. "Sure."

As we walk the path to my front door, Damien looks around and says, "This is cute."

"Thanks." I unlock and open the door, gesturing for them to go in.

"You guys should check out her back deck while you wait," Tahnee calls as she heads to my bathroom.

Stifling a sigh, I say, "Come on," and then lead the guys to the deck, purposely leaving the lights off inside my house and not offering a drink so they don't get too comfortable.

Justin and Damien each take a seat while waiting for the bathroom, probably intending on leaving right afterward, but because Tahnee settles into one of the chairs and makes herself cozy when she comes out, they follow suit and return to their seats once they're done with the bathroom as well.

I guess my plan didn't work.

I had been leaning against the railing, but when they start chatting amongst themselves, I curse under my breath and go sit in the only space left, on the chaise next to Damien.

It's not like I told Jacob I was coming over, I guess. He knew I was going out with Tahnee and a couple of guys. But I had *wanted* to go see him, especially after thinking I saw him outside the bar, *and* after the way we left things this morning.

My head snaps to the side when I feel Damien's hand land on my arm. "You don't mind us chilling here for a few minutes, do you?"

"It's fine," I reply with a smile.

Facing forward, I notice Tahnee shifting her gaze between the two of us, a smirk on her lips and a look that says she still thinks I should give him a shot. But there is zero part of me that is even contemplating seeing him after this. Maybe if I hadn't met Jacob, I'd be willing to give him a chance.

Poor Damien. He seems like a good guy and has been trying to get to know me all night, but I've kept it surface-level and have only asked him a few questions in return. I really do feel sorry for him.

Finally, half an hour later, they decide to leave. I politely take Damien's number when he offers it and tells me to use it if I ever feel like hanging out again. Then I hug each of them goodbye.

When they're finally far enough away that I don't think they'll be coming back for any reason, I quickly walk back out onto my deck and down the side steps to make my way to Jacob's house, hoping he's not already in bed.

The second both of my feet hit the ground, my hand is being pulled to the side, causing my whole body to fall sideways.

But then hands are gripping my waist, and I'm being spun around until my back hits the side of my house. When I'm steady again, I look up to see Jacob standing in front of me, jaw clenched and looking intense.

"Jacob," I breathe out. "I was just coming to see you." I attempt a smile, but my eyebrows furrow when he doesn't return one back. "What's wrong?"

Jacob roughly rubs a hand over the back of his neck. "Do you have any idea what it was like watching that . . . *guy* ogle you and put his hand on you?"

He begins pacing in front of me, bothered by what he saw, but his words and the jealousy they imply stoke a fire already building inside me after just seeing him. Heat travels the length of me before settling into the juncture between my legs.

"I came here to apologize about this morning, hoping you were done with your drinks, but when I got here and then saw him touch your arm, I wanted to storm over and slap his hand away from you." He shakes his head as if clearing a thought away. "I don't like this feeling."

"You mean jealousy?" I question.

"I don't like it," he repeats. "I was going to leave you be. Let you go out tonight and realize it will never be like that with us. But I couldn't stand another second sitting at home, knowing you were out with another guy and maybe upset with me. It was driving me fucking mental."

He's like a wild animal pacing back and forth in front of me, looking all sorts of pissed and distressed. Part of me feels bad for him—he's most likely never experienced these feelings before.

But the other part of me . . . that part, is extremely turned-on by it.

"Were you outside the bar tonight?" I ask, thinking back to the person I saw.

He gives me a confused look and pauses his pacing. "No. Did something happen there?"

The confusion on his face turns all scowly, and I fight to hold back a smile. I guess it wasn't him that I saw outside the window. And right now, by the look on his face, he's probably thinking I'm talking about something happening with Damien there.

"No, nothing happened."

"Are you—"

"Jacob," I say, cutting him off. I feel like the only way to calm him down and wipe the scowl off his face is probably to kiss him. It's something I'm dying to do, anyway.

Reaching out, I pull him until he's standing stiffly in front of me.

"What?"

Angling my chin to look up at him, I whisper, "Just kiss me."

His mouth slams into mine, both his hands coming up to rest on either side of my head on the wall. He's not pressing into me, but he's close enough for me to slide my hands up his back and tangle my fingers through his hair.

The kiss is fierce and full of fire from the second our lips touch. All his pent-up anger from the jealousy is being poured into it.

His lips move firmly over mine while our tongues tangle softly with one another. There is nothing tentative about this kiss, and if I didn't know any better, I would never guess that he only had his first kiss several days ago.

"What else did you want to do?" I murmur against his lips.

"What do you mean?"

"You said you wanted to slap his hand away. What else?"

He presses his forehead against mine, taking a deep breath. "I wanted to walk up onto your deck and sit you in my lap so they'd know you were mine. But I don't even know. . ."

His sentence drifts off into the night, carried out with the tide of the sea, and he pulls his head back and looks down at me. It suddenly occurs to me what he's trying to say. I feel bad that he didn't know already, but we haven't exactly talked about it.

Cupping his cheeks, I say, "I am yours."

A relieved puff of air escapes him, but then he shakes his head again.

"I'm not experienced in relationships. At all. I'm bitter. My life isn't nice. At all. I can't buy you nice things or take you to nice places. But fuck, I don't want to stay away."

He goes to say something else, but I'm in desperate need of feeling his lips, his body, everything. I pull his head down to my mouth and let my kiss be an answer to him. I want him, regardless of anything. Jacob kisses me back with as much fire as before, turning my insides to liquid heat.

I tangle my fingers in his hair, tugging at the strands, before dropping a hand down to the front of his jeans and cupping his hardness through the material. He's still not pressing into me, holding himself back, but as soon as I reach for the button of his jeans, he moves in closer.

His hands finally leave the wall beside my head to cup my jaw in a firm grip as he continues his delicious assault on my mouth, and my fingers fumble with his button and zipper before I'm finally able to slide my hand inside.

Jacob groans into my mouth when I grip his length, rubbing my thumb over the tip and spreading the pre-cum around. My pussy clenches around nothing, desperate to be filled by him. I nip at his bottom lip, tugging it back as my hand strokes him.

"I want you to fuck me," I murmur into his mouth and then use my free hand to slide my panties down my legs. I feel feral with need, knowing he's as affected by me as I am by him.

It's as if those words were the permission he was waiting for. Wild, heated eyes stare down at me when he lifts his head slightly, and then one hand leaves my jaw to move down my body, sliding over each curve until he reaches between my legs. His eyes darken with pure want when he feels how wet I am.

"Is that for me?"

"Yes," I breathe out.

His lips are on mine again, kissing me with urgency, pressing into me like he can't get close enough. The hand on my pussy leaves to tug his jeans down just enough to free himself, and I lift my leg up to rest on his hip. He holds it there, tight against his side, while he thrusts up into me.

We both let out a gasp, and I throw my head back, hitting the wood siding. Jacob doesn't take a moment to compose himself at all this time; he continues sliding in and out at an almost frenzied pace, and all I can do is hold on as feelings of pure ecstasy overtake me.

There's something so hot about the fact that his pants are barely below his ass, like he had that primal urge and was just as desperate as I was for him to be inside me as quickly as possible. Jacob kisses along my jaw and down my neck while my fingers hold him close to me by the back of his head.

"It feels different." His voice rumbles against my skin. "Why does it feel different?"

It really does, like *more,* somehow. Thoughts of how our feelings have grown, how we're even closer now, and how the jealousy probably sparked something in him come to mind. Plus, there's the fact that he's slightly more experienced than the first two times.

But then I realize it's not just the feelings that are different. The actual *feel* of him inside me is different. And then it suddenly occurs to me.

"You're not wearing a condom." Jacob pauses his movements mid-thrust, lifting his head from my neck. "It's okay. I'm on the pill," I add.

"Are you sure?"

He pushes the rest of the way into me again like he just can't help it, and I let out a moan. "Mm-hmm."

"Thank fuck."

He continues his movements once again, pushing me closer to the edge. His dick rubs against my inner walls while his pelvis grinds against my clit, creating a delicious combination of pleasure that sparks through me.

"Oh god, Jacob. Keep going."

"You feel so good," he groans into my neck.

The vibrations against my skin are the tipping point for me. Tingles reach out to every point in my body before culminating in one spot and exploding. I come hard, moaning loud and clenching tightly around his dick.

"Oh fuck. Hold on," he grits out right before he grips my ass and scoops me up, carrying me up the few steps to my deck while still buried inside me.

My hands fly up to his shoulders, and I hold on tight until he lays me down on the chaise lounge.

Jacob's lips land on mine once more, our tongues tangling together.

He begins moving his hips again, but his movements are erratic this time. He's losing control and being pulled into the throes of pleasure, and I'm ready to join him again.

I grab hold of my knees, drawing them back while he holds onto my shoulders and slams into me for maximum depth.

As soon as I hear his groan and feel him thicken and pulse inside me, my second orgasm is triggered. I release my knees to wrap my arms around his back, holding him close as we come together.

He continues gliding in and out slowly, riding out both of our orgasms. After a few more thrusts, he lifts his head to look down at me, his forehead shiny with perspiration.

"Feel better?" I can't help asking with a smile between breaths.

"Yeah." He places a soft kiss on my lips. "Did I hurt you at all?"

"Not even a little." I slide my hand over his chest, feeling his still heavily beating heart. "I feel better now, too."

When he finally withdraws and pushes back onto his knees, he glances down between my legs and lets out an appreciative sound from deep in his throat.

"Shit, that's really hot."

"What?"

"Seeing your pussy with my cum dripping out of it."

Oh goodness. There's something about the way he says things so bluntly. No one else ever talked to me that way, and I love it. I love every filthy word out of his mouth, as well as the sweet stuff.

"Unfortunately, I can't stay like this forever." Closing my legs, I move to stand. "I need to get cleaned up."

Jacob stands up quickly before me and helps me to my feet. Then, looking over his shoulder toward the ocean, he says, "I've got an idea." Gently tugging on my hand, he starts toward the water, but when I begin pulling away, he stops. "What's wrong?"

"I-I haven't been in the water . . . since that day."

His whole face softens in understanding, and it's the gentlest I've seen him look, probably ever. It almost makes me want to cry.

"We don't have to go in there if you don't want to, but if you do, I won't let go of you. And we won't go out very far."

Chewing on my lip, I look past him at the water and then back at his face. There's nothing but genuineness there.

He's nothing like the monster this town has painted him out to be, and I want to show him that I trust him completely.

"Okay," I answer quietly. "Let's go."

"You sure?"

"Yes."

Chapter Nineteen

Remi

It takes a little longer than usual to get my bearings when I wake up, my eyes slowly adjusting to the dim light. It appears to be early morning, but there is a heavy cloud cover that makes it difficult to tell the time, along with rain pattering against the window. A window that is *not* in my bedroom.

Turning over, I find the bed empty and cold behind me. Jacob must have already left for a fishing trip, even in this type of weather.

Warm, fuzzy feelings spread throughout me when I think about last night and how Jacob had reacted to seeing me with someone else. I appreciate that he told me how it made him feel, and I kind of love knowing that he was burning with jealousy.

And then the sex? *Phenomenal.*

But what really hit me in the feels was when he held my hand when we walked toward the ocean and didn't let me go as we waded into the water up to our asses. Under the moonlit sky, he held me close and promised he would teach me how to swim whenever I was ready to learn.

I had been attracted to him before, but now, I'm absolutely *loving* this side of him he's letting me see. It's the sweet side of him that was probably more prominent when he was a teenager before everything happened.

He's definitely still got his rough edges—prison will do that to you—but it's not nearly as bad as it was before. At least, not to me.

After being in the water, we walked back here to Jacob's place, where I ended up spending the night sleeping next to him for the second time, this time in his bed. I had simply gotten under the sheets while he was in the bathroom and then waited for him to join me, which he finally did after a short moment of hesitation.

I noticed he didn't look up at any of the cameras the entire time we were back here last night, and I don't think it occurred to him at any point when he was at my house that there weren't any there, either, so I'd say that's good progress.

I let out a contented sigh as I roll onto my back. There's still so much we have going against us in the outside world, but right here and now, I'm happy.

I just wish there was something more I could do for him to make his life better. To somehow make up for some of the wrongs that have been done to him.

My gaze lands on Jacob's laptop on the nightstand when I turn my head to the side. He told me that he keeps all the videos from the cameras on there, but I can't help wondering what else he keeps on there.

Would I find information about his case on it?

Information about his parents?

And if I were to look at the videos, would I see people from the town come and go, doing deplorable things to his property?

I shouldn't invade his privacy; I really shouldn't. Turning away from his laptop, I hope that by not looking at it and focusing on something else, the temptation to open it up and look through it will go away.

I know full well it won't, though.

* ~ * ~ * ~ *

The rain has long since stopped by the time I'm walking across the puddle-filled parking lot toward *Peaches*. The sky is still a gloomy gray, which does nothing for the anxious energy I'm feeling right now.

But it's the sight of about six people, including Jolene and Tahnee, standing in a group around the cash registers, that has the anxious feeling in my body heightening to a Defcon 5 status, only for different reasons.

I walk through the door to the store slowly and undetected, doing my best to keep quiet and find out what's going on without being noticed.

"The tire slashing isn't working," Jolene comments. "So you might as well give up on that. He just rolls out with a new tire every single time."

Tim lifts the worn cap off his head and runs a hand through his hair before returning it. "He'll run out of tires, eventually . . . or money to buy them. I'll keep it up for now, but we have to come up with something else to try to drive him away."

It appears that I've just walked in on some sort of impromptu meeting about getting rid of Jacob, and it has my stomach twisting before dropping to the floor.

"We need to hit him where it hurts most."

"His boat?"

"Can't fish if he hasn't got it."

My chest tightens and aches at what they're implying they might do to Jacob. I can't let them do it. I can't let them devastate him like that.

Jolene lets out a sigh. "No. We can't stoop that low. I wouldn't feel right."

A silent breath of relief passes my lips. Thank goodness Jolene still has a conscience when it comes to destroying Jacob's life . . . for the second time. The others let out quiet grumbles as if they don't necessarily agree with her, though.

If only I could just *tell* them he was innocent and have them believe me.

"Well, we gotta think of something," Luke mumbles, running a finger over his mustache.

Tahnee, who has been tossing a candy bar in her hand, speaks up. "I still say we trick him into trying something with a girl again."

She doesn't know, I tell myself so I don't hate her for what she just said. *She doesn't know.*

"No woman should be put in that situation, Tahnee," Wendy says in a disapproving tone.

"I agree," Tim adds.

Tahnee throws her hands up and grumbles, "Whatever," before moving away from the group to put the candy bar back on the shelf.

The rest of the group carry on talking amongst themselves, not paying attention to anything else, so I take the opportunity to walk over to Tahnee, grab her arm, and pull her down an aisle.

"Oh, hey, girl. I always knew you secretly wanted to get me alone," she jokes. But the humor in her eyes disappears when she sees the look on my face. "What's wrong?"

I remember saying those exact words to Jacob last night.

"This," I start, almost getting choked up. "This has to stop."

"What does?"

I gesture to the group near the front of the store. "This thing . . . with Jacob."

Tahnee crosses her arms and furrows her brows. "What are you talking about? Why?"

I don't know why I feel so nervous telling her this; she's always seemed to be a reasonable type of person. I just have to trust that she'll hear me out and that she'll believe my words. But if she doesn't, then I might lose her friendship and likely the others, too.

Dipping my head, I close my eyes briefly before facing her again. "I've been spending time with him."

"What?" she says in disbelief, taking a step back.

"No, Tahnee, listen to me." I close the gap she just made between us. "He didn't do it."

She scoffs. "Let me guess, he told you that he didn't do it?" I think back to the night that I found out. I don't think he ever would have straight out said it to me; I had only heard him through the bathroom door. When I don't reply immediately,

Tahnee continues, "And you actually listened to him? I can't believe you, Remi."

"Look, I know it sounds crazy, but it's the truth. It's a long story, but he really didn't do it." My mind goes back and forth, contemplating how much to tell her, wondering whether his possible feelings of embarrassment are worth it to gain her as an ally. After some thought, I decide that they *are* worth it. "He hadn't even had sex with anyone when he went to prison."

A humorless laugh passes her lips. "Again, this could be something he's just saying to you."

"No, Tahnee. I *know* he was still a virgin."

She shifts her feet a little, narrowing her gaze. "And how do you know that?"

I hold her stare, not speaking a word but saying everything with a look.

Her eyes widen. "You fucked him?"

"Shh, keep your voice down." I turn my head to the others, but thankfully, they're not paying us any mind.

Tahnee shakes her head and then stares at the ground for a long minute like she's thinking everything through.

Thinking about everything she's ever heard about him.

Thinking about every encounter she's ever had with him over the past five months or what she's maybe done to him.

Then finally, still looking at the ground, she speaks. "You said you've been spending a lot of time with him?

"I have."

"He looks like sex walking."

"He does."

"But you were his first?"

"Yes."

She chews on the tip of her thumb. "And he went to prison, even though he was innocent?"

"For ten years."

"Shit." She finally looks up at me with the most serious expression I've ever seen her wear. Then she nods slowly. "Okay. I believe you."

I let out a heavy breath and feel my shoulders relax, the relief flowing through me like a wave. "You do?" I didn't realize just how tensely I had been holding myself while waiting for her to reply.

"Yes. But I'm not sure how we're going to stop this. They're not likely to just take yours or even my word for it."

"I know."

I don't tell her that I have a sort of idea in mind, because I really don't want to have to do it, and I have to talk to Jacob about it first as well.

"Fuck, now I feel like a real bitch. I've only spat on his truck twice, but I've talked a lot of shit about him." She rubs a hand up and down her arm in a way that indicates remorse, and I truly believe she does feel bad. "Poor guy." I nod in agreement, although I think "poor guy" is an insufficient description for him. "How did that even happen in the first place?"

"It's a long story, one for another time, maybe." I blow out a breath. "I really hope they don't try to do anything to his boat. He makes barely any money as it is using it for fishing."

"You're loaded, aren't you?" Tahnee points out. "Why don't you just give him some of your money?"

"I would give him every last cent I had if I thought for one second he'd take it. He still has enough pride that he wouldn't accept any cash from me."

It's her turn to nod now. "Okay. Well, don't worry. I'm going to go back over there and try to convince them that touching his boat is the worst idea. Who knows, maybe I can somehow convince them to leave him alone and ignore him altogether."

I appreciate her saying that and offering to try, but from the look in her eyes, I can tell that even she doubts she'll have any influence on them.

"Thanks, Tahnee. And thanks for believing me."

"Sure. I mean, some people just give off honest vibes, and you're one of those people." She shrugs. But then she turns to me with a smirk on her face and a sparkle in her eye. "I can't believe you fucked him. What was it like?"

I let out a groan and start to pass her by, walking toward the front of the store to the sound of her chuckle.

"I'm just kidding. You don't have to tell me," she says. "No wonder you didn't want anything to do with Damien. I wish I knew that sooner instead of putting you through that."

I wait for her to catch up to me again. "It's okay. You didn't know." I take another step, but then pause. "Hey, listen, I'm going to be leaving town after work today. There's something I have to do." I made the decision this morning after looking through his laptop, and I just hope it doesn't backfire on me. "I should be back tomorrow, but if you see Jacob in town or anything . . ."

"Don't worry. I'm on his side now."

"Thank you."

Chapter Twenty

Jacob

I've gotten so used to seeing Remi's bright and happy face at the store whenever I walk in, even when I pretend not to notice her, even when I pretend that just seeing her isn't the fucking highlight of my day.

She's become like a safety blanket. No, more like a piece of wood I can float on in what feels like dark, shark-infested waters.

So when I walk through the door to *Peaches* and don't see her smiling face, I feel on edge, like at any moment one of those sharks is going to attack. I'm thrown back in time to before she came to this town and before she pushed herself into my life.

Remi told me she had to go out of town for something. Actually, she left me a note yesterday morning while I was out on the boat, so I couldn't even ask her why she had to go, how long she was going for, or even where the hell she was going.

So now, I just feel alone. But it's more than just having someone with me in the darkness. The strings tied around my heart, cutting off circulation, further loosen whenever we're together.

Every time I look at her beautiful smiling face, especially when she's directing it at me, my chest swells, and I feel good.

Every time I see her, the eighteen-year-old boy in me, the innocent one who once had hopes of getting the girl, tries to fight his way out of the shit I've been through.

But the man I am today just keeps on expecting something bad to happen.

Good things do not happen to me, and she feels really fucking good.

My dick twitches as I remember how good it felt fucking her up against the side of her house.

I had been going out of my mind thinking about her with another guy, and then when I saw him put his hand on her when I was walking up to her house from the beach . . . I told Remi that I wanted to slap his hand away, but really, I think I had to muster all my willpower to keep from storming over there and knocking him out. And I am not a violent guy.

The feelings were all so foreign to me, but it was exactly as Remi had said. I was burning with jealousy. Add in the fact that I know I can never claim her as mine publicly, and it had me all sorts of messed up. Then I had to stand along the side of her house, fucking fuming, while I waited for them to leave.

I pass by the teenager at the checkout, who I've probably seen here in the evenings before but never really paid any attention to. I guess he doesn't have school today since he's here filling in for Remi. His gaze is bored and indifferent, probably wishing he was anywhere else but here.

I grab the loaf of bread and milk I need and head back toward the counter, feeling grateful that it seems pretty empty in here. That feeling is short-lived, though, when I make it back to the front of the store and see Jolene standing beside the teenager, talking to a woman with bright red hair.

I place my items on the counter, trying to ignore the thick waves of hatred radiating from the store owner.

"You can go ahead and take your break now," Jolene mutters to the kid, but she continues staring at me with pure disdain.

He shrugs and saunters out the front of the store.

I pull my wallet out of my pocket and take out a five-dollar bill, wanting to get the hell out of here as quickly as possible. But a hostile thickness fills the air as Jolene stands there, *not* scanning my items.

"We're not taking cash right now."

My jaw ticks as I stare back at her, knowing full well she's just saying that. Retrieving my wallet again, I pull out my bank card instead. I usually just withdraw all my money once I cash my check, but I'm pretty sure I still have enough in my account to pay for these.

"Bank machine is down, too."

What the fuck?

My insides burn with humiliation, but I don't want her to see it and know that she's won. I don't want her to see how much she and the rest of them get to me. So, I keep my face stoic.

This is a harsh reminder of why I shouldn't be getting involved with Remi. I shouldn't be dragging her into this fucking hell hole where she'd be treated the same.

I look around the immediate area to see who else is witnessing and enjoying my degradation. But the only other person around is the redhead, and she's looking off to the side while fiddling with a thread from her top.

Turning back to Jolene and her malevolent glare, I can see she's not going to let me buy my milk and bread. Like I've said before, she'd rather watch me starve.

Calmly placing my wallet back into my back pocket, I turn to walk away and leave the store empty-handed. As I'm going, I hear the redhead say in a cheery voice, "I actually needed some milk and bread. I'll take these, Jolene. Thanks!"

Once I make it back to my truck, I brace my hands above the door, sucking in deep lungfuls of air, trying to fight the sudden urge to punch through my window.

"Jacob," a quiet, hesitant voice says from beside me. I turn to my left to see the redhead standing there, shifting her weight back and forth. Then, after a quick glance over her shoulder, she lifts her hand and says, "Here."

Grasped between her small fingers is what I'm guessing to be the same bread and milk carton I had just tried to buy. When I don't make a move to take them from her, she gives the bag a shake. "Take them, please."

I'd love to say I'm so appreciative of her generosity and that her kind-sounding voice and the tentative smile on her face are a welcome change, and that it makes me feel good.

But I'm jaded and filled with suspicion now. It laces my blood and pumps through my veins.

It had taken a little while to trust Remi. And even now, I hate the fact that there is still a tiny part in the back of my mind that thinks she might turn on me. It's barely there, like the softest touch of a feather tickling at the back of my mind. But it's there nonetheless, despite my feelings for her.

I don't know the girl in front of me in the slightest, so I have no trust for her at all.

Wanting to get her to hurry up and leave, I take the items from her without a word. I'm not sure if the cameras reach this part of the parking lot, so the longer we stand here, the tenser my shoulders get.

She looks over her shoulder once again, possibly to check if anyone is watching.

Maybe they're standing in the shadows, waiting for her signal.

Is this where she makes her move, whatever that may be?

But no. All she does is lift her hand in a little wave. "Have a good night, Jacob."

I stand in the same spot, staring at her for another ten seconds after she walks off before getting into my truck and heading home. I have no idea what to think about what just happened.

Once I'm home, I get a fire started and take a seat facing the vast ocean. Without Remi here, I feel fucking lost, and I don't know what to do with myself. I don't even know when she'll be back.

I should be getting used to this shit again, though. But does the desert ever get used to being without the rain, or does it just deal with it because it has to? Because I feel like I was a desert living through a drought for years, starved of human interaction and affection, barren, and then I finally got a downpour.

I've been filled with life again, but I know I will have to face the drought once more.

She doesn't belong in this life.

She's too kind.

Too vibrant.

She hasn't just been the rain; she's also been the rainbow after the storm. Those bright, hopeful colors that indicate that the worst has passed. I just don't know if it has, though.

Just as quickly as I decide it's best if I leave her alone, she walks around the side of my house toward me as if I conjured her with my thoughts.

She looks like a beautiful breath of fresh air with her hair blowing softly in the breeze, and all thoughts of letting her go drift away on that same breeze.

Soft, warm, hazel eyes find me, and it suddenly feels like so much longer since I last saw her. My chest physically aches at the thought of having to give her up. I don't know if I can.

Especially not now, when I know what it feels like to have her in my arms.

What it feels like to be *inside* her, and what she sounds like when she comes on my dick.

And the look she's giving me right now, like I actually mean something to her. Like I'm not dirt under her shoe.

Her steps increase as I stand from my chair. Those same feelings of being *alive* unfurl inside me. My heart ricochets in my chest, beating faster the closer she gets. She doesn't even stop when she reaches me, continuing forward until she's barreling into me and wrapping her arms tightly around my waist. It's as if it feels like it's been a lot longer for her as well.

My arms hold her close to me as I breathe in the floral scent of her hair. I want to ask her where she's been and why she left, but I don't want this slice of heaven to end.

Remi tilts her head up to me in what I've learned is an invitation, so I lean down and press my lips to hers. Kissing her has become one of my favorite things to do, and I can never seem to get enough.

But all too quickly, she pulls away and leans back to look up at me again. "I kind of missed you."

Her voice is soft, like a caress to my soul, and even though I missed her like crazy, I can't seem to force the same words out. She doesn't seem to mind, though, offering a warm smile while lifting a hand to my cheek.

"I have a surprise for you."

"I don't really like surprises."

That seems to amuse her at first, but then she takes a step back from me and begins gnawing at her bottom lip. I catch sight of her thumb rubbing along the tips of her fingers at the same time. I've seen her do it before, and I know she does it when she's nervous or something.

A sudden look of uncertainty crosses her features, instantly putting me on edge.

She looks over her shoulder to the area she just came from, and I follow her gaze there.

My insides twist with confusion when I see a man walk around the corner and then in our direction.

What the hell?

Is this some sort of twisted joke?

Is this part of the scheme I thought she was involved in at the beginning?

I turn back to her, not sure what I'm expecting to see, but it's not the soft, hopeful look on her face she's wearing as she waits for my reaction.

Looking back at the guy, I watch as he approaches, and the closer he gets, the more familiarity tugs at the back of my mind.

The guy is in his late twenties. Black hair sits messily on his head, like he's been running a hand through it multiple times. He's got a neatly trimmed beard, and he's wearing jeans and a T-shirt.

As he steps toward us, I feel Remi's hand squeeze mine, as if trying to reassure me. I don't even know when she grabbed hold of it.

"I thought you could do with another friend."

I don't look back at her, but keep my narrowed gaze on the man in front of me.

"What the fuck are you doing here?"

"It's good to see you, too." His lips lift in a half-smirk before he drops it again.

"This isn't fucking funny."

A flicker of guilt or something crosses his face at the harshness in my voice. "I know." He nods. "I'm here because when Remi turned up at my place last night, she tried to tell me something that I already knew."

The most ridiculous feelings of jealousy hit me when I think about the fact that she was at *his* place last night and not mine.

Huffing out an irritated breath, I push away the thought so I can deal with one thing at a time, like why the fuck Campbell is here, standing in front of me right now.

"And what exactly was that?"

"That you were innocent. I already knew you didn't do it."

I let out a scoff and run a hand over my jaw. The irritation boiling up inside me turns to anger.

"Yeah? Then where the fuck were you the last ten years, Campbell? Where the fuck were you when I was scared shitless about what was happening, and everyone was turning their backs on me? *Where were you* at the lowest point of my life when I wished I was *dead*?" I turn away from him, my chest heaving with anger mixed with deep feelings of hurt. "I didn't have a single fucking soul on my side."

Taking a seat, I shove a hand through my hair and briefly look up at Remi to see a tear slide down one cheek. I have to look away before I see more fall. I can't handle that.

"Shit, you think I didn't *want* to be there for you?" Campbell asks, pacing a few steps. "My parents practically *forbade* me from leaving the house. They took away my car and my allowance to make sure I couldn't make the forty-five-minute drive to the courthouse. I found a way to get there anyway, and sat in the back corner. But then they moved us to the other side of the *fucking country* to keep me away from you." He plonks down angrily onto the sand next to the fire, staring at the flames. "I cannot even begin to imagine what you've been through, Jake, or what it was like for you. But don't think for a fucking second that no one else's life was affected by what happened.

"I lost my best friend, and all the other guys drifted apart almost immediately. I lost my freedom for a long time. My parents kept looking at me like I was capable of doing what you were accused of, as if I'd been influenced by you or something. They thought I was involved in it somehow, and they were just waiting for me to do it again. Everything was shit for a long time."

I sit quietly, looking at my old best friend for a long moment, because it's true that I didn't think about how it might have affected anyone else's life. I thought they had simply turned on me.

"They told me you said you thought I was capable of doing it," I say with a lot less steam than before.

"I didn't say shit. *Mase* was the only one who said that you'd do anything to make her yours."

I should have known Mase would be the one to say that. He never did know when to shut up.

"I'm so sorry, Jake, about all of it. But just know that I never believed it, not for a second. And I've felt like shit ever since because I didn't do anything to help you."

I take a moment to mull over everything in my head. It's hard to switch off the anger and hurt I've felt for ten years, but looking over at Campbell now, I find that it's no longer directed at him.

"I'm sorry, too," I finally mumble.

I can actually see the weight lift off his shoulders, and it makes me realize that this has been something he's been carrying around for a long time. And knowing that he never doubted me, well, that has my shoulders feeling a tiny bit lighter, too.

Just like in the past, Campbell is quick to cool off after getting worked up and relaxes back into the sand.

"I just moved to the West Coast with my wife and kids about six months ago. I didn't know where you ended up, but I would have come sooner if I had known it was here. I'm really glad Remi showed up. It's good to see you."

My eyes drift to where Remi has been silently standing off to the side, watching us with tears in her eyes. A warmth fills my entire chest just from looking at her.

I didn't realize just how much I needed this, and she's the reason for it. She's the reason for every good thing in my life.

I hold out my hand, pulling her to sit on my lap when she takes hold of it, and whisper "Thank you," into her hair. The overwhelming need to be close to her and wipe the tears from her face suddenly feels more important than my next breath.

A couple of months ago, I had no one. I had nothing but an empty existence.

Now, sitting here with two people who don't think the worst of me . . . well, it feels like I've won the fucking lottery.

Holding Remi against me, I turn back to Campbell. Now, with all that said and done, I think we can finally start putting it behind us.

"It's good to see you, too," I answer quietly. "So, you have a family now?"

A goofy smile pulls at his lips, the same I remember from when we were younger. "Yeah, Jasmine and I got married a few years ago. We have two little girls."

"That's . . . that's great. Congrats."

He smiles. "Thanks."

I try to imagine him as a father, doting on two little humans, taking them on play dates and whatnot, but I just can't see it. He was someone who couldn't stand little kids. And I think he even said at one point that he'd never have any of his own.

The look of pure adoration on his face as he thinks about his family paints a different picture, though. A picture of a Campbell I no longer know, but one I would like to.

He starts telling me a little bit more about them—what his wife does, and how old his daughters are—but as much as I try to push it away, a bitterness sweeps through me when I think of the fact that I'll probably never experience that feeling he has for his family.

How could I ever bring a child into this fucked-up life of being ostracized and black-listed?

That's yet another reason why I really need to set Remi free. My throat tightens, almost suffocating me.

More time. I just want a little bit more time.

Squeezing her tighter to me, I shove those thoughts to the side for now and work at getting to know my old friend again instead.

~~*~*

After a few hours, we say goodbye to Campbell, who walks down the beach to spend the night at Remi's place while she stays at mine. We'll meet up with him again in the morning for breakfast.

I have a lot of questions for Remi, like how she found out about him and how she knew where he lived, but when we step inside my house, she makes a beeline for the kitchen.

"Hey, you left your milk out."

She makes a move to put away both the milk and the bread still sitting on the counter from when I got home. I had totally forgotten about it after she and Campbell arrived earlier.

"Wait . . . I'm not entirely sure it isn't poisoned or something."

"*What?* Why?"

I don't really want to get into the story about my humiliation at the store, but she has a way of making the words come out with just a look from her pretty eyes, which look browner tonight.

Indignation covers her face as I tell her about the refusal to serve me at the store, but when I tell her about the redhead, it morphs into a smile.

She puts the milk away and walks over, stopping when she's barely an inch in front of me. "It's not poisoned."

"No?"

"No. The redhead was Tahnee, and she's my friend." Then, sliding her hand up to my chest and resting it above my heart, she adds, "And she's on your side, too."

"Really?" I ask with skepticism. "How did that happen?"

Moving the hand that was resting over my heart around to my back, she leans into me for a hug. "I told her the truth. I had to convince her a little, but she thought it over and believed me."

I'm amazed by this woman. Absolutely amazed at how loving and kind she is. How passionate she can be when it comes to what's right and wrong.

I'm not used to having anyone be so *for* me that it takes me a while to respond.

At a loss for words and feeling so much right now, I end up just hugging her back as I rest my head on top of hers and quietly say, "Thank you."

But even as I hold her close to me, I know I'll have to let her go.

Chapter Twenty-One

Remi

With my tense shoulders almost reaching my ears, I gnaw at the corner of my bottom lip. This is quite intense, and I have no idea what the outcome will be.

I think I'm the only one taking it so seriously, though. Jacob seems more amused than anything, especially when his player manages to take the ball from *my* player and scores.

"Ugh!" I toss my controller onto the drawers under the little TV and pout.

"I didn't take you for a sore loser, sweetheart." Jacob chuckles from beside me and then grabs a lock of my hair, absently twisting it around his finger. I'm not sure he notices he's doing it, but I do, and I have to resist the urge to lean my whole head toward him.

"That was the *sixth* time in a row you've won."

"Well," he says, placing his controller on the floor and then scooting back so he's lying on the pillows. "I spent a lot of my teen years playing these games."

I glance up at the photo of him and his four teenage friends. I now know that Campbell is the guy standing directly beside him.

I wasn't sure what to expect when I turned up at Campbell's house a few days ago. He was actually the one who lived closest and was first on the list of people I intended to visit.

After hearing his version of what happened and knowing he and Jacob were best friends before all of this, I'm so glad it was him I saw first, especially since I don't know if the others would have been as receptive and willing to come see him immediately.

I just wanted to do something for Jacob. When I saw that file on his laptop labeled "old photos" and found that it listed the full names of all the people in it, I created some fake social media accounts—since I don't have any—and went deep diving to find those people.

Now, knowing he somewhat has his best friend back . . . well, it makes me feel really good inside.

Shifting back on the bed a little, my hand brushes along Jacob's leg, and I turn to look at him. Today he brought me fishing. He was so patient with me, even when I managed to accidentally throw one of his fishing rods over the edge of the boat.

While I did enjoy it, I started to get a little bored after a couple of hours. I don't know how he does it almost every day, and by himself, for that matter. At least now I can say that I've tried it.

Jacob suggested we come down here, in the cabin, for a bit when he noticed me losing interest in the fishing.

So now, we've been playing video games like a couple of teenagers for the past hour, which is another thing I'd always wanted to do but never had the opportunity.

Seeing Jacob leaning back on his bed has me suddenly wanting to thank him properly for all that he's done for me. I slowly crawl the short distance over to him and then stop once I'm straddling his thighs.

Leaning forward, I brush my lips over his. "Thank you for teaching me to fish today." I nip at his bottom lip, earning a rumble from his chest. "And for playing video games with me, although you didn't let me win." I bite his top lip a little harder and then soothe it with my tongue before pulling back with a smile.

"Was I supposed to?" he asks in a husky voice, while his heat-filled eyes stare back at me.

"No," I respond quietly, running one of my hands up through his hair. "I like that you don't pretend to suck at it."

He lifts his head, capturing my mouth with his before I can say another word. My body is quick to respond, grinding against his growing erection, with the area between my legs already wet and beginning to pulse with need.

It's always this way with him.

There's an impatient want from within that demands me to be as close as possible to him, as quickly as possible.

A vibration runs through his chest to mine as he lets out a groan. I *love* that sound.

Jacob's hands find the hem of my tank top, and I sit up so he can slide it up over my head. Next, my bra is thrown to the side.

His eyes darken when they land on my bare breasts and stomach, causing my nipples to harden.

But even though he's made it to this point, where he'll undress me without being prompted, there's still a feeling that lingers inside, telling me he's still holding back.

And I don't want him to.

I want it *all*.

He lifts his arms up so I can take his shirt off next, and then I run my fingers over the hot, smooth skin of his chest, dipping between the grooves of his muscles. I still can't believe I'm the only one who has touched this. The only one who has kissed and loved it.

Leaning down, I press close, so we're chest to chest, lips to lips. I kiss him deeply, igniting a fire between us. His hands trail up my back, goosebumps following along with them.

"I want you to let go," I whisper against his mouth.

His brows furrow. "I am."

"Mmm. No, you're not."

He shifts below me, moving so he's in more of a sitting position with his back against the wall, looking slightly frustrated and shaking his head. I'm forced to sit up a little further as well with the movement.

"I want it all from you," I add. "I want you to lose control."

His eyes shoot to mine. "I *don't* want to lose control."

"Why not?"

I can't read the look on his face as his gaze travels over my lips and cheeks and then lands on my eyes. "I don't want to ever do anything that makes me feel like I'm . . . like I'm . . ."

Raping you.

He doesn't say it, but he doesn't have to. I feel like a jerk for not realizing sooner that he would feel that way. Gosh, *of course*, he would.

But I know to my very core that he would never hurt me.

"I would never want to make you do anything you weren't comfortable with. But there are still plenty of things you can do without going *that* far." I lean into his space again, trailing light kisses all over his face.

"There are some things I've thought about trying," he whispers, closing his eyes. "But I don't know if they're okay."

"Do them."

He seems slightly irritated by my flippant answer, a gruff sound coming from his throat. "And what if I hurt you?"

"You won't."

I swallow down his next protest with a kiss, annoying him even further.

He grabs my jaw, trying to control the kiss and sliding his tongue into my mouth, but I pull back again. "Let go, Jacob."

A mix between a growl and a groan comes from him right before he takes a fistful of my hair and pulls my head back with it, exposing my neck to him.

Sliding his nose up the length of skin bared to him, he takes a deep breath as he goes, sending a shiver through me.

"Like this?" His hot breath against my neck turns my insides to liquid heat. "Or like this," he says, right before sinking his teeth into my skin. The gravelly sound of his voice has me letting out a moan.

Yes.

A mix of pleasure and pain skitters from my neck and shoots all the way down to my pussy, causing me to squeeze my legs against his thighs.

Warm, wet lips kiss over the area he just bit and then trail up to nip along my jaw, all the way to my lips, sucking my bottom lip into his mouth before kissing me deeply.

I had been goading him earlier, knowing he needed a little push to get him to do whatever it was that he wanted, and now that it seems like he is, I'm more turned-on than ever.

His free hand slides down my body and undoes the button to my shorts before sliding in and settling between my legs, rubbing my clit in a leisurely way. The hand in my hair loosens and moves so he's gripping the back of my head, holding my mouth to his.

This is his show. I feel like all I can do is metaphorically sit back and enjoy the ride.

I rock my hips along with his fingers, feeling so greedy I can't get enough.

When he inserts two fingers inside, I have to grip his shoulders for purchase and let out a breathy moan into his mouth.

He continues fingering me, pumping in and out while rubbing a thumb over my throbbing bud. I'm sure my nails are close to puncturing his skin, but I can't seem to loosen them. He's hitting all the right spots, driving me wild to the point of release.

This time, when I orgasm, he doesn't slow down to let me catch my breath. He flips me so I'm on my hands and knees, and then tugs down my shorts. I free one leg from them and then feel his chest press into my back.

I'm still so worked up and continue to pant while one of his hands reaches around and squeezes one breast while the other works to pull his pants down.

Once he's freed, his hand slides up from my ass to my neck, goosebumps forming on my skin in its wake. Then, gathering my hair in that hand, he pulls my head back, and I decide that I *love* having my hair pulled by him.

"I've always wanted to try it this way," he whispers in my ear. "Are you ready for my cock?"

A puff of air escapes my lips when he nibbles on my lobe, and I do my best to nod.

Jacob rubs his dick along my ass before lining himself up with my pussy and thrusting into me in one go.

"Oh!" My hand flies up to the wall in front of me, stopping me from falling forward. "Yes," I hiss out.

I start pushing back as he moves his hips forward. Skin slapping skin and our heavy breathing are the only things that can be heard. The gentle rock of the boat is barely noticeable through our movements.

Warm lips skate across my shoulders and neck, and although he's still gripping my hair, holding my head back, it's not hard enough that I can't lean into his touch and rub his cheek with mine.

Then, releasing my hair, he grabs my jaw and turns my face so he can kiss me, groaning deep in my mouth.

After another couple of minutes, he sits back, pulling me with him and holding me flush against his chest while his dick is still buried inside me.

"Fuck, Remi. You're going to make me come too quickly."

Both of his hands move up to my chest, where he squeezes and plays with my nipples.

"Jacob," I breathe out, dropping my head back against him, enjoying every feeling he's gifting me. "So good."

"I want you to come again before I do."

The glide of his hand as he moves over the skin of my stomach, going lower and lower, has my breaths coming out in short puffs. He doesn't stop until he reaches my clit, then his fingers start to move in quick circles, increasing in pressure, doing everything I taught him and more as he pumps upwards from beneath me.

It takes no time at all before I'm clenching tight around his cock and moaning out his name.

Jacob thrusts up a few more times and then holds me tighter against him with an arm banded across my chest. Vibrations shoot through me as he groans into my neck and releases inside me.

A few seconds pass as we catch our breath, his hold on me never loosening. It feels warm and comfortable to be held by him like this. It makes my chest tingle and expand at the same time.

"I fucking love—"

Everything seems to go deathly quiet when he cuts himself off, and his words hang in the air between us. I find myself holding my breath, waiting for him to finish that sentence.

It feels like forever when, in actuality, it's probably only a few seconds before he speaks again.

"Coming inside you," he finally finishes. "I love coming inside you."

I exhale slowly after hearing his words, unable to tell if I'm disappointed or not.

I wasn't exactly expecting him to say *I love you* tonight—and in reality, it's probably going to take him some time to get there.

He's already come a long way, and I can't let myself be disappointed.

I grab one of his hands and bring it to my mouth for a soft kiss before he pulls out and disentangles himself from me.

Neither of us says a word as we gather our clothes, and he passes me some napkins to clean myself.

An uneasy tension starts to fill the cabin the longer we're silent, though, and I notice that Jacob is avoiding eye contact with me while we dress, and *that* has me starting to worry.

I don't understand. Is he angry that he almost said *I love you*?

Or is he angry that he feels that way in the first place?

Now that I think about it a little more, was he even going to say that?

Or did I just assume because I wanted to hear it?

His eyes are usually windows into what's going on with him, but they're hidden from me right now, making it impossible for me to read.

The sex we just had was a little more intense. Maybe I'm just being overly sensitive now because of it.

After we're both dressed, I stay down in the cabin for a moment to myself while Jacob goes up to start the motor. I sit on the edge of the bed, staring ahead at the two photos on the wall once again, while listening to the sounds above me.

I should just ask him if there is anything wrong. It's not like I've ever held back with my questions in the past.

I wait a few more minutes before I get to my feet and head for the stairs.

"Fuck! No." I hear in a tone from Jacob that I haven't heard him use before when I'm halfway up.

It has me moving that much faster to see what's going on. But when I first make it up to the top step, I can't see anything noticeably wrong.

It's not until I'm standing next to him, looking toward the shore, that I see it, and my stomach drops straight to the ocean floor.

"*Oh my god*," I gasp, grabbing hold of Jacob's arm.

He is completely silent as we make our way back to the shore, and we watch helplessly as his truck is engulfed in flames. Fire covers every inch of it, leaving no part unscathed.

Although we're still standing next to each other, it feels like the space between us is growing, and the air around us rises with tension.

The second we arrive at the dock, he's mooring the boat at lightning speed, and I'm watching him take off running, all the while feeling sick to my stomach.

I take a little longer getting off, making sure I'm not going to fall into the water, and then I'm running as well.

By the time I make it to where he's standing, he's already got a hose in one hand, trying unsuccessfully to put out the flames. His other hand is shakily rubbing his jaw.

I can see his chest heaving with barely contained anger or frustration, and the vice around my chest tightens. The whole scene is just so surreal.

"I'm so sorry, Jacob."

I don't need to ask him what happened; we both know this was done intentionally by someone in this town. I just cannot believe they'd actually stoop to this level.

When I heard them mention doing something to his boat, I had hoped they'd never really follow through with something like that, especially after Tahnee was going to talk to them.

Now, after seeing this, I'm not so sure they won't go after it next.

I'm just glad his truck was far enough away from the house that it didn't catch fire as well.

Even though the water from the hose is barely doing a thing to stop the fire—which must have been burning for quite some time—Jacob continues spraying it on the skeleton of his truck like there's still something to save.

My heart aches and then cracks wide open as I watch his head bow, and then he finally drops the hose to the ground in defeat.

Eventually, he angles his head in such a way that I catch the shine lining his eyes before he turns it away again. If my heart was cracked a moment ago, it's now in a million little pieces.

"Jacob," I murmur, trying to get his attention. "Talk to me."

"What do you want me to say, Remi?"

The tone he uses is not friendly, it's not kind, and it has me standing a little straighter.

"I . . . I don't know."

He stabs a hand into his hair. "Fuck. This is what my life is like, okay? And like I've said before, you . . . you don't belong in it."

"Don't say that." I shake my head, not wanting to hear it. "We can talk to them or something. Maybe find—"

"No. I'm done, okay? All we did was fuck a bunch of times, anyway. It's not like there's anything special going on. You just need to leave."

His words feel like a slap to the face, and my head rears back as if he did actually slap it while tears gather and pool along my lower lid. This isn't the Jacob I've come to know and love. This is an imposter, someone I don't know.

"That's not true."

"Please." The half-laugh, half-scoff he lets out is completely devoid of any emotion whatsoever. "You were the first available pussy. Use that pretty little head of yours to figure out what that means. You were all too willing to put out."

No.

This whole time he's been talking, his face has been hidden from me, staring off somewhere past his truck. Right now, I *need* to see his eyes. I need them to tell me the truth.

They'll tell me he doesn't really feel that way.

They'll tell me he's *lying*.

"Jacob, please." I reach for his shoulder, wanting him to turn around and face me.

But all he does is shrug my hand off and take a step away. "I said fuck off already!"

I take one step back, two steps, unable to accept what he's just said to me and how he's discarding me like I'm nothing.

But he's not turning around and apologizing, begging me to forgive him, telling me that he didn't mean it.

The hurt I feel isn't just limited to my chest. I feel it all over.

"You're an asshole," I cry as the first tear slips free. "And you're going to die all alone."

I spin around and start back to my home, covering my mouth to try to hold in a sob. But it breaks through when I start thinking of how we went from what happened on the boat to this.

Chapter Twenty-Two

Jacob

I didn't mean it.

I didn't mean it.

Sliding down the side of my house, I draw my knees up and hang my head.

Even through the crackles of the flames and the constant sound of the waves, I heard her sob. I *keep* hearing it over and over in my head, and each time is like a stab to my chest.

"Fuck!" I lift a shaky hand to wipe the wetness from my eyes.

The heat from the flames is burning the front of my legs, but I can't find it in me to care right now.

My head feels heavy as I lift it up and drop it back against the wall behind me, staring at the fire eating away at my truck, reducing it to a handful of burnt metal pieces.

I've been through *a lot* over the years. I've been spat on, pissed on, and even had shit thrown on me. I've been threatened, attacked, and abandoned. But nothing, and I mean *nothing*, compared to the worry that hit me when I thought about what could have happened if they had done it to either my house or my boat instead, and Remi happened to be inside it at the time.

I wouldn't be able to live with myself if she got hurt because of me.

Back on the boat, I almost ended up blurting out that I loved her. At the moment before I opened my mouth, it just felt so right to say. But that's the last thing I should have been doing, and the second it started to leave my lips, reality sunk in and stopped me.

I've been selfish for keeping her around as long as I have.

On top of all of that, there are days when I wonder how much more of this *I* can take. Why would I possibly want to subject her to the same thing?

Like I've said from the beginning, she is better off staying away from me, so she won't be in any danger, and she won't have any issues with the people in town.

I was so fucking angry and upset when I saw what they had done to my truck, and I ended up channeling it all onto her—hating every second of it.

But I knew that if I didn't do it, she would stay, and she would try to help me in any way she could.

She is *such* a good person.

And I do not deserve her.

Pulling myself together, I get to my feet, spray the side of my house and the surrounding area to make sure the fire doesn't spread, and then head inside my empty home.

The sound of hurt in her voice will haunt me for some time to come. I absolutely deserved to be called an asshole.

Chapter Twenty-Three

Remi

Taking a sip from my wineglass, I try not to let another tear drip from my eye.

Some people around the bar have been giving me curious glances ever since I started crying while telling Tahnee what happened a few days ago, and I don't want to continue drawing their attention.

"And you haven't seen him since?"

I shake my head, placing my glass down on the table. "No, I went to his house yesterday, but he didn't answer. His boat was there, so unless he was out for a walk, he was ignoring me."

Tahnee's mouth opens and then closes and twists as if she wants to say something, but then changes her mind.

"What?" I prompt.

"Well, I just think that *he* should be the one chasing you and seeking you out to apologize, especially after what he said. From what you've told me, you're always the one making all the effort."

"For starters, that's not true."

I mean, every single time I went over to his home, he stepped out of his comfort zone to entertain me.

And then there's also picking wildflowers for me all the time once he knew that I loved them, cooking dinner for me, and several other things.

He also spent the time teaching me to fish and then played video games with me simply because he knew I wanted to.

Those are the things I appreciate.

"And secondly," I continue. "He has had everything, and I mean *everything*, taken away from him. And still, things are being taken away. Like his truck." I place a hand on my chest. "I have so much to give, willingly. And I have no problem giving him my time and energy. *My love*. Because if anyone deserves it, it's him. And then, thirdly, I know he didn't even mean what he said."

"Shit, you're right," she says, leaning back into her chair. "God, I'm such a bitch sometimes. If anyone deserves to have you, it's him." She picks up a fry and points it at me. "But you did call him an asshole."

"I know." I deflate a little into my seat. "I feel bad about that. But emotions were running high between both of us, and I just lashed out after what he said to me."

Taking her glass in her hand, she shakes her head, her red hair swishing over her shoulders. "I just can't believe they actually set his truck on fire."

"Oh, Tahnee, you should have seen the look on his face. He was *devastated*. And I'm sure I saw tears in his eyes at one point. Ugh, just thinking about it makes me tear up." I swipe under my eyes again and pick up my drink. "Let's talk about something else for a bit. What's happening with you and Justin?"

She gives me a look of sympathy and contemplates whether she wants to change the subject or not. Eventually, she gives in, realizing it really is what I want, and with a small smile tugging at her lips, she starts. "Things are . . . good."

I give her a skeptical look because that is not the typical answer from Tahnee that I've come to expect. "Just good?"

Her smile grows. "Okay, well, do you want the toned-down version or the Tahnee version?"

"Is there a middle option?"

She runs a finger over her top lip and idly plays with a piece of her hair, contemplating. "All right, well, he fucked me with his giant dick, and now I'm ruined for other men, and I can't stop thinking about him. He and his python left my place this morning, actually."

"Oh my goodness." I cover my eyes and let out a chuckle. "Do I even want to know what the 'Tahnee version' would have been?"

"Hmm, probably something like—"

"No!" I cut her off, holding my hand out and laughing. "That's quite all right." Then, after another beat, I sigh. "Thanks for making me laugh. I needed that."

"I know." She places her hand on top of mine. "But seriously, I think things will work out with you guys. He probably just needs a little time."

I look down, fiddling with the bracelet on my wrist. "I don't know. I guess we'll see." Then, looking back at her, I add, "Do you think I'm a coward for not confronting anyone about it yet?"

"Hell no. It's not an easy situation, and there is a lot to factor in."

She's right. There's definitely nothing easy about this situation, that's for sure.

After swallowing the last of my wine, I hold my hand up and signal the waitress walking past for another one.

* ~ * ~ * ~ *

A couple of hours later, Tahnee and I walk arm in arm down the streets back toward my home.

This feeling right here, the feeling of being comfortable and being free to be me, spending time with a true friend, is what I always dreamed of having while growing up.

She takes the lead in talking about whatever the hell comes to her mind, being almost successful in keeping me distracted.

"Are you sure you don't want me to stay the night?" she asks when we reach my place.

"I am, but thank you. I might just take a bath and then go to bed."

"Okay. Hey, it looks like someone left you something." I look to where she's indicating and see a bottle of wine by my front door. My *favorite* wine. "Who would have left that?"

"I'm not sure."

"Is there a note or anything?"

"No," I reply after lifting it up and turning it in my hands.

A little bit of hope takes root and begins to bloom in my chest when I think about it possibly being from Jacob.

I try not to let it grow too much, but I *have* mentioned my favorite wine to him before. In fact, it's the same wine I had given him that time, along with the cheese and bread.

"Well, it's a nice little gift from whoever gave it." She leans in for a hug and then whispers, "Goodnight, sweetie." And then she walks off.

I take the bottle into the kitchen with me, dumping my purse next to it on the counter. Then I eye the glasses sitting on the drying rack, thinking about whether I should open the bottle up now and if it really is a peace offering from him.

I can't help but wonder what Jacob is doing right now. Has he been going fishing?

Shit, he doesn't even have a vehicle to get the fish to the market. My insides squeeze tight, thinking about it again.

Tahnee said he probably needs time, but I'm having a hard time not walking down the beach right now and pounding on his door until he answers.

Grabbing a clean glass, I decide to have just one drink. I already have a slight buzz going, but I don't have to work in the morning, and I have nowhere I have to be.

After pouring it almost to the brim, I carry it with me out to the deck, choosing to sit on the chaise lounge that we fucked on.

Visions of Jacob, whenever he graced me with one of his rare, incredibly beautiful smiles, flood my mind.

Because his smiles were so rare, I stored each one of them in a special place in my mind, keeping them locked up but ready to access anytime I want.

I swallow a few large mouthfuls and lay my head back on the lounge. I try to resist the urge to turn in the direction of Jacob's place, but it's hopeless. After another thirty seconds, my head flops to the side to face his direction.

I know in my heart that everything from the other night was mainly him trying to protect me. I'm just not sure how to convince him that he doesn't need to.

Ugh, how can something like this be fixed?

There's no way I can convince the whole town without showing them some sort of evidence.

I take a few more mouthfuls and then get to my feet, making the quick decision to go see him.

My head spins a little as I walk the few steps down the side of my deck, making me think I must have drank more than I realized. But the walk will do me good.

After a few more steps, I take one more sip of the wine in my hand, pour the rest out, and then drop the glass to the sand as well. I'll have to remember to pick it up when I come back this way.

As I walk farther along the beach, I find that my head doesn't clear up like I thought it would.

In fact, it becomes even foggier with every second that passes. I try to shake it away, but it continues to get worse. And then there's a heaviness that starts to settle into my muscles.

With each step I take, it becomes increasingly difficult to move my legs and hold my head up.

Something isn't right.

Collapsing onto the sand, I decide to take a little break.

"Are you all right?" a voice says from somewhere.

I try turning my head, but everything starts spinning, and I can't seem to focus on the person standing nearby. "I juss . . ." My words come out slurred, so I try again. "Not feelin' good."

When my head becomes too heavy to hold up, and I feel my mind being taken under by something, I flop back onto the sand with a groan.

"Shh, it's okay. Just lie back."

What are you doing? I want to ask the person, but I can't even find the energy to open my mouth anymore.

Even my eyelids feel heavy, and it feels like a fight to keep them open. Finally, I lose the battle, and they slowly lower despite my efforts.

I'm sure it's a familiar face I see crouching next to me right before my eyes shut completely.

But then it's dark, and only the laps of the waves reach my consciousness.

Jacob comes to my mind, and then there's nothing.

Chapter Twenty-Four

Jacob

The two hours I've been out here on the water have been a total bust.

A broken line and an amateur slip of the hands had me losing the two fish I had managed to catch, leaving me with nothing.

Not that I have any idea of how I'd be getting them to the market, anyway. I hadn't gotten that far yet.

The full moon tonight makes it so you can see for miles out into the empty, distant ocean. It gives off an eerie yet beautiful, ethereal glow to my surroundings.

If only it weren't tainted by the black cloud hanging over me, surrounding me.

Being on *Grace* hasn't had the same calming effect it usually has, either.

Frustrated, I kick at an empty bucket sitting by my feet, sending it flying over the edge and into the water. But as I watch it bob up and down on the surface, slowly drifting away, I start feeling guilty about adding more shit to the ocean.

I grab my pole with the hook and scoop it up out of the water, dumping it back onto the boat by my feet again.

Deciding to quit and call it a night, I turn the boat around and head back to shore.

The last few days have been shit. I've been replaying the hurt look on Remi's face over and over again. And I don't just mean in my imagination.

I captured the perfect view of it on my cameras and decided to put myself through more torture by forcing myself to watch it. I needed to remind myself that the asshole she called me is what I am to her now.

The thing is, I hate more than anything that *she,* of all people, thinks of me like that. The rest of the world can fucking hate me, but I don't want her to.

She's the kindest, sweetest, beautiful, one-in-a-million type of person who was actually on my side for once.

And now it's ruined.

Pulling up to my dock, I stare at the empty space where my truck is usually parked. I know I still need to call the insurance company to see what I can do, but I've just been wallowing in self-pity and self-loathing.

No charges can be made since you can't see the face or the vehicle of the person who did it. Plus, the cops aren't particularly on my side, either.

I moor *Grace* and walk along the dock toward my place, glancing once in the direction of Remi's home, and I note that one of her lights is on. She's home.

I can't help but wonder what she's doing or whether she's with anyone tonight. And damn, just knowing she's there has the desire to walk over and see her ramping right up.

Turning away, I walk in my front door and just stand there, staring.

I've been alone for ten years now, but this emptiness in my home has the feelings of loneliness amplified by a hundred. It's so much worse after having had Remi inside of it.

I can't stand it.

Fuck, I need to see her.

The thought of her going through life without knowing what she meant to me, and thinking I just used her for a fuck, is something I can't live with.

I turn back around, walk through my front door, and start walking along the sand to Remi's house.

All the reasons I said I'd stay away can't seem to hold me back right now.

There aren't usually any people on this section of the beach between our homes other than Remi, or the odd time, me. So when I see what looks like a couple lying near the dunes up ahead, illuminated by the moon, I move a little closer to the shoreline to try to stay out of their view and not disturb them.

At first, I try to keep my eyes averted, giving them the privacy I'd want to have, especially at this time of night. But as I get closer to passing by in front of them, curiosity gets the better of me.

I peek at the couple again, but something doesn't look quite right now that I'm closer.

It's bright enough to see it's a man straddling a woman underneath him, but what has my hackles rising is that the woman appears to be unmoving.

I can't tell if it's just my past experience that has the worst-case scenario coming to my mind first and I'm just seeing things that aren't really happening, or if I'm completely right and something terrible is going on.

I find myself changing course and walking toward them instead. At this point, I don't give a fuck if it turns out to be nothing and they see me. I just need to make sure everything is okay.

A wave of anger builds and explodes inside me as I come up behind the guy and watch him tear open the unresponsive woman's dress. And she *is* unresponsive. I can't see her face, but her limbs haven't moved once the entire time my eyes have been pinned on the couple.

"What the hell are you doing?!" I shout.

"Care to join in?" the guy asks over his shoulder when I'm barely a couple of feet away.

A red haze covers my vision, and I grab hold of his shirt, throwing him to the side with as much force as I can, and then I jump on him a second later. The whole irony of this situation isn't lost on me.

But I can't let it happen.

"You're fucking sick!"

The guy is as big as me and is clearly in shape, so I expect him to fight back or do *something*, but all he does is hold his arms up to block my hits to his head and makes very feeble attempts at hitting me back.

At one point between my swings, I catch sight of the guy's face and recognize him as the guy who was eating an apple against my truck that morning. *Motherfucker.*

A kind of gurgling, choking noise draws my attention and has me looking over my shoulder at the woman.

And then all the blood is draining from my face as déjà vu hits me like a tsunami.

No, no, no, no.

I'm frozen for a moment, locked in my own head as twisted memories of finding my teenage crush in the field that night flash in front of my eyes.

Now, seeing Remi lying there in the moonlight has some sort of traumatic reaction happening to me. It has to be the reason I feel dizzy. Why I have ringing in my ears, nausea rolling around in my stomach, and I have this inability to move.

I'm snapped back to reality as if water was thrown in my face when I hear that sound again and see the white froth dripping from her mouth.

Pushing off the guy, I scramble over to her, grabbing her face in my shaking hands. "Remi," I choke out. "Remi, sweetheart, can you hear me?"

There's no response except for more of the frothing at the mouth and her eyes rolling back.

"What the fuck did you do to her?" I frantically demand from the guy, not once looking away from her.

But I get no response.

I could kill him right now, but I can't leave Remi like this.

I turn her body to the side, trying to clear her airway, but I'm not sure if it's even helping.

Panic, as great as I've never known, fills me, sinking into my bones and making them feel like dead weight, like I'm paralyzed. A decade's worth of pain and suffering pools together and converges on this very moment.

"Fuck, Remi. Please don't leave me."

My chest feels so tight I can barely breathe. I would do anything just to hear her say something to me, even if it's her yelling at me, calling me an asshole.

"Help!" I cry out. "Somebody help!"

My phone is back on the boat, and I've never been so mad at myself for not carrying it around with me. I can't leave her to go and get it. *I can't.*

A thought crosses my mind, and the tiniest bit of hope emerges when I remember the piece of shit I pulled off her. As despicable of a human being as he is, he'll probably have a cell phone on him.

That piece of hope I had dies just as quickly when I scan the area and realize he's gone.

"No!"

This isn't happening.

This isn't happening.

I feel fucking helpless as my eyes trail over her lifeless-looking body with the torn dress.

I think I hear sirens in the distance, but at this point, I'm not sure if it's from right now or from the memories that are clouding my mind.

I start talking, fumbling with my words, telling her that she can hate me if she just wakes up. I doubt I'm making any sense right now, though.

Fuck, what do I do? Do I give her CPR? She has a pulse, but it's weak.

"Remi," my voice cracks as I look around the area and finally make a decision, "I'm going to carry you to your neighbor's house for help, okay? Stay with me. *Please.*"

I place an arm behind her neck, and I'm just sliding my other arm behind her knees when I hear voices and then someone yelling, "Over here!"

Thank fucking goodness, someone is here to help.

"Help is here, sweetheart," I whisper to Remi. "You're going to get some help."

I sit back up, about to wave them over, when a flashlight shines right in my face.

"Move away from the girl."

"She needs help, please." I cover my eyes for a second, but then I get to my feet, making room for him to do whatever he needs to do to help her.

"I said—oh shit, of course, it's *you*," he spits out, pulling a gun on me in the next second. "Why am I not surprised? Get the fuck away from her."

No. Not this again. Time moves in slow motion as I'm once again thrown back in time to ten years ago in that field. I shake my head, trying to clear away the mess his words are making in my head.

That was the night that changed my life forever.

The night that *ruined* my life.

Ruined everything.

And it was all because I tried to help the girl I liked.

Now . . . now I need to help the woman I love.

Focus.

God, why isn't he doing anything?

"Seriously, you have to do something to help her!" My heart pounds restlessly in my chest.

Right now, he's not doing a damn thing other than standing there, too busy giving me shit about something that didn't even happen. And every second that he's not helping her is a second closer to losing her forever.

The cop keeps the gun trained on me as he shuffles his weight but stays planted in his position several feet away. "I'm helping her by getting you away from her."

Over his shoulder, I can see flashlights waving back and forth as others run along the dunes toward us. I just hope they're not as stupid as this guy appears to be. *Come on, come on.*

Movement from the ground between us has both of our eyes dropping to Remi. At first, it's just her arms twitching, but then her whole body starts convulsing as well.

"Remi!" I shout at the same time the cop says, "Shit." And then he's lowering his gun.

I drop to my knees, trying to reach for her jerking body, but then the gun is right there, pointing directly in my face, stopping me in my tracks.

"Back the fuck up, now!"

"Can't you see she needs help?!" The sound of my voice conveys the level at which I'm freaking out, but it's like he can't hear me or doesn't want to.

I can't believe he's still just standing there, doing absolutely nothing.

Finally, the others reach us.

People who appear to be paramedics approach Remi, and I stand to get out of the way, ignoring whatever the hell the cop is saying to me. My focus is on Remi and what they're doing to her, thankful that *someone* is helping her now.

When my arm is grabbed and yanked behind my back, I shrug free and spin around to face the guy. "Don't fucking touch me."

Another cop appears beside me and starts grabbing at my other arm. I manage to pull it free once again, but then the two of them are on me while I wrestle against them.

"You're going back to prison, asshole," one of them grunts.

"No! I didn't do anything!" I continue struggling, trying to fight against them, but it's no use. "Remi!" I call out as if she can help me.

When they shove me to the ground, pressing my face sideways into the grains, each of them digging a knee into my spine, the air gets forced from my lungs and sand makes its way into my eye.

They're telling me things I can't hear right now.

The sand scratching at my eye, the pain in my back, the metal digging into my wrists . . . none of it matters right now.

Because right now, my face is aligned with Remi's.

I'm looking directly at her.

She's no longer convulsing.

She just looks . . . dead.

Chapter Twenty-Five

Jacob

Time creeps by at an excruciatingly slow pace. Every single loud tick from the clock on the wall feels like ten.

I don't know what time it is.

I don't know how long I've been sitting here with my forehead resting against the cool metal table.

I don't even know how long I've been in this place or what day it is.

Mentally, I'm still back on that beach, watching as Remi convulses in front of me and then turns lifeless before my eyes.

I don't *want* to see it.

I'd rather watch her upset and angry with me through the cameras a thousand times than what I keep seeing.

But even if I'm able to force the image of her smile to appear, it still ends up morphing, and she becomes lifeless in front of my eyes once again.

And I'm still stuck in here, not knowing whether she's alive or not.

So, I keep sitting here with my head on the table and my eyes closed, hoping I'll wake up from this horrible nightmare any minute now, and I'll be lying back in my bed with Remi beside me.

The door clicks open and then shut, and my head shoots up.

I catch my reflection in the mirrored glass along the wall: red eyes with dark circles beneath them and wild hair sticking in every direction. It matches my insides perfectly.

"Is she alive?" I blurt out the second I see the guy who walked in.

He ignores me, taking a seat in the opposite chair. Then he starts talking about some bullshit that I don't even hear because he didn't say *yes* or *no*.

"Is she fucking alive?!" I yell, interrupting whatever he was saying.

"Watch your mouth," he snaps with a curl of his lip that I'm all too familiar with.

"Just tell me, *please*," I beg quietly.

"Yes, she is awake. No thanks to *you*."

Relief rushes through me like a tidal wave, and I close my eyes.

She's alive.

The world hasn't been robbed of her kindness or her smile that is like the sun on a cloudy day, warm and inviting.

But somewhere through the respite, my subconsciousness catches onto something, telling me not to get too excited just yet. He said, "*No thanks to you.*"

"What do you mean?" I ask, flicking my eyes open and looking at him. "Did she tell you what happened?"

Through all of this, I had ignored what was happening in my own situation. I wasn't *really* sitting here in this small interrogation room at the police station as a suspect, being accused of drugging a woman and attempted rape.

The only thing different from now and a decade ago is the word *attempted*.

But Remi is alive. She's awake, and she'll set things straight.

"Yeah, she did," he says, looking down at the file in front of him. Then his eyes swing up to meet mine, and the hateful smile he sends my way has me sitting up a little straighter. "And she told us what *you* did to her."

* ~ * ~ * ~ *

I've spent the last week trying to understand what the fuck happened to her.

At first, I thought for sure it was a mistake, a misunderstanding that would be rectified. No way would she tell them I did that to her.

But here I am, a week later.

I bring one of my knees up and rest my arm on top of it. I remember the concrete floor being a lot more uncomfortable the last time. I guess that's what happens when you're numb all over and dead inside. I don't feel anything right now.

Betrayal of the deepest kind by the woman I love, no . . . *loved,* killed everything inside me that cared.

She *knew* I didn't attack Jennifer. At least, I thought she did.

So what the hell happened?

Was this part of some long scheme she was in on with the town that I had suspicions about from the beginning? What I saw on the beach *wrecked* me, and I can't believe someone would be willing to do that to themselves, that *she'd* be willing to go to those lengths for them. But maybe I'm wrong.

Or maybe she really was attacked, and she genuinely thought it was me who attacked her? But how could she think I was capable of that unless she still believed I did it to Jennifer?

Or maybe she just decided to blame me for what happened to her because of our fight? A fight the cops happened to know about, which means she would have told them.

Regardless of whatever fucking reason it was, she told them I did it. And here I am.

I feel like a fool because even though I had planned to let her go, even though I didn't want to bring her into my world... she made me hope, she made me *love*, and she made me not feel alone.

Then she ripped it all away in the cruelest way.

This past week, I've been in a state of shock and confusion because I thought she...

I guess I was wrong.

And now, I'm just left with bitterness.

My thoughts have spiraled so low that I don't think I can get them up again. They've pulled me down along with them, chaining me to the dark depths of this pathetic existence.

I shouldn't have left my fucking house with the security of my cameras. I knew something bad was coming.

The smell of this vile place burns a path through my nose to my insides.

I *hate* it.

I hate the sounds.

I hate the food.

I hate the people.

I can't stand being in here again.

This is no life. There is nothing for me in here.

I guess there's nothing for me out there, either.

My mind flicks to Campbell, and sure, we just reconnected, but we aren't *friends.* And I would never want him visiting me in here, either.

One thing is for sure. I don't plan on being the guy everyone treats like shit. I don't plan on being the guy who barely sleeps because someone will sneak in for an attack at any moment.

I'm done.

And so I wait. I wait for the psycho, who everyone calls Stitch. The psycho who runs this area. I want him to cross paths with me and do his worst.

I wait, and I wait.

Everything around me is a blur of movements and a mumbling of voices as I sit here, looking ahead, not paying attention to any of it.

Finally, the man I've been waiting for comes into view. I'm surprised he's not surrounded by his guys, but whatever. He's lethal enough by himself.

I watch as someone unknowingly gets in his way and then is grabbed by the collar and shoved into the wall.

Looks like he's in a bad mood.

Perfect.

I wait until he's a little closer before getting to my feet, and then I walk into his path, stopping right in front of him.

Unlike the other guy he just shoved into the wall, I've got a couple of inches on him, so he doesn't go for the same move.

"Got a problem, *bro*?" he asks, taking a step closer.

From this close, the guy's eyes have a weird look to them. Like they're dead inside or something. Empty. There's nothing behind them.

And I wonder if that's how mine look right now.

My heart isn't pounding in my chest.

My blood isn't pumping through my veins from adrenaline.

My shoulders aren't tense.

I'm just . . . ready.

"Yeah," I scoff, looking him up and down. "Your fuckin' ugly mug in my face."

Stitch's lip twitches before turning into a sneer.

Out of my peripheral, I see him reach for something in his waistband.

And then I move.

Chapter Twenty-Six

Remi

My mouth is so dry that I can barely get it open. Even when I try clearing my throat, I find it to be just as scratchy.

What is going on?

Finally opening my eyes, I have no idea where I am.

I look from one side of the room, where I note some medical equipment, a door, and a whiteboard, and then to the other before my eyes land on . . .

"Dad?"

My voice is quiet and strained, but he hears me. Looking up from his phone, he unfolds his leg from the other and stands.

There's a look in his eyes I haven't really seen before as he steps closer. A hint of, dare I say, concern? But by the time he's standing next to the bed, it's gone.

"Remi." He pours some water into a cup and pops a straw in before bringing it to my mouth.

"Thanks," I whisper after taking a sip. "What's going on? Where am I?"

"You were attacked."

"Attacked?" Okay, so I'm probably at a hospital, but in an expensive private room, by the looks of it.

"Attempted rape." At my wide eyes, he adds, "Don't worry, the man has been dealt with."

Attempted rape. Squeezing my eyes shut again, I try to draw out some memories of what he's saying happened.

I try to remember something, *anything*.

Tahnee.

We went out for a couple of drinks. She walked me home. And then . . . nothing.

No, wait. There was a bottle of wine at my door. I drank some of it.

"I remember feeling really dizzy after I drank some wine that was left for me."

He folds one hand on top of the other, looking like he's standing at the head of a conference table rather than here with me.

"You were drugged," he states bluntly. There's nothing fatherly or gentle about his tone. I must have been imagining the flicker of concern I saw in his eyes earlier. There is something there in his voice, though, irritation maybe? "As I said, the scumbag has been dealt with. He'll rot in prison."

I guess I'm grateful for that. It's a small town, though, and unless they were just passing through, I would most likely know the person. I just can't imagine any of them being capable of doing it.

"Who was it?"

"That's not important."

There's no mistaking the dismissive way he answers. It's his 'this line of questioning is over' tone.

Turning away from him, I look around the room and wonder how long I've been in here.

And then another flicker of memory. Jacob. I think I was on my way to see him.

Yes.

I remember that now.

I wonder if he knows what happened to me. Would he have somehow heard it around town? I can't even imagine how he would feel about it, something hitting so close to home.

Is he okay?

I shift in my hospital bed as uneasy thoughts start running rampant. I know he's been living on his own and dealing with everything himself for the past decade, but I can't help but feel like something like this would push him too far.

I care about him so much, and love him so—

"When you're released," my father starts, cutting off my thoughts, "I'll be taking you home."

My eyes swing to him. "Home? As in, my home?"

"That place is not your home. You belong in San Francisco with your mother and me."

"What? No!" I sit up straighter in my bed. "My life ... I have a job–"

"Job," he scoffs. "That *job* is done. You've been in here a week. We've already called and taken care of that."

"A week?!" My stomach twists and turns at the thought.

"I got them to keep you under for longer to make sure you were okay."

No. I can't believe this is happening. It's exactly what I was afraid of.

I feel like I have no control over the situation, no control over my life.

Not only are my wings being clipped once again, but they're going to be bound close to my body.

"Where is Mom?" I croak, noting she hasn't made an appearance yet.

"She had an event back at home that needed organizing. You know how she is."

I do know how she is. Her image is most important, and she'll never miss something that will make her look good. Not even for her own daughter, who is in the hospital after being attacked.

"Listen, we'll talk about this later," he says, starting for the door. "Get some rest."

"Wait. Um. Where's my phone?"

He looks at me over his shoulder, and there's a beat before he answers, "Must have gotten lost on the beach." And then he's gone.

Alone, I lay my head back and stare at the ceiling.

I can't believe I was attacked, that I've been in here a week, that my father is trying to drag me back to San Francisco, and that I have no way of contacting anyone without my phone.

I can't check on Tahnee to make sure she's okay and ask her what she knows about what happened that night after she left.

I can't check if Jolene has been managing okay without me at the store... The store. Maybe if I get the number for *Peaches,* I can call her.

I don't see any phone in here, but I could ask the next nurse who comes where I can find one.

And then there's Jacob. I never got his number. But I probably wouldn't have it memorized even if I did. Plus, he rarely uses his phone anyway, usually leaving it on the boat.

How am I going to get in contact with him? My heart hurts thinking about how we left things. I know that he didn't mean the words he said, but does he know that *I* didn't, either? I wish I could see him right now and tell him.

The town was so concerned about him being a threat that they didn't pay attention to the actual threat they had lurking in their midst. Although, admittedly, I still don't know if it was a local or not. I just hope they back off Jacob now.

God, I *cannot* go back to San Francisco with my dad. I just can't.

I need to figure out a way out of it.

A nurse comes by a short while later, does her thing, and tells me that I'm being discharged tomorrow.

Before she leaves, she kindly searches the number for *Peaches* in Google and then lets me know there is a payphone down the hall and around the corner.

Instead of going straight there, I shuffle into the small private bathroom and take a long hot shower for the first time in a week, apparently, making me feel a hundred times better. I didn't realize just how awful I felt beforehand.

Food is waiting for me when I step out of the bathroom, which has hunger pangs hitting me like a ton of bricks. I devour everything, regardless of the bland taste.

As much as I've slept over the past week, the shower and the food leave me feeling drained, like I need to lie down again.

Once I've rested, I'll make that call.

~~*~*

A couple of hours later, I'm making my way down the empty corridor of the hospital toward where the nurse said the phone was, when I hear angry, hushed voices from around the corner.

One I recognize as my father's, and although the other one sounds kind of familiar, I can't quite place it.

"It was too much, and you know it."

"It all went according to plan," the other guy answers in a bored tone.

"You almost killed her," my father practically hisses. "I didn't pay you for that."

"No. You paid me to move there and follow her around the whole time."

"Yeah. Follow her around. *Not* start fires and *not* kill her."

"Oh, please. When I told you she was hanging around with that scum, you made me set this whole thing up so he'd get arrested, *which is what I did.* And she's *fine.* Shit. Besides her having a reaction to the drugs, it went perfectly. I couldn't have timed his walking by to go see her any better."

The breath I was exhaling freezes in my throat. It suddenly feels like a vice just tightened around my neck, making it hard to breathe.

No way did I hear that correctly. No way did my father have someone follow me around and then set up this whole attack to have Jacob arrested.

Oh, god. *Jacob.*

I inch forward to peek around the corner, hoping and praying that I'm wrong, that it's not even my father speaking, but someone else who sounds like him, talking about something else entirely.

But when the two men come into view, that hope shatters completely, and my insides revolt against me.

There stands my father, hands stuffed into his pockets with a deep frown crinkling his forehead, and the guy he's talking to is none other than Grant.

Thoughts of how I always felt uncomfortable around him come to mind. How whenever he came into the store to buy a single pack of gum or a candy bar, it must have been him just keeping tabs on me. Then there was the figure in the window of that house, the figure in the window at the bar, the feelings of being watched . . .

It was probably all him.

This is real.

They really did it.

Jacob has been put in prison *again*.

He's been falsely accused *again*.

Wronged *again*.

Covering my mouth, I stumble back to my room, where I empty the contents of my stomach into the toilet.

What am I going to do?

What *can* I possibly do?

Dread fills me as the reality of the situation sinks in further.

There's absolutely no way I can let Jacob take the blame for this.

What must he be going through right now?

The door to my room opens and closes, and after rinsing my mouth and sucking in several deep breaths, I step out of the bathroom to face my father.

I've always known he wasn't exactly a nice man, and I know he's done some shady things over the years. But *never* did I think he'd be capable of something like *this*.

"Dad," I choke out. "What have you *done*?"

Thick, salt-and-pepper eyebrows that match his hair quirk up as if he has no idea what I'm talking about. "What do you mean?"

"You . . . you set this up. I'm here because of *you*."

The stoic expression on his face never falters as he undoes the button of his suit jacket and takes a seat in the armchair near the window, as if my finding out is no big deal.

Meanwhile, I'm close to crumbling to pieces, and I can't seem to hide it.

"Well, I hadn't planned on you being in here for quite this long."

I move over to the bed and grab hold of it for support, not feeling like I can rely on my own strength right now.

"How could you do that to me?"

"How could *I* do that? What do you expect me to do when I find out my daughter is running around with a fucking *rapist*." He shakes his head, and the derisive scoff he lets out seems to be filled with barely contained loathing. I'm not even sure who it's directed at, me or Jacob. "Doing it this way took care of two things at once," he adds after reining in some of his anger. "You'll be coming back home, and he's off the streets."

"No. Dad, you have to fix this!"

The panicked shriek of my voice rings through the air between us. I feel like I'm being consumed by thick emotions while my father is calmly seated in the chair with nothing but an annoyed look on his face.

"Why would I fix it?"

"Because he's *innocent*."

"Because he's—" Shaking his head with a humorless laugh, he stands and adjusts his sleeves. "*This* time, maybe. It doesn't mean he doesn't deserve to be in there. It was only a matter of time before he did it again."

"*No.* I mean that he's completely innocent. As in *both* times. He didn't do it, and he absolutely does *not* deserve to be in prison."

"Enough!" he scolds, turning to look out the window. "I never thought you'd be so stupid, Remi, but here you are, proving me wrong. Believing a sexual predator like an idiot."

Closing my eyes tight, I grip the sheets on the bed like they're the only things stopping me from falling. I'm barely holding myself together, but somehow, I manage to compose myself enough to be able to speak calmly and clearly.

I need to convey to my father just how serious I am about what I'm about to say.

"I have proof," I state, which has his gaze swinging from the window to me. "A video of us together, for the first time. It was his first time *ever.*" I pause, making sure I have every last shred of his attention on me. "And I will blast it all over the internet and news if you don't fix this."

I'm so far beyond the point of caring that I'm actually threatening my father with a *sex tape* right now. I will do whatever is necessary to have this whole situation undone.

"You're not serious."

Finally, I see signs of the slightest kink in my father's armor. He goes to great lengths to portray the perfect image—he and Mom both. So, to have a video of me having sex with a *convicted sex offender*, regardless of whether he's innocent or not, circulating *everywhere* would be completely unacceptable. And I can see it concerns him.

"I am one hundred percent serious. You need to get him out of prison, or I'll be releasing it right away."

He holds my glare for a long moment, like a challenge, or maybe even trying to read whether I'm bluffing or not. And then he's reaching into his pocket and pulling out my phone, the phone he said was lost on the beach.

I'm floored once again by the depth of his lies and manipulation.

I remember at one point trying to see Jacob as the monster everyone said he was, but now I can see the only monsters in my life are the people who raised me.

"Might be a little hard to do it without this."

I stare at the phone in his hand, contemplating what my odds are and how quickly I could move to tear it away from him. But I know I wouldn't be able to get there in time before he held it out of reach or destroyed it.

My eyes flick back to him, and I hope like hell he can't see the worry on my face before I come up with something on the spot.

"I don't need my phone to do it. The files are on an online server. All I need is the internet just once, and I doubt you'd be able to keep me away from it forever. Plus, my best friend Tahnee has a copy."

Please don't let him see that I'm lying. I sent the video to myself the morning I got the names of Jacob's friends off his laptop, keeping it as a last resort, for maybe if Tahnee hadn't believed me.

I had also thought about using it as something to show the people in town as proof and have them finally start treating Jacob better. I wouldn't have shown everyone, just one or two people who would then convince the rest.

I would never have done it without Jacob's permission, either, but I hadn't gotten around to asking him about it. I really didn't want to show it, but I was almost that desperate.

Like right now, I'm really not comfortable having it out there for the world to see, despite what I've just implied to my father. But desperate times call for desperate measures.

Finally, my father shakes his head and tosses my phone onto the bed. "I can't believe what you're willing to do to your own family, Remi. I'm more than a little disappointed in you."

His words don't have the same effect on me that they probably would have in the past.

I still can't believe I've stood up to him like this, but right now, I'm too upset with him to let it really sink in.

"I'm willing to do what it takes for you to get him out because he's innocent, and it's the right thing to do."

He gives me a look that I'm sure is used to intimidate his business associates, but it doesn't work on me. I hold my ground, steady and determined.

And then I watch as he reaches into his pocket again, this time pulling out his own phone.

He lifts it to his ear and then walks toward the door, giving me one last glance over his shoulder and shaking his head before walking through the door.

The second the door closes behind him, I collapse onto the bed with my face in my hands, crying. My body is shaking with all the emotions I've been trying to keep a hold of.

Every time I think about Jacob in prison again, *because of me*, sharp pain slices through my chest.

It's all too much.

I continue letting it all out until there's nothing left but an anxiousness that has made its home inside me.

A short time after I've finally gotten a hold of myself, my father steps through the door to my room once more.

"Well, it looks like you might be too late."

Chapter Twenty-Seven

Remi

"I'm sorry," Tahnee tells me once again. "I just . . . I should have insisted on staying with you that night or made you sleep at my place or something."

I swipe away another group of tears that have slid down my face and gathered along my jaw. "Stop apologizing. If it didn't happen that night, it would have just been another night."

"I guess you're right. I just feel so terrible for you. And him. Ugh, the poor guy."

At the mention of Jacob, another tear spills over, and I drop my head back against the wall I'm leaning on. "Yeah. Um, so, were you able to move all the stuff?"

"Yep. Got everything emptied out of your old place and moved it over to the new pad."

Exhaling a breath, I close my eyes and let the feelings of relief and sadness linger for a moment. I put my little beach house up for a quick sale and bought a different one farther up the coast.

I loved my home, but it had been defiled and violated. I learned that Grant, AKA *Michael*, had followed me almost daily—including the night Jacob and I fought. He had been in my home and had gone through my things. I couldn't stand the thought of living there while knowing that.

Plus, I just can't see the town, or rather, the people in it, the same way I used to. I know it wasn't them who set Jacob's truck on fire—*that* was Grant. But all I see when I think about them now is how cruel they've been to Jacob for the past few months. I can forgive Jolene for her behavior because of her past, but I definitely need more time for the others.

I would have moved all his stuff out of his beach shack as well if I could have, but it's not my decision to make.

"I can't thank you enough for doing that for me. Seriously. You and Justin. Was he okay doing it?"

"Please," she scoffs. "I have him eating out of my pussy."

The laugh that cuts through my tears feels good. I knew if anyone could cheer me up, it would be Tahnee. Her crass talk and carefree nature has always been something that I love about her.

"I'm going to miss you."

She sighs into the phone. "Me, too. But it's only an hour and a half away. I'm already planning my next weekend trip."

"Can't wait," I murmur, gripping the phone tight against my ear.

"I gotta get back to work now, but listen to me, he's going to be okay. I just know it. He didn't survive ten years of hell just to quit now." I nod, even though she can't see me. "And you know, I think Jolene may actually come around, too. I think she's feeling guilt more than anything right now."

I hum in response. After I was discharged from the hospital, I called Tahnee to let her know everything that had happened. She, in turn, had relayed the whole story to Jolene, who apparently didn't say a word and has been quiet ever since. I'll give her space for now, but I know I need to talk to her, eventually.

"I'll talk to you tomorrow, okay?" The noise of chatter and clanking dishes mixes with Tahnee's voice, meaning she must have walked back inside *The Big Five*.

"Okay. Love you."

"Love you, too."

We hang up and I take a deep breath, then I push through the door to his room, coming to a complete stop when I see eyes land on me.

"You're awake," I breathe out.

My feet are on the move again, rushing me to the side of his bed. I gently rest my hands on his cheeks and look him over again, as if I haven't been watching him for the past few days.

The doctors told me that he was going to be okay; Tahnee told me he was going to be okay. But I just couldn't let myself relax and believe it until this very second when I saw him awake.

My thumb runs over the crease line forming between his brows. "I was so worried about you."

The look on his face is as if he's trying to figure something out. A thousand questions lay waiting there. Maybe he's trying to figure out what happened to him and why he's here, much like what I went through when I first woke up in a hospital bed.

Before he tries to open his mouth to speak, I press a finger to his lips. "I'll explain everything to you, but you can't talk." I slide my gaze down from his lips to the shallow wound below. "You were stabbed near your throat. You're okay. You'll be able to talk. They just want it to heal a little more before you start speaking."

He was actually stabbed in three different places, but luckily, no major organs were hit.

I don't realize my finger is still pressed to his lips until he's pulling his head back to turn his face away from me. My eyes flick up to his face, trying to get a read on him, but it's just . . . blank.

Emotionless.

I can still see enough of his eyes and face, even though he's turned away from me, and something isn't right.

I mean, I guess he could still be mad at me about what I said the night of the fire. But he was coming to see me when the incident happened, so I don't think that's so.

I can't help but wonder if what he's just been through, if this whole experience, is the thing that has finally made him break.

Maybe it was too much.

The tipping point.

"I'm so sorry, Jacob. This was all my fault. You got arrested because of me. You're here because of me."

I watch as his eyes close, like he doesn't want to hear this, like he doesn't want to listen to my words. But I need to explain to him what happened that night; I need him to know what my father did to us and how bad I feel about it.

Before I'm able to speak again, the door to his room opens, and a nurse walks in. Jacob opens his eyes again, turning his attention to her.

"Oh, good. You're awake," the nurse says to him before she looks over at me. "I'm sorry, you're going to have to leave for a moment."

I want to argue with her, demand that I should be allowed to stay here while she checks on him and does whatever she needs to do, even though I'm not family.

But I don't.

Instead, I stand outside the room, thinking about the way he just looked at me, or rather, the way he *didn't* look at me. I'm worried that it's too late, that I've lost him.

I have no idea what my father did exactly, and to be honest, at this point, I don't care, but somehow, he managed to get the whole situation erased, as if it had never happened. As a result, there are no police officers standing guard outside Jacob's room, and he won't be going back to prison once he's released from the hospital.

He wasn't able to do anything about the original charge or being on the sex offenders list. Although, I'm not really sure he even tried to do anything about it. But I'm okay with that. Jacob is alive, and he's free again. And I'm able to be with him right now.

I'm just about crawling out of my skin several minutes later when the nurse finally steps out of the room. "He has a pen and notepad now," she says to me. "So he'll be able to talk to you if he wants to." Then she walks away down the hall to continue with her other patients.

After taking a deep breath and releasing it slowly, I make a few swipes of my thumb over my fingertips and then walk through his door again.

Jacob's eyes are closed when I walk in, and although I'm pretty sure he's not sleeping, I don't want to be talking to a man who clearly isn't in the right head-space to hear me.

Instead, I lean in to kiss his forehead, pick up the pen sitting on the table by his bed, and write "*I'll be back*" on the notepad. I'll go for a walk and then when I come back, I'll be able to explain everything.

After walking outside the hospital doors, I text Campbell that Jacob has woken up, and he replies that he'll come visit him tomorrow.

He was totally shocked when I told him what had happened over the past two weeks. He had wanted to come to the hospital right away, but I told him that it was a long drive to make when Jacob wasn't even awake yet and that I'd let him know once he woke up.

* ~ * ~ * ~ *

When I walk back into his room an hour later, Jacob is facing off to the side, looking out the window. I have no doubt that he knows it's me that just came through the door, even without looking. I drag the chair as close to the bed as possible and take a seat.

"How are you feeling?" I ask. "Did they say when you can start talking again?"

I get no response from him. It reminds me so much of back when I first met him. Those early days before the talking, before the kissing and the smiling—before I knew him.

I didn't expect him to actually speak right now since he can't, but maybe turn toward me in acknowledgment or maybe write something on the notepad that's right there. I notice the page I had left the message on is gone, which means he read it.

Deciding not to wait any longer, I prepare myself to tell him, regardless of whether he's looking at me or not.

Okay, here it goes.

"It was my father." That statement seems to catch his attention. He doesn't look at me, but his eyes shift sideways as if he's waiting for me to continue. A slight curiosity fills his face now instead of the total blank look from earlier. It's a start, so I continue, "He hired someone to follow me around and then to fake an attack on me and have you framed for it. That way, you'd return to prison, and I'd return home. *Their* home."

Those blue-gray eyes now swing over to me, a heavy crease forming between his brows as he appears to think it over. There's no sign of the emptiness I saw before. Instead, a mixture of thoughts and emotions cross his face, filling in all the voids.

Now, there's a little bit of life in his eyes, a spark.

He drops his gaze down for a second, and then he reaches for the notepad, writing something down. When he's done, I look at the paper.

"*You didn't tell them I did it?*"

"What? No!" I practically yell. "Did you honestly think that?"

His behavior now makes so much more sense if he was actually thinking that.

"*They told me you did.*"

I'm already shaking my head before I finish reading it. "No way. Jacob, I would *never*. It kills me enough to know you went through it once already when you were innocent. I can't believe this whole time . . . you thought I betrayed you like that."

It hurts my heart to think that. He spent a week in prison, the whole time assuming I'd put him there.

Now, it's guilt I see reflected on his face. Maybe because he had let himself believe it when he should have known better, he should have known *me* better.

I don't want him to feel that way, though. We've both been through enough as it is, him especially.

He writes again. "*You said he faked an attack on you? But what I saw wasn't fake.*"

This time, when he looks at me, there's pain there, and it makes me wonder what he saw that night. I wonder what he experienced. I know I had a bad reaction to what was used on me, but they didn't go into detail.

"He drugged me," I say, shifting in my seat. "He was supposed to make it look like attempted rape. But I had a reaction to the drugs, and apparently a little too much was used. I was in the hospital for a week."

Both of Jacob's fists clench tight, along with the narrowing of his eyes. His nostrils flare while his mouth flattens into a thin line. The anger radiating off him is as clear as day, a complete contrast to what he was like earlier.

Then he writes again. "*Are you okay?*"

I let out a short chuckle because *this* is the guy I've come to know. He's back.

"Am I okay? You're the one laying in a hospital bed with three stab wounds." I move up to sit on the edge of the bed and softly trace around his wounds. "What happened?" I ask softly.

"*You answer first.*"

I let out a sigh.

I know Grant didn't actually assault me, but knowing that he *could* have and that I'd have had no way to stop it and no memory of it doesn't sit well in my stomach at all.

But sitting here next to Jacob, well, that makes things better. I lift one of his hands to my lips, kiss his split knuckles, and then smile. "I'm okay now."

Using the same hand I'm still holding, he pulls me in close to hug the side of him that's not hurt.

Finally, I think, closing my eyes and snuggling in close.

God, it feels good. I missed him. I missed his touch. I missed his warmth.

He exhales a heavy breath that makes me think he's feeling the same way, too.

"Your turn," I mumble into him.

I stay close but angle my head so I can still see the notepad when he starts to write again.

"*The thought of looking over my shoulder for the next ten years was unappealing. So, I took matters into my own hands.*"

I twist around to face him directly. "What do you mean?"

He pokes his tongue into his cheek and then winces as if it hurt. He must have felt it in his throat.

"*I was going to become the psycho that everyone stayed clear of. I just didn't give a shit anymore.*"

"Oh, Jacob." I lean into him, pressing my face into his neck, but being careful not to hurt him anywhere. "I'm so sorry."

He gives a slight shake of his head before writing more.

"*I almost had him. But then three of his guys turned up and pinned me down.*"

I close my eyes, trying not to picture it, but no matter what, I see him being held down while some crazy guy stabs at him and then leaves him there to bleed out.

"*I just don't know what to expect when I go back.*"

"Go back?" I sit up so I can face him again. "Jacob, you aren't going back. You're free." Then, at the completely bewildered look on his face, I add, "I made my father undo everything he did to you."

For a full minute, he just stares. He appears shocked, speechless, and relieved.

I can't believe that since he woke up, he's been sitting here expecting to be sent back to prison, but *of course,* he wouldn't have known all that transpired while he's been in here.

"I'm sorry. It should have been the first thing I said to you."

He shakes his head at me with a slight smile beginning to form, lifting his cheeks. It feels so good to see it again that my heart flutters, feeling light and *happy.*

"*I was wondering how you were able to be in here with me and why there were no handcuffs.*"

For a moment, we just sit, smiling at each other while I play with his fingers in my hand. The relief coming from him is almost palpable, contagious.

"I'm just sorry he couldn't do anything about your original charge or the registry you're on."

His smile falters for a moment. Like he only just remembered all the shit from the past ten years, what his life is like, and the root cause of this whole situation. It's as if a dark cloud slowly develops over us, dimming the brightness from his eyes that was there moments ago.

But then he focuses on the notepad again. *"How did you get him to undo what he did?"*

"Uh, well . . ." I start and then fidget with my own fingers a little.

Firstly, I tell him how I ended up with the video to begin with. Then I tell him the whole conversation I had with my father and how I didn't actually *want* to go through with it, but I was desperate.

And while he's not thrilled that I had to threaten to use the video of us, and he's glad that I didn't release it, I think he's more happy that it worked and that he won't be going back to prison.

I also tell him how I most likely won't be hearing from my parents again, and that I was told not to come crawling back to them when I need help. I'm okay with that.

We continue to chat, me talking and him writing things down. We both apologize for the things we said but never meant the night of the fire.

But ever since I brought up the fact that my dad was unable to change anything from before this incident, there has been *something* there.

He keeps looking at me almost as if it's the last time, every time.

His hugs are a little tighter.

His touches linger a little longer.

His smiles are a little sadder.

And I just can't shake the odd feeling.

Chapter Twenty-Eight

Remi

Those feelings are still lingering in my mind a couple of days later as I walk from the hotel I've been staying at to the hospital, choosing to leave my car in the underground parking lot and instead get some fresh air.

The nurses have been quite strict when it comes to letting me stay at the hospital any longer than the specific visiting hours *and* not freely giving me any information about Jacob, like when he can talk again or when he'll be discharged.

I think they only informed me that he couldn't talk because of the stab wound so that if he woke up when I was with him,

I would be able to tell him right away not to try to talk, which is what ended up happening.

Any other information I've gotten was from sneaking a look at his chart.

I half wonder if my father had a hand in making them act this way just to make it that much harder because he's angry with me. Who knows.

I take the elevator up and walk down the familiar halls of the hospital toward the room I've been coming to for the past few days.

I gently open his door just in case he's still sleeping, but find his bed empty.

Standing over by the window with his back to me is Jacob . . . *talking* on a cell phone.

"Thanks. Yeah. I'll see you later." His voice is raspy sounding, almost like it has to pass through gravel before making it out.

He hangs up, stares at the phone in his hand for a second, and then presses his forehead to the glass in front of him.

"Jacob?" He spins around at the sound of my voice with a surprised look on his face, obviously not realizing I was standing here. "You can talk now?"

He nods and then takes a few steps in my direction. "Yeah, they got me to say some shit last night after you left and then told me I could continue talking after that. I should start sounding normal again in a few days."

"That's great," I reply, feeling happy for him that at least one thing is going back to normal. My eyes drift to the phone he's sliding into his back pocket. "When did you get that phone?" As far as I knew, his phone was still back on his boat.

A look of guilt flashes across his face before he answers, "Uh, Campbell brought it for me yesterday. It's just a pay-as-you-go one to use right now."

I never saw Campbell give it to him, so I assume he must have done it one of the times I left them alone, or he came back at some point afterward.

Jacob shifts on his feet like he's a little uncomfortable, making *me* uncomfortable, and since I've never been one to hold off on asking questions, I do just that.

"What's going on, Jacob?" I watch as his shoulders droop and he exhales a long, quiet breath. It's only now that I catch on that he's fully dressed, with shoes on, and the room looks as if he'll no longer be staying in it. "Were you discharged?"

"Uh, yeah . . . this morning." It's now that he looks me directly in the eyes, and I just know he's about to say something I'm not going to want to hear. "Campbell is going to come and get me."

"What? Why?" Confusion mixes with hurt in my tone. "Why would he come when I'm right here?"

Deep down, I know what he's planning before he's even spoken it. I need to hear him say the words, though.

Jacob moves to stand directly in front of me, now looking as devastated as I feel, then lifts a hand to palm my cheek gently.

Is that moisture in his eyes?

Actually, I change my mind. I don't think I want to hear what he's going to say after all.

"Don't say it," I whisper.

"Sweetheart," he says softly, and that one word has tears pooling in my eyes. "I love you more than anything, but our story is still the same as it was before. You've seen firsthand some of the fucked-up things that happen in my life. And I can't ask you to endure that as well."

I shake my head, trying to stop him from talking, unable to speak myself.

"You have the biggest heart, Remi. You feel *so damn passionately* about what's right and wrong. And I *love* that about you." His words come out choked, filled with emotion. "But I don't want your heart to get fucking beaten because of what *will* happen to me on a regular basis, and even to *you* if you stick by me."

His thumb rubs along my cheek, then his free hand takes hold of one of my limp hands while I stare at a random spot on his chest.

"I am *so fucking grateful* for everything you've done for me, Remi. You'll never know just how much." He lifts the hand he's holding and presses it to my chest above my heart. "Take care of this for me." Then he's pressing a kiss to my cheek, walking past me and out the door, out of my life.

I stay standing in the same spot, staring at nothing.

Feeling gutted.

Shocked.

Numb.

I can't believe that after everything we've been through, he's still doing this.

I can't believe that he told me *he loves me*, and it was part of a fucking goodbye.

I continue standing here, taking in one deep breath after another.

Filling my lungs with life.

Regrouping.

Gathering my strength.

And then, I'm running.

Down the halls. Past the nurses. Past the patients. Taking the stairs instead of waiting for the elevator. And then out the front doors.

I don't stop until I'm standing in front of Jacob, preventing him from going any further.

"No!" My chest heaves from the run, but also from all the emotions swarming through my body. "You don't get to decide that."

"Remi–"

"No!" I cry out. "I am not a delicate flower, Jacob. *Yes*, I may be passionate about what is right and wrong and feel it deep within. I feel the pain. I feel *your* pain." I slam my hand to my chest. "But don't underestimate what this heart can handle."

I move into his space that tiny bit more and lift my hands to his jaw. "You're not *asking* me to endure anything . . . because *I love you,* and I've already decided that I'll go through every bit of pain and suffering right alongside you. We'll face every shitty thing that comes our way *together*."

He closes his eyes, dropping his forehead to mine as he slides his arms around my back, letting my words hang in the air a moment before he absorbs them and whispers, "God, I don't deserve you."

"Yes, you do. One day, you'll see that." I angle my head up so I can press my lips to his and then linger there, basking in his warmth and the comfort of feeling him holding me. "Please don't ask me to stay away."

His grip tightens as he looks down at me. I can't imagine that his wounds aren't hurting as his body presses into mine, but he's been through so much that it mustn't faze him at all.

"I always knew you were stubborn."

I smile despite myself. "When it comes to the important things, yes."

He lowers his head so his cheek is resting on top of my head and then sucks in a deep breath, releasing it slowly. "Are you really sure you want this?"

"Yes. With all my heart." There is no delay in my answer, no doubt in my voice. I know what I want.

And it's him.

After pulling back, his beautiful ocean-colored eyes search over my face before he slowly nods and then answers quietly, "Then I won't ask you to stay away."

I grip his shirt, dropping my head gently to his chest and breathing out a sigh of relief. And for a while, we just hold each other close, soaking in the moment as if time isn't a factor, as if the hurdles ahead are tomorrow's problem and not ours.

Eventually, I pull back. "If you want to keep your home, that's fine; we'll make it work. But I think you might like where I've moved to a little better."

Nodding, he says, "We'll figure it out."

"Okay. Where do you want to go now? Are you hungry?"

He fingers a lock of my hair before answering, "I think I could eat. How about you?"

"Yeah. Let's go get something." I step to his side, taking his hand in mine, ready to walk wherever this world takes us—probably to the hotel to get my car. "Where do you want to go afterward? Are you able to come see my new place? Oh, do you need to let your parole officer know beforehand?" At the look on his face, I add, "I know, I know. Me and my questions."

"It's okay. I kind of like your questions."

I smile, and we slowly walk along the path. Everything looks much brighter than before. Maybe it's just this feeling of being truly free.

Free to love him.

Free from my parents.

After a couple more steps, I tug on Jacob's hand to stop him. "Wait." He turns to me with a raised brow. "Can you tell me again? Can you tell me that you love me? This time without the goodbye?"

His lips do that twitching thing before finally giving up and turning into one of his rare smiles. And then his mouth crashes into mine.

Epilogue

Jacob — Nine and a half years later

It takes all I have not to go in and wipe away the tears I can see Remi swiping at through the crack in the bathroom door. I know she's trying to hide them from me, trying to hide her heartache. It still kills me to see her tears.

So, I stay sitting here on the edge of the bed, watching as she grips the counter, trying to pull herself together.

But truthfully, right now, I'm trying to hide *my own* cracking heart from *her*.

When she steps out of the bathroom, she does a double-take when she sees me sitting here. I try to send a comforting smile her way, but shit, she must see right through it because she changes course and heads straight for me.

Stepping between my legs, she wraps her arms around my head and holds it close to her stomach.

For a brief moment, as I lift my arms and slide them around the curve of her body, I wonder if there's a little piece of me growing inside of her right now. A precious life, just waiting to have me in the palm of their hands.

The corners of my mouth twitch with a smile that's trying to appear just thinking about it, a nice distraction from the pain.

"It's just so unfair." Remi sniffles, unable to keep her emotions out of her voice.

"I know, sweetheart, but we've known this would be the case all along." I slide my hand up and down her back, moving in circular motions.

"I know, I just . . ." She takes a deep breath and releases. "I just thought with only two weeks left, they'd be more lenient. You know?"

I know she thought that. But I try never to let myself get too hopeful when it comes to things like that.

"It's okay. Two more weeks, and we can start to put it all behind us. Right?"

Remi has been my gift, the priceless reward for all the injustices I've faced. She's been everything good in my life . . . up until five years ago, that is.

She pulls back, looking down at me with all the love in the world in her eyes. And that look right there, directed at me, *that* has me feeling like the luckiest son of a bitch in the world, despite all the shit.

"Two weeks," she whispers, palming my cheek.

The moment is broken when I'm being propelled forward in the next second, and two little arms come around my neck. Thankfully, I stop myself from falling forward and knocking Remi over.

Swinging my arm around behind me, I scoop my baby girl up and pull her around into my lap. "Hey, Popsicle."

"Poppy," Remi scolds. "You've messed your hair up already." My daughter and I exchange wide eyes before she starts giggling, and Remi goes to get a brush. "I'm going to do two braids. That way, they shouldn't come undone. Sit still on Daddy's lap."

I watch as Remi starts running the brush through Poppy's dark hair, which is so much like her mother's. Besides the color of her eyes, which are just like mine, she's a perfect replica of Remi, even down to her big heart of gold.

"Are you ready for your first day of school?"

"Yup," she answers with a bounce, causing Remi to place a hand on her shoulder in silent warning. Then, as if just remembering, her excited smile turns into a kind of pout. "Why can't you come with us to see my classroom?"

That crack in my heart widens just a little further when I see the sadness in her eyes. I smooth a hand over the first finished braid and try my best to give her a carefree smile. "I really wanted to, Pop, but I have to get out on the boat this morning with Uncle Campbell."

The crease between her eyes deepens as her lower lip drops further. Shit. I wish I didn't make it sound like she wasn't important enough to miss going out fishing.

We made it so Campbell and I would be going out on the boat in the mornings for the next two weeks so we wouldn't have to lie about why I wasn't allowed to go to the school.

I hate that I don't get to go with her this morning. Hate that I don't get to her hand as we find her desk, or watch as she makes a new friend or two.

But knowing that in two weeks, I'll finally be off this fucking sex offenders list, well, it's what's keeping me going, and it has me reaching forward to tickle my little girl, pulling some more giggles out of her and turning that frown upside down.

"Daddy!" When the smile starts to drop again, I go for another tactic.

"Uncle Campbell is driving an hour every morning, and if I make him wait any longer, he'll be a big cranky pants." I have no problem throwing Campbell under the bus. She loves him almost as much as she loves me, and he can do no wrong in her eyes.

It works, of course, and she nods.

"Mommy's going to take lots and lots of photos for me."

"Maybe I can even Facetime," Remi adds. "Then it'll be like he's right there."

"Yes!"

"Then after school, maybe we can have ice cream on the beach and look for some pretty shells," I say, tugging on the end of one braid.

Her eyes blow wide with excitement, and she launches herself at me for a hug. "Today is going to be the best day." She snuggles in even closer. "I love you, Daddy."

And just like that, everything is okay again.

God, these two women sure know how to melt me from the inside out. I close my eyes, holding her little body close to mine.

There have been *plenty* of hard times over the years, but I can't deny that there have also been plenty of good.

And then there have been times like all those years ago, when we went back to our old town a short time after I was let out of the hospital, so I could deal with my house. Jolene had turned up at my door, came to me and collapsed in my arms, crying and begging for forgiveness.

After a few long, tense moments on my end, I told her that I forgave her. But I don't think she forgave herself for quite some time.

"I love you, too, Popsicle."

I've come to realize over time that when we suffer through pain and badness, we need to keep a part of that with us so when the good comes along, we'll recognize it for what it is and truly appreciate it. We'll take hold of it and cherish it.

Opening my eyes again, I find Remi leaning against the bathroom doorframe, watching us as she wipes away another tear. And now I'm really thinking, *and hoping*, that she's pregnant again. She's definitely been on the more emotional side lately.

I hold her gaze over the top of Poppy's head leaning against my chest, the moment only breaking when a horn blares outside.

Poppy is off me in a second, bounding for the door. "Uncle Campbell is here!" And then she's gone.

Shaking my head, I get up from the bed and step toward Remi. "If I didn't know that he bribes her with candies, I'd be jealous."

The small laugh she gives is full of amusement as I enclose her in my arms. "Plus, you know very well that you're her favorite . . . and mine."

"I do know that." Nuzzling into her neck, I smile against her skin. "And you guys are my favorite, too. My best friends."

"Mmm." Remi hums. "So, you don't still think I'm a delirious *space filler* in your life?" she asks, referring to one of our earliest conversations from many years ago. I can hear the smile in her voice.

"Yeah, I do." When she starts to push at me in protest, I keep her held close to me and chuckle. Then, turning more serious, I add, "You fill all the best spaces in my life, Remi. And in my heart. I love you."

I feel her melt into me again.

And because I want to keep her mind off things, I begin kissing the delicate flesh of her neck, sliding my lips over her skin until I reach her mouth. Then I'm taking it and kissing her as passionately and as deeply as always.

She was my first kiss, and she'll be my last.

Only her.

I'm still as ravenous for her as I've always been. In fact . . . "I'm hungry for your pussy," I whisper after pulling back. "Maybe I should have a taste."

"Jacob!" Remi sputters. "We both have to leave. And Poppy and Campbell are just downstairs."

Despite what she said, her body still arches into mine, her hazel eyes go half-lidded as she licks her lips. Lips that I can't resist tasting again and again.

Gripping her hips, I draw her in closer to grind against me, letting her feel exactly how much I want her.

"Hey, Jake! I found a monkey down here. I think it's yours!" Campbell's voice, followed by Poppy's giggles, travel up the stairs, putting an abrupt end to our moment.

Resting my brow against hers, I chuckle. "I guess I'll have to wait until we're back for a taste." Then, with one last nibble on her lip, I pull back, smile down at her hazed-over eyes, and then wink before heading for the bedroom door.

Before I'm able to walk through it, Remi speaks again. "Don't think I don't know what you were doing." Raising a questioning eyebrow, I watch as she walks over to me. "Getting me all worked up so I'll be distracted thinking about your mouth on me."

"Did it work?"

She moves so she's standing right in front of me and then slides her hand up my abs, over my chest, and around to the back of my neck. Then she's pulling my head down until it's barely an inch from her mouth. "Absolutely. But just so you know, your mouth isn't the only one that's going to have fun when we're both back."

After the faintest brush of her tongue across my lip, she pulls back, winks at me, and then turns to head for the stairs, leaving me to adjust myself.

With a smile on my face, I follow her down the stairs to be with the people I love the most. The people I love with all my heart.

THE END.

THANK YOU!

Thank you so much for reading my book!
If you enjoyed Remi & Jacob's story, please consider leaving a rating and review. Ratings and reviews help the book and authors like me get noticed.
Curious about Campbell? Read his story in Wrecked, also available on KU

CONTACT ME

CONTACT ME :

Instagram

Facebook Group: Rin's Romance Readers

Email: rin.sher.author@gmail.com

Tik Tok

Website: https://www.rinsherauthor.com/

Other Books In This Series

Wrecked

***Wrecked*. It's how Jasmine Delaney found me.**

The truth was, I'd been heading down a one-way street to destruction for a long time.

I raced - *illegally*. I drank - *excessively*. I slept with women - *indiscriminately*.

There was no escape in sight.

That is, until I met *her*. She made me feel whole again, nurturing my heart right along with my soul. But right when I had a reason to be a better man...I did what I always warned her about.

I wrecked it.

She should have stayed away.

***Orchids*. It's how Campbell Baxter crawled into my heart.**

The truth was, I'd been walking down a lonely path for far too long.

I loved - *passionately*. I gave - *freely*. I cared - *easily*.

There was no one worth the risk.

That is, until I met *him*. He lit my insides on fire, engulfing me in a love like I'd never felt before. But right when everything was in our favor and I'd found what I was looking for...he did what he warned me about.

He wrecked me.

I should have believed him.

Shattered

One text and I was curious.

One conversation and I was intrigued

One revelation and I was Shattered.

The mysterious stranger I was texting should never have been her—**my best friend's little sister,** and the one girl I couldn't have.

Behind the screen, she was the one who kept my world from falling into darkness when everything seemed to be collapsing around me. *My sunflower.*

But in the light of day, she was my ruin. I couldn't be with her, especially after what happened to one of my best friends.

In a moment of desperation, I irrevocably changed our lives.

Years later, when I've buried the past and am focused on being the best single dad to my son, I find myself face-to-face with my past once again.

Little by little, she starts lighting my world again, stirring up long since dormant desires. She says we're not those same teenagers anymore.

But she's still my best friend's little sister.

She's still my *sunflower*.

<u>Shamed</u> coming in 2025!

ALSO BY THE AUTHOR

The Woman

A companion.

A slave to my every desire.

That's what she's meant to be, whether I want it or not.

Being granted the ability to choose my woman at a younger age is supposed to be an honor, a privilege in our society. And though it's against my own desire, I follow through with my grandfather's wishes and pick a female from a selection that is shown to me.

There's something different about the woman with the violet eyes I end up picking.

I try to ignore having her in my home, in my space, but something is intriguing about her behavior. No matter how much I try, I can't stop thinking about her.

She messes with my head and makes me lose control, and I'm

a man who needs it.

By the time the reason for her peculiar behavior comes to light, I'm in too deep.

Now that I know the truth, I have a choice to make: go against society's expectation and risk it all... or lose her forever.

See You Again

Riley

While on a week's long trip in a small town for one of my best friend's bachelorette getaway, I did something I never do . . . I had a one-night stand.

But I was left with more than just the amazing memories of the beautiful man I spent the night with.

With no numbers or last names exchanged, I can't exactly tell him about it either.

For all I know, he could live on the other side of the country.

Jasper

I spent an amazing night with a woman who made me feel things that I never did before. Months later, she's *still* on my mind.

But then I meet a woman who looks exactly like her, and she reminds me of her in so many ways.

Only it's not her.

Not only does she have a different name, but the biggest difference?

She's blind.

Oh, and she's pregnant.

Acknowledgements

Thank you so much to all of my wonderful book friends and readers who have given me support along the way. The book community is such a great thing to be a part of.
FELLOW AUTHORS AND READERS, **YOU ROCK!!**
To my beautiful friends who have given opinions or have been a sounding board for me, and put up with all of my ups and downs along the way, **THANK YOU!** I appreciate you guys so much!!
Steffanie Blais, Chloe Wong, Tiffany Ross, and Denise Reynolds- LOVE YOU GUYS!!!
Lastly, I'd like to thank Justin Dube' who did an amazing job on the book cover. It's awesome!
There are many, many more people I could mention, but it would take up too much space. So, thank you to everyone :)

Printed in Great Britain
by Amazon